Series

KOBO's Best Children's Book of the Month Selection

"Swashbuckling abounds in this fun-filled series opener."
—*KIRKUS REVIEWS*

"This fantasy series debut has everything that readers could want: magic, used for both good and ill; dragons; a quest; a rebellious and brave princess; life-and-death adventure; and a cliffhanger ending. Highly recommended." —*SCHOOL LIBRARY JOURNAL*

"In this invigorating trilogy opener, Kagawa conjures an atmospheric setting populated by eclectic characters and fanciful creatures."
—*PUBLISHERS WEEKLY*

"A solid read for any fans of dragon fantasies, this makes an easy sell for fans of Alex London's Battle Dragons or Anne McCaffrey's *Dragonflight*." —*BOOKLIST*

"A swashbuckling adventure of airborne proportions with a dragon-sized heart. I flew through the book as if riding my own True Dragon, and ahoy, me hearties! The second book can't come fast enough!"
—GRACI KIM, *New York Times* best-selling author of *The Last Fallen Star*

"*Lightningborn* will hit you like a bolt of lightning! It will make you forget where you are, what time it is, and all the homework you have to do. What a ride!"
—RIDLEY PEARSON, author of the Kingdom Keepers series

"Think you know dragons? Think again! Kagawa's world-building is extraordinary and the stakes beyond sky-high."
—SARWAT CHADDA, author of *City of the Plague God*

STORM DRAGONS

BOOK ONE
LIGHTNINGBORN

JULIE KAGAWA

Disney • HYPERION
Los Angeles   New York

Copyright © 2024 by Julie Kagawa

All rights reserved. Published by Disney • Hyperion, an imprint of Buena Vista Books, Inc. No part of this book may be reproduced or transmitted in any form or by any means, electronic or mechanical, including photocopying, recording, or by any information storage and retrieval system, without written permission from the publisher. For information address Disney • Hyperion, 7 Hudson Square, New York, New York 10013.

First Hardcover Edition, April 2024
First Paperback Edition, March 2025
10 9 8 7 6 5 4
FAC-025438-25239
Printed in the United States of America

This book is set in Adobe Caslon Pro/Monotype
Designed by Marci Senders
Interior illustrations by Aliva/Shutterstock (1729573654)

Library of Congress Control Number for Hardcover Edition: 2023932250
ISBN 978-1-368-09211-1

Visit www.DisneyBooks.com

To Kieran, Nick, and all fellow dragonlovers

PART I

CHAPTER ONE

It was a risky jump.

Not the type where, if you missed or miscalculated, you might scrape your knee or knock a tooth loose. Not the type where a fumble could result in broken bones, a bloody nose, or even a minor concussion from landing on your stupid, why-did-you-think-you-could-do-this? head. No, this was a fall-into-an-endless-void-filled-with-arcane-lightning-that-will-fry-you-to-a-crisp type of jump. This was a plummet straight into the Maelstrom. Fail to stick the landing, and there was no ground to break your fall, your pride, or even your bones. There was nothing below to save you. Slip off the edge of the island, and you'd keep tumbling through a roiling, angry storm forever. Or until you were inevitably disintegrated by purple lightning. Obviously, most sane people stayed as far away from The Edge as they could.

But then, most sane people didn't steal from sky pirates, either.

"There he is!"

Remy winced, glancing over his shoulder. The trio of pirates was stalking down the mud-filled plank passage between shanty huts, swords bare and glittering in the dim light. One of them spotted Remy and pointed a rusty curved blade in his direction.

"Little rat thief!" he bellowed. "Swipe my purse, will you? I'll string you up by your toes and dangle you off The Edge for the storm gulls to pick at!"

"Uh, no thanks; that sounds painful!" Desperately, Remy looked around, searching for another escape route. Rickety houses of wood and corrugated metal lined either side of the muddy road, leaning against or sitting on top of each other. Behind him, the path came to an abrupt and sudden end. At one point, before Remy was even born, there had been a fence between the road and The Edge to keep the brave, intoxicated, or foolish from lurching past it into empty space. But time and apathy had reduced the barrier to a few rotting sticks lying in the weeds. So there was nothing between him, the open sky, and the Maelstrom below.

Beyond the edge of the island, a single floating chunk of dirt and rock drifted slowly past, almost as if it were taunting him. It was one of the thousands of smaller landmasses that circled the whole, like planets orbiting the sun. Although they'd once been part of the land itself, either time or nature had broken them loose, but they seemed to share the magic that kept the islands aloft and did not plummet straight into the Maelstrom. Most of them were tiny, head sized or smaller. A rare few were so large, huge chains had been sunk in them to anchor the masses to the island, with houses or shops built on any available space. But some, like the chunk drifting past, a single dying tree poking out of the top, were just large enough to hold one person. Definitely a skinny, mop-haired street urchin like Remy.

If he could make the jump.

"Nowhere for ya to go now, little rat!" The pirates were sloshing toward him through the mud, lantern and torchlight gleaming off their blades. The one who had spoken first, a lanky man with stringy yellow hair and three gold teeth, flashed a glittering smile. "Here, I'll make it easy on ya. Chuck the purse to me now, and I'll only run ya through! It'll be over fast. Or you can choose the hard way, and I'll dangle ya upside own over the Maelstrom so storm gulls can peck at yer eyes!"

"You mean this?" Remy held up his fist, a small leather pouch clutched between his fingers. A tiny rabbit had been inked into the leather, a strangely cute choice for a rough-looking pirate. "This is yours?"

The pirate's eyes bulged, and he scowled. "Yes, it's mine!

Hand it over, and I'll be sure to gut ya fast!" He raised his cutlass with an evil smile. "It'll be quick, I promise."

Remy, tossed the pouch in the air, caught it, and gave the pirates a cheeky grin.

"Thanks, but I'm gonna go with choice number three. You want this?" He raised the coin purse, shaking it enticingly. "Come get it!"

And he whirled, sprang into the weeds at the end of the road, and began running straight toward The Edge.

The end of the island loomed before him, and beyond it, tantalizingly close, the small land wedge spun lazily by. A gust of wind roared up from below, tossing his hair and clothes. Remy hit the end of solid ground just as the chunk was sliding past, and launched himself into open air.

Don't look down, don't look down, don't look down.

A roar much louder than thunder boomed from below, and a rogue strand of purple lightning sizzled up from the clouds, almost as if it were reaching for him. Remy felt all his hair stand on end, and for a moment, he was floating, weightless, in the open sky.

Then he was falling, hitting the edge of the land chunk and lurching forward to grab the tree. His arms circled the rough bark, the air driven from his lungs as he slammed into the trunk, scraping his cheek and his arms. The ground beneath him bobbed a bit, spinning in place, but even with his added weight, it didn't sink or fall into the Maelstrom. It simply continued to float lazily in the air.

Panting, Remy looked up, seeing the trio of pirates at The Edge where he had leaped off. None of them looked keen on following his leap of faith, and one pirate hung several paces back from the drop-off, reluctant to step any closer. The pirate with the gold teeth glared at Remy as he drifted past, shaking his cutlass in helpless rage.

"I won't forget this, rat! You wait! When I find ya, you're gonna wish I had just run ya through!"

His voice grew fainter, threats and promises fading into the distance. Remy gave the pirates one last wave as he floated away, watching as they grew smaller and smaller, and finally disappeared altogether.

According to Crusty Bart, the white-haired, shriveled old man who was always found at the Salty Barrel tavern, two thousand years ago the land had been whole. There were no floating islands, no sky ships soaring through the clouds, no Maelstrom raging below everything. There were towns and villages, cities and hamlets, but people traveled the land by roads, from one kingdom to the next.

Then came the Shattering, the Undoing of the World. No one knew how or why it happened; some said it was a natural occurrence, some theorized that a cabal of mages discovered something deep below the earth that they should have left alone. However it happened, the result was the same. One day, the world exploded in a torrent of magical energy that ripped it apart. Kingdoms crumbled. Cities were toppled in an instant. Everyone thought the end of the world had come.

"But the world survived," Crusty Bart would finish with a grin and a wink. "The world survived, because we humans are too darn stubborn to lie down and die, even if everything else is blown to smithereens. We found other ways to thrive. We built new cities on the world remains, the islands that float above the Maelstrom. The great storm crystals at the heart of every island keep us afloat, though don't ask me how they got there; that's a mystery that was lost to the Shattering. The sky ships were the end to our isolation, as we could now travel from island to island. And of course . . ." And here, Bart would lower his voice so you really had to lean in to listen. "Of course, there were . . . the dragons. The mighty winged lizards that soar the winds and breathe fire hot enough to melt steel. But, if you want to hear more about *them*, I'm afraid my mug is empty, and only a copper will refill it."

Dragons. Remy rolled his eyes. Sitting against the tree, he gazed at the evening sky through the gnarled, withered branches. Far overhead, the last rays of sun caught the sails of a distant sky ship pulling away from Cutthroat Wedge, the floating island he called home. Everyone wanted to hear about dragons. Remy had seen a lot of sky ships in his life, but never a dragon. Oh, he knew they existed. The king's sky knights, his elite royal guard, all rode on the backs of mighty dragons. And he would hear tales sometimes when he was at the tavern, of sailors who saw dragons in their travels across the kingdom.

But there were no dragons this far out in the Fringe, the ring of islands farthest from the capital. And no way to ever see one. Dragons were rare and extremely expensive; only the wealthiest and most important people in the kingdom could afford them. If you paid for enough of his drinks, Bart would tell grand tales of wild dragons in the days before the Shattering. But nowadays, every dragon was marked from the egg with a special, magical tattoo. This tattoo conveyed ownership, bloodline, and hatch date, so no dragon was ever unaccounted for.

Looking down at the pouch in his hands, Remy gave the drawstrings a tug and pulled it open. A handful of copper coins and a few pieces of silver glinted inside, making him smile sadly. He could steal a thousand of these, a million, and still not have enough to buy a dragon. And even if he did, dragons were only sold to those with the highest status. Those who lived close to the capital and owned stables bigger than his entire neighborhood. A poor street rat with mud-colored hair, mud-colored eyes, and no future couldn't even dream of seeing much less buying one.

The floating rock eventually circled closer to The Edge, and Remy was able to spring off the chunk onto solid ground. Quickly, he took a few large steps back from The Edge, putting a safe distance between himself and the Maelstrom, before relaxing and gazing around to get his bearings. The rocky, mud-covered chunk of land called Cutthroat Wedge wasn't a large island, more of a sky town than a sky city. Not like the capital, where he'd heard there were places you could stand and not see the edge of the island. Here on Cutthroat Wedge, there was one high point where the airships docked that held the tavern, the warehouses, the gambling den, and all the other places that attracted the type of crowd that gave the island its name. Stilt homes and shanties were built on whatever available space was left, crammed together or piled atop each other, sometimes three or four high, so some portions of town looked like they were about to topple over at any moment. The resulting maze of narrow alleys, tight corridors, wooden walkways, and rickety bridges spanning the roads were what Remy called home. It was perfect for a mud rat like him.

Remy hefted the purse in his hands, feeling the weight of the coins through the leather. In reality, it wasn't much, but it was still a fortune to someone who had virtually nothing. For a moment, he stood there, fighting a battle within himself, before his shoulders slumped and he gave a gusty sigh.

Tucking the pouch into his pocket, he headed into the labyrinth.

The Salty Barrel tavern sat on a point called the Jut, a large chunk of rock stretching out over open sky. It was the closest building to the airship docks, not counting the warehouses that held all sorts of illegal goods, so it was the first thing sailors glimpsed when they left their ships. Obviously, it was a popular place, a haven for smugglers, gamblers, sky pirates, and anyone else trying to avoid the law.

"What are you doing here, mud rat?" Ferus scowled at Remy as he slipped through the broken doors, gazing around the beat-up tavern. The owner of the Salty Barrel was a thin, twitchy little man with greasy black hair and dark, beady eyes. He wasn't fond of Remy, mostly because Remy had no coin to spend on drinks and, sometimes, unattended items or forgotten bits of food went missing when he was around. Ferus didn't really care if Remy stole from his customers, but he hated that Remy was often able to pocket any loose coins before *he* could get to them.

"Keep your sticky little fingers to yourself, boy," Ferus warned, jabbing a bony finger in his direction. "I swear, if even a crust of bread goes missing, I'll have Lod snap all your fingers, one by one. Then we'll see how well you can pick up anything."

"He'd have to catch me first." Remy smirked. Lod was the tavern cook, but due to his immense size, he doubled as a bouncer if the customers got too unruly. He was also, not to put too fine a point on it, about as quick as the potatoes in his stew. Besides, Ferus made that particular threat at least once a month. Remy would be more worried if the tavern owner *wasn't* threatening him with violence. When he was silent, that's when he was plotting things.

"I'm just here to see Bart," Remy said. "I'll leave right after I talk to him."

Ferus rolled his eyes and started wiping the counter with a wet rag. "He's in his usual spot," he said, waving a hand at the far wall. "Old windbag is in one of his sulky moods, though. Said he doesn't feel like telling stories tonight. Bah. What's he good for, if not that?"

Remy glanced at the fireplace. A white-haired old man in a tattered captain's coat sat by the fire, shoulders hunched and mouth pulled into an unhappy upside-down U.

"Go cheer him up," Ferus urged. "He likes you, for some unknown reason. Get him talking. Put him in a storytelling mood before the evening crowd starts coming in. I don't let him sit there and drink for nothing."

Remy walked over to the fireplace. Crusty Bart sat in a worn leather chair, the end table beside it holding an empty mug that served as a tip jar. He stared moodily into the embers of the fire and didn't look up as Remy approached.

"No stories today," Crusty Bart muttered as Remy stopped beside the chair. "My heart ain't in it." He sighed, sinking deeper into the cushions and still not looking at Remy. "Don't get old, boy," he said in his breathy voice. "No one respects their elders anymore. You'd think people would be decent enough not to steal from an old man who has nothing but stories left to tell. But there are no decent people in the world. Or at least, not here on this blasted, forgotten rock. Makes me want to give up storytelling altogether."

Remy sighed. Digging the coin purse from his trousers, he held it out to the old man. "I think you dropped something," he said as Bart's eyes widened.

"My lucky rabbit!" he cried, snatching the purse from Remy's hand. "You found it!"

"Yeah." Remy nodded. "I saw it sitting on a table in the gambling hall and thought it looked familiar. Unfortunately, the pirate I took it from wasn't quite as drunk as I thought."

Bart shook his head. "Idiot boy," he snapped. "What do I always tell you? Pirates are thieves and cutthroats, but they don't forget who robs them. If you keep stealing from pirates, one day you'll find yourself walking a plank above the Maelstrom."

Remy shrugged. "Hasn't happened yet," he said casually. "And you're welcome, by the way. If you're feeling really generous, you might spare a coin or two. You know, for rescuing your purse and getting chased all over Cutthroat Wedge. It's not like there are a lot of places for me to go."

Bart's jaw tightened. He yanked the purse open, pushing coins around with a thin, dirty finger. "I'm missing some copper," he muttered.

"Don't look at me," Remy said. "I didn't take anything. I may be a thief, but I don't steal from people I know."

"Hmph," Bart said, closing the pouch back up. "Well . . .

you wouldn't deny an old man what little coin he has, would you?" he asked in a suddenly weak voice. "How about this: Come back tomorrow night, and I'll tell you a dragon story. Maybe I'll tell my grandest one about dragons and the world Before."

"I've already heard all your dragon stories," Remy sighed. He wasn't even angry. Bart had been around since before he could remember; he could pretty much predict what the old man was going to say in most situations. "I've been listening to you since I was five; there's no story I haven't heard before."

"Oh, is that so?" Bart's eyebrows bristled, and he drew himself up in his chair. "Then I suppose you know what happened when Duke Cloudwright's youngest son found an injured dragon in a cave below his family estate?"

"He befriended the dragon, saved the king from a pirate attack, and became the first anointed sky knight," Remy quoted automatically.

"Hmph." Bart wrinkled his nose, deflating a bit in his chair. "All right, Mr. Know-It-All. If you think you've heard all my stories, then answer me this: What became of the True Dragons, and where are they now?"

"Extinct," Remy said. "They're in storybooks and legends, but nowhere else."

"Ah, but you're wrong." Bart gave a grin of triumph. "See, boy, you don't know as much as you think you do. This old man still has a few secrets up his sleeve."

Remy shrugged. The tale of the True Dragons was one of those stories no one could ever agree on. They were supposedly the ancestors of the regular dragons, like how wolves were ancestors of domestic dogs. But unlike normal dragons, who were more akin to large, scaly horses, the True Dragons were said to be creatures capable of intelligent thought and speech. In some stories, they could also cast and use magic. In a few darker tellings, it was the True Dragons who brought about the cataclysm and the Undoing of the World. The one thing everyone *could* agree on, though, was that there were no True Dragons in the world anymore. And Remy didn't feel like standing around listening to Bart tell a story he'd heard a dozen times before.

The doors of the tavern swung open, and loud voices echoed into the room. A group of pirates lurched through, laughing and shoving at each other. Remy jumped, tensing to dart behind the chair and hide, until he saw that it wasn't the trio that had chased him that afternoon. Still, he took it as a sign that it was time to leave.

"I gotta go," he told Bart, stepping away from the chair. "See you later. Try not to lose your lucky rabbit again; I'd hate to have to do this a second time."

"Remy," Crusty Bart said, making him turn back. The old man paused, then, with a sigh, flipped him something that glittered in the light. Remy caught it with a grin: a single copper coin. Not much, but enough to buy food for the night. That was worth getting chased all over the Wedge by pirates.

"The True Dragons still exist," Bart said firmly, slipping the purse into a coat pocket. "No one believes it, but they are still here. You would do well to come back tomorrow and listen to the whole story."

"So I can drop coins that I don't have into your mug? I'll pass." Remy shook his head and turned away. Dragon stories wouldn't keep him from going hungry. "Even if I thought there were still True Dragons out there, so what?" he challenged. "They'll never come *here*, so why worry about it?"

Bart only grunted at that, and Remy slipped out of the tavern. The sun had fully set over the distant horizon, and a chill had crept into the air, smelling of mud and frost. Shoving his hands into the pockets of his ratty trousers, Remy headed for home.

Beggar's Row was a sector of Cutthroat Wedge that was as illustrious as it sounded: the poorest of the poor lived here, in shanties and huts stacked atop one another, balanced on stilts to keep them out of the wet. Rickety wooden bridges, stairs, and walkways spanned the narrow streets, and though the rotting planks hovered several feet above the ground, they were always covered in mud. As were all the residents who lived here.

Remy's "house" sat at the end of a ramshackle path, balanced precariously over a storm drain that emptied into a pool of stagnant water. He had grown up in this house, but after his mother's death three years ago, he'd expected someone to come and take it from him. But months, and then years, passed, and no one did. Perhaps no one wanted it. Perhaps no one cared. Remy didn't ask questions. The hut was small, flimsy, and a breath away from falling into the ditch below, but it was home to a penniless mud rat like him.

The shack creaked in the wind as Remy walked up, planks and boards groaning loudly. A tattered gray cloth hung in the doorway, as there was no actual door, and the windows had been boarded up to keep out the chill. Pushing the cloth aside, Remy stepped into the tiny, cramped room. A single chair sat beside a table that was missing a leg, and a moth-eaten blanket hung from a hammock in the corner. Remy needed to sleep elevated, as the floor would become soaked whenever it rained. Brutus, the large brown rat that shared the room with him, looked up from gnawing on a chair leg, twitched an ear, and went back to chewing the wood. Remy sighed.

Home sweet home.

Picking his way across the floor, Remy gently freed the chair from Brutus's incisors and sat down, pulling out a bundle he'd bought from Silas the food vendor on the way home. Opening it revealed a hard lump of bread and a pair of pigeon kabobs, which was what his single coin afforded him. The bird kabobs had been two for a single copper; Silas had thrown in the bread because he liked Remy. Unlike some of the other hungry residents who prowled Beggar's Row, Remy didn't steal from him.

Brutus the rat circled the table and sat up, whiskers trembling as he sniffed the air. Remy made a face at him.

"Nope, this isn't for you," he told the rodent. "You're not the one who got chased all over Cutthroat Wedge by pirates today. Find your own dinner for once."

The rat stared at him with large black eyes, and he sighed. "Fine. Just to stop you from chewing through my hammock ropes again." He tossed Brutus a crust, which the rat immediately snatched up before fleeing into one of the many holes in the wall. "You're welcome," Remy called after him. "And stop eating my chair."

The bread was as hard as a rock, and the pigeon kabobs were scrawny, with barely any meat on the bones, but it was food. Remy had eaten far worse. After chewing his way through the bread and sucking all the meat from one bird carcass, he wrapped the second pigeon kabob back in the greasy cloth and tucked it into his pocket for later. After all, he never knew when his next meal would be. Some days, you could steal from pirates and get away with it, but some days, luck was just not on your side. Remy knew Bart hated it when he stole things, but the old man didn't understand. No one was looking out for him; Remy had to take care of himself.

He sighed, remembering what Bart had said earlier that

evening. There was a time, a couple years ago, when dragons had fascinated him. When he would sit, wide-eyed, on the hard tavern floor, listening to every story Bart told about dragons. Remy would fantasize about stowing away on a pirate ship, or maybe joining a crew as a cabin boy and flying off to the capital, where sky knights soared on dragons and the rich held stunning aerial races to see which dragon was the swiftest. And maybe, just maybe, he would perform an act of great courage before the king, just like Sir Cloudwright, and be allowed to join the sky knights himself.

But that was before he became an orphan. Before his father departed on a ship and never came back, and his mother succumbed to some wasting sickness. His mom had always encouraged his love for dragons. When he told her his dreams of becoming a sky knight, she never told him it was impossible. When he regaled her with the stories he'd heard at the tavern, she always smiled and told him he would be a wonderful sky knight someday. After she died, Remy had been hit with the harsh reality: Mud rats like him didn't become sky knights. They didn't own dragons, and they didn't go on adventures. He never blamed her for building up his dreams only to have them brutally crushed by reality, but the day she died was when he stopped listening to Bart's dragon stories.

For a short time, he tried to leave Cutthroat Wedge, but he quickly found even that dream was out of reach. Life had been hard before, but it was harder still for an orphaned mud rat left with nothing. None of the ship crews wanted him; he was too frail, too small, too sickly. He wouldn't withstand the hardships of ship life, they claimed, so he was always passed over for stronger, hardier boys. It wasn't just Remy who wanted to see the capital. Everyone was trying to get off Cutthroat Wedge, and the sky ships were the only way to leave. Unfortunately, a pirate haven only attracted pirates and other cutthroats, who jeered at Remy at best and at worst took a swing at him with a fist or even a blade. Until one day, he stopped trying to become a pirate and started stealing from them instead.

Remy shook his head and rose from the chair. His bare feet landed with a muddy splat on the planks, highlighting his reality. Small-boy fantasies were just that: fantasies. His world was dirt and cold and hunger, scrounging for food and pocketing whatever coin he could get away with taking. Thieves and mud rats did not become sky knights. Crusty Bart's stories were the closest he would ever get to seeing a world of dragons.

Outside, a flicker of lightning lit up the sky for a moment, and a gust of wind rattled the boards over his windows, making him wince. Brutus poked his head out of one of his nooks, nose twitching as it sniffed the air.

"Storm's coming," Remy told him. "I sure hope those boards hold, or it's gonna be a really wet night."

Brutus flicked an ear and vanished back into his hole.

Remy bent down, picked up his single lantern, and hung it on a nail, then climbed into his hammock.

Pulling the tattered blanket over his head, he closed his eyes and listened to the rising wind outside the walls until it lulled him into a restless sleep.

In his dreams, he thought he heard something crying.

CHAPTER TWO

"Gemillia Sunwind Gallecia, why are you in my office again?"

Gem chewed her lip. She wanted to look down at her boots, at the floor, out the window, anywhere to avoid the exasperated glare of Headmistress Idella across the desk, but that wouldn't be proper for someone of her station. "Keep your head up," her father had told her numerous times. "Look the person you are speaking to in the eye. That will show that you have nothing to hide, and you will be able to tell if someone is lying to *you*."

Headmistress Idella raised a thin silver brow, half-moon spectacles flashing in the dim light of her office. She wasn't old, but like all storm mages, her hair, frizzy and unkempt, had turned pure white from decades of practicing magic. Gem's straight black hair was mostly untouched, except for a single silver streak growing from above her forehead. She wore it proudly, for it defined her, beyond all doubt, as someone who could wield the magic of the storm.

Unfortunately, that was part of the reason that she was here. Headmistress Idella was still watching her across the desk, waiting for an answer. Several excuses flitted through Gem's mind, but the echo of her father's voice shut them all out. "Always tell the truth," it said. "Even when it is painful. Honesty is vital if you want others to trust you."

She sighed. "I was practicing my magic, Headmistress. Outside of class hours."

"Gemillia." Headmistress Idella's painted blue nails tapped the surface of the desk. "We have already talked about this."

"Yes, ma'am. I know."

"You are a first-year student," the headmistress went on, as if Gem hadn't spoken. "Within these walls, your station and privilege are nonexistent. Your father has already informed me that you are to be instructed and treated like everyone else. Which means you are to abide by the same rules, and are subject to the same punishments, as the rest of the students. I am aware that you had private tutors before you came here, and that your grasp of magic is likely better than the others of your year. But the rules are there for a reason, Gemillia." Headmistress Idella was getting more and more agitated; the tiny crystals on her desk were starting to vibrate. "Storm magic is volatile and dangerous," she continued, pointing at Gem with a blue-tinted fingernail, "and first-year students practicing their magic without supervision is a recipe for disaster. The last thing I want is to have to send a letter to your father explaining some terrible accident or catastrophe because you believe you are above following the rules here!"

The shards on her desk trembled, then floated several inches off the surface of the wood. Gem could feel the energy in the room: like the air preceding a storm, heavy and charged with static. Headmistress Idella let out a sigh and snapped her fingers, dispelling the magic and the energy that had built up at her outburst. The crystals spun lazily in the air a moment longer, then drifted slowly back to the desk with soft plinks.

Gem swallowed. One of the second-year students had been taunting her that morning, claiming she was only there because of her father, that she had no real talent for magic. She had to prove him wrong, of course, but she knew she'd be breaking the rules to do it. As her father had told her: "The laws are there for a reason. Not even we can ignore them. If we do break the rules, we have to face the consequences like everyone else."

"I am ready to face the consequences of my decision, Headmistress," Gem said, raising her chin a bit. "But there is no clear, stated punishment for practicing magic outside of class hours. The rules only say 'up to and including expulsion.' Perhaps if I had a clearer idea of the consequences of breaking the stated rule, I could make more informed choices."

The headmistress pursed her lips. "You are your father's daughter, through and through," she muttered. "Very well. Here is your punishment, and further breaking of the rules will result in more of the same: I want a fifteen-page report on the history and dangers of uncontrolled magic and mages, from the Age of Chaos to the present day. And I want it on my desk by the beginning of next week."

"Fifteen pages?" Gem nearly choked.

Headmistress Idella smiled. "Oh, don't worry, there is plenty of information on the subject, enough to fill a whole library. And each time a rule is broken, the number of pages increases by five. Is that clear enough for you, *Miss* Gallecia?"

"Yes, ma'am," Gem said, a bit faintly.

"Excellent." Headmistress Idella leaned back in her chair, looking satisfied. "You may return to your dorm. Classes are over for the day, but I suggest you get started on that report. You have a lot of ground to cover."

Feeling a bit numb, Gem slipped out of the office into the hallway. The elegant blue-and-gold carpets, paneled walls, and large oil paintings of famous mages greeted her as she stepped through the door, still wincing over what she had to do.

A face peered around the corner at the end of the hall, a lanky boy her own age with short brown hair that had a spot of white in it, unfortunately in the exact center of his forehead. His name was Lutos, but some of the older students had started calling him Lighthouse, and the nickname stuck.

"Gem." Lighthouse waved at her, still from around the corner.

Gem rolled her eyes. "You can come closer, you know. The headmistress isn't going to pop out and eat you."

"Don't say that too loudly." Lighthouse sidled into the hall and walked up to her, keeping a wary eye on the door she had just come through. He was, understandably, terrified of the headmistress, but then again, most first-years were.

Gem was not.

"Did you get expelled?" Lighthouse asked, his eyes wide as he stared at her. "I told you just to ignore Petor. He's like that to everyone."

"No, I didn't get expelled." Gem snorted. "I just have to write a report on the dangers of uncontrolled magic. Not so bad. And Petor is a jerk. I would do it again if I had to."

"Wow." Lighthouse's voice was awed, and just the tiniest bit jealous. "Lucky you. I guess even Headmistress is scared of your dad."

Gem's irritation flared. No matter where she went, it seemed people only saw her as her father's daughter. Never her. Never just Gem.

"Regardless," she sighed, and started down the hall. "I need to go to the library to get books for this report. You don't have to come if you don't want to."

But Lighthouse shrugged and fell into step beside her. "I have nothing else to do anyway."

They walked down the long corridors of the College of Magic, passing other students, staff, and teachers in the halls. Most of the students were dressed like Gem and Lighthouse: in identical black trousers, leather boots, and dark blue tunics with billowy sleeves. Though you could easily tell what year they were by the amount of silver embroidery on their tunic. First-year uniforms were plain and unmarked, while fourth-year students had elegant swirling filigree lining their shoulders and trimming their sleeves. So the older you were, the fancier your uniform became. Gem rather liked her plain blue tunic; none of the teachers wore elaborate finery except Mage Opus, but he was over-the-top to begin with.

There were very few senior students in this part of the college; the third- and fourth-years had their own dorms on the other side of the yard, while the first- and second-years were lumped together in rooms off the main building. Gem would sometimes see flashes of light or bursts of energy from the senior side of the college, and she wondered if the older students had to follow the no-magic-outside-of-class rule.

"Hey, did you hear?" Lighthouse asked, pushing open the door of the building, wincing a moment as bright sunlight flooded in. "High Mage Alaric is leaving the college."

Gem frowned. High Mage Alaric was one of the central figures of the college, a tall mage with a hooked nose and white hair that stuck out in every direction. He was viewed as one of the most powerful figures in the college for his impressive control of storm energy. When a student reached the point where they were shooting strands of blue lightning from their fingers, you could be sure Alaric was their teacher.

"Why?" she asked.

Lighthouse shrugged. "I don't know. No one will say, but the third- and fourth-years are really unhappy about it."

Interesting. That was the second mage to leave the college in a single week. The first had been High Mage Elina, the Levitation teacher. Gem remembered the evening she left. Everyone had been in the dining hall, having dinner. The teachers and staff, of course, had their own table near the back of the room, and it had seemed like a perfectly normal end of the day.

Gem remembered seeing the doors open and a messenger slip into the room. She noticed him immediately because he wore the uniform of the royal couriers, and for a moment, she was afraid he had come for her. Perhaps her father had sent him. Perhaps he had changed his mind about her attending mage college and was ordering her home. But the messenger spotted the teachers' table and immediately started heading in that direction, much to Gem's relief.

High Mage Elina was sitting at one end of the table, her silver hair pulled into its normal bun. She looked confused when the messenger strode up and bowed, presenting a sealed envelope to her with both hands. Gem watched her face as she opened it, saw her eyes go wide behind her spectacles and the blood drain from her face. Without warning, High Mage Elina stood, causing all the teachers to blink up at her, and walked to the head of the table. Bending down, she whispered something into the ear of Headmistress Idella, who straightened and looked at her in alarm.

The two women rose and walked out of the dining hall, to the whispers and stares of students and teachers alike. That was the last time Gem saw High Mage Elina. The official announcement from the headmistress was that High Mage Elina had to return to her island for family reasons. But if that were true, why had a royal courier delivered the message? Such communications were only used by the king and the royal council for delivering news of the utmost importance. Something seemed a little fishy there, but Gem wasn't going to question it.

But now High Mage Alaric was leaving the college as well. Strange. But again, nothing she could do about it.

They had to leave the building to get to the library, which was across the yard, and the single largest structure in the whole college. It held the biggest collection of books, scrolls, texts, and tomes in the entire kingdom, and the mages were both extremely proud and protective of their stored compilation of knowledge. The library loomed over the grounds, three stories of ancient stone, brick, and mortar, the entrance guarded by two proud stone dragons whose wings made a sweeping arch over the steps. According to popular rumor, the statues actually depicted a pair of True Dragons, bigger, stronger, and far more intelligent than the beasts Gem was used to seeing. Though they were long extinct, it was said that the True Dragons were the ones who first taught magic to humans, in the days before the Shattering.

Gem loved dragons. Back home, her favorite thing to do was to ride on Cloud, her sweet white dragon with stunning blue eyes. Her father owned a huge stable of dragons, from even-tempered riding dragons like Cloud, to sleek but flighty racers as fast as the wind, to the fierce, armored, hard-to-handle battle dragons. Each dragon was different and special, and she loved getting to know all their quirks and temperaments. But gazing at the imposing statues looming over the library steps, she couldn't help but shiver. Maybe it was their size; they were at least three times bigger than the largest battle dragon she had seen, an actual representation, according to the plaque at the base of the platform. Or maybe it was their stern, unamused reptilian faces, gazing down at the puny mortals far below, that gave Gem the feeling that, had these two been alive, they would be severely unimpressed with any of them.

"So what's this report about again?" Lighthouse wondered as they climbed the steps and ducked into the cool, dim silence of the library. He kept his voice barely above a whisper; the librarians who prowled the aisles had ears like bats and could appear like a summoned demon should any shenanigans occur in their library. Their intuition was almost supernatural: Gem had accidentally dropped a heavy text onto the tiles once; before she could even pick up, she had found herself surrounded by three librarians, lips pursed as they scowled down at her.

Gem sighed. "The dangers of uncontrolled magic," she told Lighthouse, rolling her eyes. "I think Headmistress is really trying to prove a point."

Lighthouse nodded sympathetically. "Miss Hagda could find you books on the subject if you asked her," he said, referring to the ancient head librarian who sat behind the mahogany desk in the corner.

Gem winced and shook her head. "Hawkeye Hagda" always had her nose buried in a massive tome and usually ignored everything around her. But whenever Gem walked by the desk, she would peek up from the book, beady black eyes watching her, until Gem was out of sight.

"No, I'll find them myself. I have a general idea of where to look." Gem gazed around the enormous room of shelves and aisles and sighed. Her next few days were going to be spent here, it seemed. "What are you going to do?" she asked, turning back to Lighthouse.

He shrugged his thin shoulders. "There's a test in Ancient Dwarven History that I need to study for," he said, somewhat evasively.

Gem smirked. "You mean you're going to camp out in

the adventure novel aisle until the library closes," she said, "and hope the librarians don't kick you out."

"Shh! Don't say that too loud. They'll hear you." Lighthouse glanced around warily, then stepped back, clearing his throat. "I have to go study," he said, a bit louder than he had to. "Uh, you don't need any help, do you, Gem?"

"No." She shook her head and waved him off. "Get out of here. Have fun studying with Captain Madhammer and the Pirates of Tomorrow."

"The *Privateers* of Tomorrow," Lighthouse corrected. "You should really read the series sometime. Captain Madhammer doesn't just fight monsters all the time; he solves mysteries, too."

"A story about a pirate hero fighting evil mages and spell storm monstrosities, all for the good of the kingdom?" Gem rolled her eyes. "That really is a fantasy." Sky pirates existed, of course. Countless warnings had been issued about sailing too far from the capital and the ring of main islands surrounding it. The farther you got from the center of the kingdom, its laws, and the protection of its sky knights, the more dangerous the skies became. The Fringe, the lawless ring of islands farthest from the capital, was the territory of thieves, smugglers, and all manner of cutthroats. And none of them were out there fighting evil for the good of the kingdom. "Pirates are criminals, Lighthouse," Gem finished. "There are no real-life Captain Madhammers."

Lighthouse sniffed. "Well, I still like him," he said

stubbornly, turning away. "And it's better than dusty old textbooks. Have fun with your fifteen pages of research paper," he called over his shoulder. "I'm going to read something exciting."

She watched him hurry past the History aisle, take a sharp left toward Fiction and Adventure, and disappear from sight.

With a sigh, Gem turned and wandered toward the stairs. The Magic section of the library was the entire second floor; that seemed as good a place as any to find the research materials she needed.

An hour later, Gem sat at one of the long tables surrounded by three different books, the sound of her own pen scratching the paper grating in her ears. As expected, there were plenty of books that listed the dangers of uncontrolled magic, plenty of examples of mages who let their powers get away from them. Storm magic was, as all the books repeated over and over again, volatile, dangerous, and unpredictable, and the consequences of losing control were explicitly laid out. There had been several incidents where a mage had blasted a hole though the sky ship they were supposed to be controlling, and the vessel had gone down in flames. In the most extreme cases, the magic coursing through a mage's body had torn it apart, or had twisted it into something unrecognizable. Magic came from the Maelstrom, which in itself was the most chaotic, destructive force of nature in the world. To use it required the utmost skill and concentration.

Gem put down her pen and scrubbed a hand over her eyes. Though the titles and authors were different and used different words, all the books basically said the same thing. Uncontrolled magic, bad. Losing control of magic, very bad. Bad things happen when you lose control. If Headmistress Idella wanted to beat the lesson into her head with this assignment, she was doing a great job of it.

Turning the page, Gem continued reading. This book was titled *Joffrey's Accounts of Magical Mishaps, 1402–04*, and described magic-based accidents in gruesome detail. This one was an article about an infamous storm mage named Mordred who tried to send the entire crew of the ship he'd been controlling into the Maelstrom.

From Joffrey's Accounts of Magical Mishaps, *chapter seven, page 216*

It is unknown whether or not Storm Mage Mordred had already gone sky-mad when he decided to commandeer the merchant ship and send it plummeting toward the Maelstrom. Thankfully, he was stopped by his own apprentice, who regained control of the vessel and brought it safely out of the storm. When later asked why he would do such a thing, Mordred simply replied: "I saw an Ancient One in the Maelstrom."

Mordred's story was officially denounced by the college as the addled ramblings of a madman, though it was later discovered that his apprentice also claimed to have seen the Ancient within the Maelstrom. As of the time of these writings, neither claim has been taken seriously.

Gem blinked, sitting up a little straighter in her chair. An Ancient One? She had never heard that term before. What were the Ancient Ones? And why had they caused a powerful storm mage to go diving into the Maelstrom after them?

Quickly, she skimmed the rest of the tome for anything more about these Ancient Ones, or Ancients. But it seemed that single page held the only instance of it. Gem could find no more references to Ancients within the pages of the book. So, after putting it back, she started searching other books.

She found . . . nothing.

After another hour, with different tomes and texts open and scattered around the table, Gem was ready to bang her head on the desk in frustration. There was not one mention of Ancients in any of the books she had searched. She had dragged down the original book and checked the paragraph several times more, just to make sure she hadn't misread anything. She hadn't. The words "Ancient Ones" were right there, on page 216. But no matter how hard she looked, she couldn't find anything else about them.

"This is ridiculous," Gem muttered, slamming another book shut after it held no mentions of Ancients. "This is the

Great Library, the most complete source of knowledge in the kingdom. You're supposed to be able to find anything here."

She had to be missing something. Maybe information about the Ancient Ones wasn't in the Uncontrolled Magics section. Though she had no idea where else it could be.

But the head librarian might.

Gem drummed her fingers against the table in annoyance. She didn't like asking for help. "Fight your own battles," her father had always told her. "Don't rely on others to save you. Learn to save yourself."

But she wanted information on the Ancient Ones, and looking for it herself was getting her nowhere. With a sigh, she picked up *Joffrey's Accounts of Magical Mishaps, 1402–04*, tucked it under her arm, and went downstairs.

As she approached the large mahogany desk in the corner, she could see Head Librarian Hagda's eyes, already peering over a book at her. They continued to watch her suspiciously until she stopped at the edge of the desk.

"Gemillia Gallecia." Miss Hagda's voice was flat as she lowered the book, still not smiling. Gem had no idea why the head librarian didn't like her, but she wasn't going to let herself be scared off. "Is there something I can do for you?"

"Yes, Miss Hagda." Gem stood a little straighter, raising her chin. "I'm looking for information on the Ancients."

She couldn't be certain, but she thought she saw the librarian's thin lips tighten. "And where did you hear that term?" Miss Hagda questioned.

"From this book." Gem held up *Joffrey's Accounts of Magical Mishaps*. "Page 216. There was a paragraph that mentioned something called an Ancient One, but I can't find any more information about them."

"That book was misshelved," Miss Hagda snapped. Quicker than thought, she reached over the desk and plucked the tome from Gem's hands. "Students are not supposed to have access to this book," she said firmly, placing the book well out of Gem's reach. "It is from the restricted wing of the library."

"Restricted wing?" Gem didn't even know the library had a restricted wing. "Where is that?"

"Nowhere that should concern you, Miss Gallecia," the head librarian replied. "It is not a place for students."

"Why not?" Gem asked. "Isn't the library a place for learning? Why would knowledge on the Ancients be restricted? Who are they?"

"As I said, that information is not available for students," Miss Hagda insisted. "Return to your studies and put it from your mind, Miss Gallecia. You shouldn't . . ."

She trailed off, eyes going wide as she looked at something over Gem's shoulder. Blinking, Gem turned around, and her heart sank.

A man stood a few paces away, a gnarled whitewood staff in one hand, the blue storm crystal affixed to the top glittering in the dim light. He was bald, with a hooked nose and extremely bushy eyebrows that bristled like white caterpillars over his dark gray eyes. He wore simple blue robes, unembellished like the first-years' tunics, but no one in Gallecia would mistake him for a simple student. His station was unmistakable.

"A-Archmage Aetrius," Miss Hagda stammered behind Gem. "This is a surprise. We weren't expecting you." She paused as the leader of the kingdom's storm mages turned piercing gray eyes upon Gem. "I assume you are here for Miss Gallecia?"

Of course he would be. The archmage of the kingdom wouldn't be standing there, staring at her, if he were not. Gem sighed and took a few steps forward to face the ancient storm mage, the sinking feeling in her chest spreading to the rest of her body.

"Did my father send you?" she asked.

Archmage Aetrius gave a single, grave nod. "He did," he replied in a voice rustier than old nails. "And I am afraid we must leave immediately."

"Of course," Gem muttered. There was no fighting this summons. When her father called, you had to go. "Should I get my things?"

"It is already taken care of. There is a carriage waiting outside to return us both to the palace." Archmage Aetrius did not smile. A billowy sleeve lifted as he held out a withered hand. "Come, then, Princess. The king is waiting."

CHAPTER
THREE

A boom rattled the entire hut and jerked Remy awake. He bolted upright in his hammock, overbalanced, and flipped over, landing with a splat on the floor. Mud and cold water soaked his clothes, shocking him even more fully awake. Standing up, he gazed around, seeing blinding flashes of purple lighting the sky outside, making his blood chill.

A spell storm.

Normal storms were bad enough. Strong gusts of winds could blow ships off course and send floating chunks of rock careening into everything in their path. Lightning could damage homes, blast things apart, and set ship sails on fire. But a spell storm was catastrophically dangerous. Normally, the lands were safe from the Maelstrom raging below. But on rare occasions, a squall would flare up with screaming winds and sizzling lightning, sweeping across the islands for miles. This was called a spell storm, and everything in its path was at risk. Strange things would often fall from the sky or go hurtling through the air, everything from daggers to frogs to massive sky whales. Magical lightning could strike unexpectedly, with bizarre results, bringing trees to life, turning creatures inside out, or changing a house into a shambling, ravenous monster. Whenever a spell storm hit, the only thing you could do was seek shelter, preferably underground, to wait it out. And hope that everything was still there when it was over.

A flash of purple light lit up the room again, and another boom made the ground tremble. Remy rushed to one of the boarded-up windows and peered out, squinting and shielding his eyes against the constant flickering light. Through the slats, he could see the roiling sky above, the flickers of purple lightning crawling in the belly of the clouds. The dark edge of the storm was coming right for him, and his stomach clenched. If any of those lightning strands hit his tiny hovel, it would blow the house, and probably him, to pieces.

I have to get out of here!

Staggering from the window, he fled outside.

A vicious gust of wind nearly blew him off his feet as he rushed out, and drops of rain pelted him as he sprinted toward the edge of the pool of water at the storm drain.

Behind him, the sky flashed and pulsed with purple light, and thunder howled as the storm crept closer.

Suddenly, there was a roar, different from the sound of the storm, directly overhead.

Something flashed by in the clouds. Something big and dark, with a long tail trailing behind it. It was gone so quickly, Remy wasn't certain of what he'd seen, but a few seconds later, the clouds parted and a massive sky ship burst through the storm after it, making his heart seize up. The hull of the vessel was armored and enormous, and the painted image of a terrible, grinning, sharp-toothed fish made the ship itself look like some huge predator.

Remy knew this ship. If not by sight, then by reputation. It was called the *Windshark*, and it belonged to one of the most dangerous, infamous pirates in the Fringe. Probably in the whole kingdom. A man named Jhaeros, who was famous not just for his ruthlessness and cruelty, but also for the fact that he himself was a storm mage. Mages were common aboard sky ships, but they were usually belowdecks, powering the ship crystal that enabled it to fly. A ship either hired a storm mage for the journey or they had their own on hand at all times, but mages usually worked *for* ship captains as part of the crew. Jhaeros was an exception to this.

The sky ship continued on, soaring into a cloud bank and vanishing from sight. A moment later, though, a tremendous boom rocked the earth at Remy's feet, a red flare igniting the clouds near where the *Windshark* had passed.

Cannon fire? Remy gasped and stumbled forward, the echoes of the cannons ringing in his head. *What is it shooting at?*

A bucket went spinning by his face, barely missing him. The spell storm was nearly there. Remy lunged forward, stumbled, and fell to his hands and knees at the edge of the pool. Cold mud soaked his trousers and coated his arms as he pulled himself upright, panting and looking around. In the ominous flickering, he suddenly spotted the stone drainage pipe across the water. His feet sank into the mud, but he pushed his way through the reeds toward the distant safety of the pipe.

A cry made him pause. It sounded like something in pain. Remy stopped, gazing around as the wind tore at him, wondering if anyone else was out in the dangerous weather.

Something dark fluttered down from the sky, landing with a splash in the center of the pool, and Remy's heart jumped. The creature, whatever it was, let out a cry, weakly flapping its wings against the water. It was larger than any bird he had seen, more the size of a terrier or the big, scarred alley cats that prowled Beggar's Row looking for fights. The wings of this bird were also strange—smooth and almost... leathery?

Whatever it was, it was obviously hurt, and probably close to drowning if it couldn't fly. Remy splashed into the pond, pushing his way toward the distressed creature. For him, the water wasn't very deep, only coming up to his waist. But it was cold, and the mud sucked at his ankles, so it took him a few seconds to wade out to the center of the pond.

The large bird, or whatever it was, still struggled weakly to keep afloat as Remy reached it. Without thinking, he stretched out an arm, and the creature immediately latched on, digging into his skin with tiny talons. Remy sucked in a breath at the pain.

"Ow, ow! Hey, take it easy; you're okay now. Calm—"

The creature's head twisted up to look at him, and Remy was suddenly pinned by a pair of bright purple eyes.

It wasn't a bird staring at him. No bird had horns sweeping out from its skull. Or a reptilian muzzle with the tips of fangs poking out of its jaw. Or a pair of large, bat-like wings flaring from its back and shoulders.

This . . . was a dragon. Remy was holding a baby dragon.

Overhead, a blinding purple flash lit up the sky, and a boom of thunder caused ripples to shake the pond. Dragon or no, they couldn't stand here, staring at each other, with the storm about to break on top of them. Pulling the dragon to his chest, Remy cradled it gently as he sloshed through the water. The dragon clung to his shirt with tiny claws; he could feel its heart beating through its scales as it shook against him.

Remy scrambled into the pipe just as the skies opened up and the rain poured down in sheets. As the purple lightning flickered and the thunder roared, he sat down with his back to the wall and gazed at the creature in his arms.

A dragon. His eyes hadn't been playing tricks on him; it was a real dragon, curled up and shaking in his lap. It was dark, and with the eerie flickering light Remy couldn't tell what color the dragon's scales were, but it did have a silky white mane running from between its horns all the way to its spade-tipped tail.

A dragon was sitting in his lap. Remy wondered if he really was dreaming, after all.

A clap of thunder boomed overhead, reverberating through the pipe, and the dragon flinched, trying to burrow into him. "Ouch!" Remy exclaimed as those sharp talons dug into his skin. "Hey, calm down," he said, putting both hands on the dragon's side, feeling its heart fluttering like a bird's against his palms. "It's all right; we're safe here. The storm can't get to us, I promise."

He didn't know if the dragon could understand him, but it stopped trying to dig its way into his clothes. It craned its head around, peering back at him with glowing eyes the same color as the lightning overhead. Its jaws opened, showing a flash of tiny teeth, and it made a sound almost like a baby bird.

Remy let out a shaky breath. In that moment, with the dragon's luminescent purple eyes staring him right in the face, he would've done anything to protect it. Maybe because it was so tiny and defenseless. Or maybe because the dragon was an orphan like him, left with no parents and all alone in the world. He knew what that was like.

Carefully, he gathered the dragon in his arms, holding it close to his chest so his body heat could warm it up. The baby made another squeak, then tucked its nose into the crook of his elbow and wrapped its tail around itself. Leaning against the cold stone, Remy hunched his body over the dragon and felt the tiny creature relax.

"It's okay," he whispered. "I've got you."

The dragon shivered. Outside, the storm continued to rage across Cutthroat Wedge. Lightning flashed, wind howled, and rain beat against everything. Debris went hurling by the pipe's opening, spinning and tumbling with the storm, but inside, Remy felt safe with the dragon.

Storm. That would be a good name for him, all things considered.

Remy looked down at the dragon, its head buried in the crook of his arm. This wasn't *his* dragon, of course. Even hatchlings like this were far too valuable and expensive to just let go. Obviously, this was someone's baby from one of the dragon stables around the kingdom, though Remy had no idea how it had gotten this far by itself. He was a thief, but he knew better than to steal something as precious and expensive as a dragon. Egg smuggling was one of the most serious crimes you could commit, and those who tried selling dragons on the black market were immediately and violently put out of business.

He sighed, remembering one of Bart's stories about dragons and how the rich kept track of them. "Every dragon stable has their own unique tattoo," Bart had said. "When a dragon lays an egg, the tattoo is magically branded onto the egg. When the dragon hatches, the tattoo is already in place. That's why you can't just steal an egg to raise your own dragon. All someone has to do is lift up the right wing to see the brand, and you would be arrested for false ownership."

As much as Remy hated it, there was no way he could keep this dragon. He could *not* get attached. He could not be thinking of names, or where it would sleep. Having a dragon in his possession would cause *all* sorts of trouble; dragons weren't exactly subtle creatures that you could just hide away. Eventually, everyone would know about it.

No, the best thing to do was to take the baby dragon to the Salty Barrel in the morning, and have Ferus or Bart hand it over to the proper authorities. They would be able to track down its owner and return the dragon to where it belonged. That would be best, for both of them.

"Storm," he whispered. "That's what I'd call you, if you were mine."

The dragon curled its claws into his sleeve, buried its nose farther into his arm, and went to sleep. Sitting in the cold mud with his back to a stone pipe, Remy listened to the wind and rain hammering around them, and wondered if he would wake up from this dream.

⚡

Something was tugging at his hand.

Remy groaned, raising an arm to shoo it away. Brutus probably, crawling into his hammock again to nose around for scraps.

"No," he muttered. "Go 'way."

The tugging came again, followed by a squeak that didn't sound like a rat. More of a chirp, actually. That was weird. Had a bird gotten inside? Also, why was his hammock soaked?

Remy's eyes flew open, and he jerked up, bashing the back of his head on the stone pipe. Grimacing, he slumped forward, rubbing at his skull, as everything from the night before came flooding back.

He turned his head, looked down, and met the gaze of the baby dragon.

"Okay," he breathed as the hatchling gave a chirp and crawled into his lap again. "It wasn't a dream."

The dragon garbled something, turning in a circle and nosing his clothes. Now that the storm had moved on and the sun was shining again, Remy could see it clearly. The dragon's scales were a deep cobalt blue, its horns shiny black.

Bright silver markings like lightning strands crawled down its back and neck and crept over its wings, so it would look like a stormy sky when the wings were fully extended. Its white mane, now that it was dry, was fluffy and spiky at the same time, and its spade-tipped tail, like its sweeping wing tips, was tinged with purple.

It was an absolutely beautiful dragon. Even Remy, who had never seen one before, could tell that much. Certainly, whoever this dragon belonged to wanted it back.

Remy stared down at the dragon, still nosing around in his shirt. He already hated the thought of giving it up. But the longer he put it off, the harder it would be.

"All right, little . . . dragon," he muttered, and the hatchling immediately looked up at him with glowing purple eyes. Remy set his jaw and tried to ignore its cuteness. "Don't look at me like that," he told it, averting his eyes from its gaze. "Come on, I need to see who you belong to."

Gently, he hooked two fingers under the dragon's right wing and lifted it away from the body. According to Bart, the tattoo would be bright, easily visible, in the membrane of the wing. But Remy didn't see anything unusual, marking or otherwise. He lifted the wing higher, tilting it toward the light, to try to glimpse the dragon's tattoo, but all he could see were scales and the veined, slightly rosy membrane of the wing.

"Huh, guess it's on the other side," he muttered, and

the dragon cocked its head at the sound of his voice. "Sorry, dragon, I have to move your other wing now. Don't bite me."

He peeked under the left wing but couldn't see any markings there, either. Thinking that maybe Bart was wrong about tattoo placement, Remy checked the dragon's whole body: neck, back, head, underside, even its tail. The dragon made confused squeaking noises as he poked and prodded, even turning it on its back to look at its stomach, but it didn't nip or try to bite him. When he was done, Remy sat back, gazing down at the creature still in his lap.

The dragon had no tattoo.

He had checked every possible place for one, and there was no ownership tattoo anywhere on the dragon's body. Which meant—and Remy's heart beat faster at the thought—could this be a *wild* dragon?

Wild dragons, according to Bart, were like sky sirens and harbinger stags: myths that existed in old sailor tales. Every airship captain knew someone who claimed to have seen a glowing, ethereal stag bounding through the clouds in the distance or heard a faint melody drifting over the wind. And every sailor was terrified of Tendril, the great monster that lived in the Maelstrom itself. It was a myth, of course, but every so often, a story would emerge of a huge black tentacle reaching up through the clouds, curling around a ship, and dragging it back into the Maelstrom. Whenever a ship vanished or went missing out in the great unknown, the hushed whispers would say it was Tendril, claiming another vessel for its own.

Wild dragons were extinct; everyone knew this. But, like the harbinger stag and the sky sirens, sailors would boast that they had seen a glimpse of one, flying through the clouds or perched on a tiny piece of rock in the middle of the sky.

The dragon's impatient chirp brought Remy out of his musings. Blinking, he gazed down at the creature, now tugging at his shirt in a more aggressive manner. It shoved its muzzle into the pocket that held the food package from the night before, and Remy winced at his own cluelessness.

"Oh, you're hungry, aren't you?" he muttered as the dragon continued to root around in his clothes. One sharp little claw caught on his skin, and he flinched. "Ouch! Okay, hang on, hang on." He picked the dragon up, holding it at arm's length, and it immediately stopped burrowing to gaze up at him expectantly. Its wings flared out, silvery lightning bolt markings almost seeming to glow in the dimness of the pipe. Remy's breath caught again at how striking it was.

If this dragon had no tattoo, if it was really a wild hatchling, could he . . . keep it? No one would be looking for it. None of the dragon stables would notice one of their hatchlings was missing. No dragon bounty hunters would be called after him. The only problem would be keeping it hidden from the other residents of Cutthroat Wedge.

But if . . . if he could keep it hidden long enough, once it grew up a bit, Remy could finally leave the island and fly away to wherever he wished. Maybe he would even go as far as the capital, away from the Fringe and his tiny hovel, to a new life in the city.

Once *it* grew up a bit? Remy paused, realizing he had never thought whether this could be a male or female baby dragon. However, gazing into the dragon's face, he suddenly knew. The hatchling was a male dragon, and his name was . . .

"Storm," Remy whispered.

The dragon cocked his head, blinking, then opened his jaws and let out a strident squawk.

"Right, you're still hungry," Remy said. "Come on, let's go back inside, and I'll get you something to eat."

The pigeon kabob he'd tucked away was cold, and grease had congealed over the meat, turning it into a slimy mess. Remy unwrapped the slightly unappetizing lump and offered it to the dragon. He didn't know what dragons ate, if Storm would want cooked, extremely greasy meat, but the dragon snatched up the bird and started bolting it down, bones and all, narrow jaws working frantically as he chewed.

As Remy sat back and watched the hatchling tear through the meat chunks, Brutus poked his head out of the wall, nose twitching. Smelling the meat, the rat crept toward the carcass, only to have Storm immediately cover it with a claw and emit a tiny growl, causing the rat to squeak and puff up with indignation.

Remy chuckled. "I wouldn't pick that fight," he told the rat, tossing him a bread crumb he'd found in his pocket. "He's only going to get bigger."

Brutus paused, seeming to weigh the free bread against the meat he would have to fight for, then snatched up the crumb and vanished back into his hole. Remy leaned on the wall, frowning slightly as Storm finished the last of the pigeon. How fast *did* dragons grow? Storm was little and easy to hide now, but according to Bart, adult dragons were as big as horses and twice as long. The hatchling wouldn't be able to fit in this hovel if he grew that large.

Also, how was Remy going to feed it? Some days it was hard enough finding food for himself, much less a hungry baby dragon. Was it okay to give it cooked meat, or did it need something . . . fresher? Was the rodent and feline population of Beggar's Row going to be in danger once Storm grew big enough to hunt?

Were normal people going to be in danger if there was a dragon living right next door?

Remy winced. Despite all the stories he had heard over the years, mostly from Bart, he really didn't know that much about dragons. Or at least, not enough to raise and care for one as a baby. If Remy wanted answers to the million or so questions running through his head, he was going to have to talk to someone who knew dragons better than he did.

Storm finished the last of the pigeon kabob. He gave a tiny yawn that showed a flash of needle teeth, then crawled across the floor into Remy's lap. Curling up like a cat, he tucked his nose under his wing, closed his eyes, and started to snore. Remy waited a few minutes, until Storm's tail began to twitch in his dreams, then slid his arms under the dragon, walked across the room, and placed him gently in the hammock. For a moment, he held his breath as he pulled away, waiting to see if Storm would wake. But the hatchling seemed dead to the world, warm and with a belly full of food. He didn't even stop snoring.

Remy tiptoed across the floor, avoiding the squeaky planks, and paused in the doorway. A dragon, *his* dragon, slept peacefully in his hammock. If Remy could somehow keep him safe, and hidden, they could both someday leave this place and not look back.

But first, he had to know what the heck he was doing.

He ducked out the door and started to sprint.

CHAPTER FOUR

"The island crystals are failing."

Princess Gemillia Sunwind Gallecia heard the gasp that went around the council chamber, as every noble, councillor, chancellor, and politician reacted the way anyone would when hearing such news: with horror, disbelief, and genuine fear. She herself felt an icy shiver run up her spine and was only able to keep a serene expression on her face because Aetrius had told her the terrible news in the carriage. Even then, she couldn't break down. A princess had to remain calm and composed, even in the face of utter disaster.

Even when hearing that the literal end of the world could be nigh.

In the center of the chamber, Archmage Aetrius stared around, eyeing the two dozen people in the seats surrounding him. Gem was seated next to the largest chair in the room, the throne upon which her father, King Gallus Gallecia XIV, sat with his fingers laced beneath his chin. His black hair and piercing iron-gray eyes made him seem intimidating to most, but though he rarely smiled, Gem had never seen him lose his temper. The king of Gallecia remained in complete, icy control of himself at all times.

"Archmage," King Gallus said into the stunned silence, "please explain what that means in detail for the rest of the council. I'm afraid that most of us are not as versed in the storm crystals as you."

"Of course, Your Majesty." The archmage gave a small bow before turning to the rest of the chamber. For a moment, he looked annoyed, as if he were speaking to a crowd of unruly toddlers. "The islands," he stated in a clear yet rusty voice, "are sinking. By an approximated three to five inches a year. That may not sound like much, yet even if there is no accelerated decay, the lowest islands could drop dangerously close to the Maelstrom in as little as ten years. But the real danger is that the crystals that keep this island afloat are giving out."

He raised a hand, the shard of a bright purple-blue crystal held between two sticklike fingers. A tiny fragment of a much larger whole. Gemillia hadn't seen the great storm crystals at the heart of the island, but she had been told they were the size of airships. Light flickered and glowed within the shard, sputtering like a candle flame. "Every island," the mage began, moving the fragment he held slowly through the air, "from the capital to those in the farthest reaches of the Fringe, is kept aloft by storm crystals. These crystals are ancient, enormous, and have worked on their own for centuries.

"But now the crystals are going dark," Aetrius went on, holding the shard even higher. "The magic stored within is fading. And if they continue to fail, we won't have to worry about a slow drift into the Maelstrom. Once the crystals are gone . . ." He opened his fingers, and the shard immediately fell to the marble floor, shattering at his feet.

The effect was devastating and instantaneous. Council members were on their feet, shouting, protesting, asking a dozen questions at once. Gem sat in her chair, gazing at the glittering shards on the floor, feeling a cold fist slowly squeezing her insides.

"Enough."

Her father rose, and as usual, his imposing presence was enough to quiet even the most disorderly room. The shouting quieted, questions fading away, as the king gazed around the chamber, his steely eyes demanding silence without a word being said. "Obviously, we will find an answer," King Gallus told the room. "This is, of course, the highest priority now. We will not let this kingdom sink into the Maelstrom. Archmage Aetrius," he continued, turning to the storm mage in the center, "what can we do to stop, or perhaps slow, the degrading of the crystals?"

"The College of Mages has been looking into it," Aetrius replied. "We haven't been able to discern much, but what we know is this. The magic stored in the crystals is either leaking or simply failing as a result of age and time. We have long believed that the crystals are charged and recharged by the Maelstrom itself, but over the course of two thousand years, the crystals are simply getting old."

"Replace the crystals, then," someone called. A small man with curly blond hair and a soft face, he was the youngest person in the room save for Gem herself. The archmage turned and gave the council member a scathing look.

"Replace them?" Aetrius's voice was flat. "Do you know how large the crystals are that keep this island afloat, Councillor Wick?" he asked the young council member. "Do you know how many storm crystals lie at the heart of not only the capital island, but all the islands in the kingdom? Where would we find more crystals? Where would we take them from? The other islands? So *they* might fall into the Maelstrom sooner?"

"There must be an excess of crystals somewhere—"

"There is not," King Gallus said, his voice hard. "And even if there were, I am not willing to risk the lives of everyone on any one island by taking their storm crystals. There is no way to get more; we must make do with what we have."

"There is, however, a temporary solution," Aetrius went on, gazing around the room. "I assume everyone here knows how sky ships work?"

There was an awkward pause, and Gem bit her lip to keep a snort contained. That would not be fitting for a princess. But she guessed no one on the council knew anything about sky ships except how to ride in one.

"Sky ships are powered by storm energy, much like the island crystals," Aetrius continued. "They also use storm crystals, albeit much smaller, weaker ones, to keep the airships afloat. However, to fly the vessel through the air requires a storm mage to power the crystal. This is why nearly all sky ships have at least one storm mage as part of the crew; without a mage, the ship must rely on the wind currents to get where they are going."

"I don't understand," another council member said. "Why does a sky ship have anything to do with the island's storm crystals?"

"Because, Councillor," Aetrius snapped, his patience completely gone now, "if storm mages can power a sky ship, it stands to reason that they can do the same for the failing storm crystals. Not permanently, of course. But enough to keep them charged while we search for another solution."

"Which brings us to the reason for this council meeting," King Gallus said, gazing around. "Aetrius has spoken to the senior mages at the college, and they have all agreed to what must be done. The College of Magic will temporarily be shut down, and all available storm mages will be summoned to power the crystals."

Gem sat straight up in her chair as several council members began talking at once. Shut down the college? That meant there would be no more magic classes. What would happen to all the students? What would happen to the mages in training? If all the storm mages were being called to power the crystals, they would have to figure out a solution before the college could open again.

"I know this is a drastic measure," King Gallus said as the fervor died down a bit. "And it is one I would not consider if I did not think it was absolutely necessary. I am not shutting down the college to send the senior staff on vacation. I am shutting down the college to buy us time. We must figure out how to preserve and save the crystals, before it is too late."

"How large are these crystals?" asked another council member. "How many mages are we talking about?"

"Too many," Aetrius sighed, sounding tired. "Already, my senior mages have exhausted most of their energy trying to keep the crystals charged, and it has not made even a dent in the magic that is needed. The crystals continue to fail. I am afraid that if I continue pushing the mages beyond the limits of their strength, some of them will start to burn out."

"And what does that mean, exactly?" asked a portly council member. "Will they simply lose their magic for a time? Or forever? A small price to pay to keep the capital afloat."

"No, Council Member. It means they could expend so much of themselves and their magic trying to keep the crystals charged, they could literally be torn apart and die," Aetrius said in a deathly flat voice. "Storm magic is of the Maelstrom; it is volatile and unpredictable. Learning to harness it safely can take years, but even so, if the mage is tired, or expends too much, they can lose control of the magic. You don't see it happen often in the capital because we at the college emphasize caution and self-control over all else, but when a mage loses control and the magic goes wild, it can have catastrophic consequences."

"Which is why we need to start pulling mages from other areas," King Gallus said into the somber silence that followed. "The college cannot be solely responsible for such a monumental task. Other storm mages must be willing to step in. For our survival.

"Tomorrow, I will make this decree," King Gallus went on, making Gem's stomach turn anxiously. Her father didn't make decrees often, and when he did, it was always for the good of the kingdom, but it still made her slightly nervous every time. "By order of the crown, all available storm mages must stop what they are doing and return to the college, where they will be given an undisclosed task."

"Undisclosed?" The young council member Wick looked confused. "That seems very deceptive. Am I to understand that we are not going to tell anyone about the state of the kingdom?"

"Of course not, Councillor!" Aetrius shook his head in utter disbelief. "This must not get out to the citizens. If it becomes known that the islands are sinking, there will be kingdom-wide panic! I will be at the college to personally explain the situation to the mages, and they will be furtively escorted to the heart of the city to lend their magic to power the storm crystals. But we must not, under any circumstances, let this information become public. The chaos and panic it would cause would be catastrophic."

"What about the other islands?" asked a council member, a steely-haired older woman who had been silent until this point. Her name was Beatrice, and she had been on the council as long as Gem could remember. "Their crystals could also be failing."

King Gallus nodded. "I have sent word to the dukes and governors of each island," he replied. "I have warned them of the need for secrecy, but they will each have to be responsible for collecting the storm mages needed to power their island's crystals."

The portly council member blew out a gusty breath. "This is going to affect . . . everything," he muttered. "The kingdom's sky ships cannot run without storm mages. This will ground countless ships, ships that import and export supplies across all of Gallecia. Citizens will be unable to travel between islands. Countless sailors will lose their jobs. The maritime industries will suffer a huge blow. If you proceed with this plan, the kingdom might never recover."

"I am well aware, Flauvius." Her father now sounded tired, and Gem clenched her fists in her lap. "I know what this will do to Gallecia. Aetrius and I have debated and argued and discussed possible solutions for days. Were there another way, I would take it." His voice hardened once more. "But this is not a minor catastrophe. The storm crystals that keep this kingdom alive are failing. The islands are sinking into the Maelstrom. I am not thinking of fishing as much as the millions of lives that will be lost should the worst happen. Imagine what would happen should any of the islands fall. It would be . . ." King Gallus shook his head. "Absolutely devastating."

Councilor Beatrice raised her head. For a moment, she seemed hesitant to say anything, but she then continued in a firm, calm voice. "What about the Ancient Ones?" she said quietly.

Gem's stomach clenched. A gasp nearly escaped her lips, and she bit her lip to keep it down.

"What about them?" Aetrius said in a flat voice. He did not, Gem noted, immediately scoff at the idea of the Ancient Ones. Which meant that everyone at the council knew or believed that the Ancient Ones, whoever or whatever they were, were real. That they weren't just the addled ramblings of pirates and madmen.

Councilor Beatrice frowned at the mage's deliberate ignorance. "The Ancient Ones have knowledge of the world's magic," she said patiently. "They were around before the world broke apart. They were there when the crystals were formed. If anyone knows how to restore the storm crystals, it would be them."

"The Ancient Ones are lost," Aetrius said. "How do you expect to reach them? No one knows where they are. No one has seen an Ancient in hundreds of years."

"I am aware of that, Archmage," Beatrice said calmly. "But I thought that, given the dire circumstances, exploring all possible solutions would be a prudent idea. The Ancients are wise, powerful, and supposedly immortal. Seeking their help seems like a logical decision. We could at least *try* to find them."

"No," said King Gallus.

Surprised, Gem glanced at him. The king's tone was final, and she wondered why. If the Ancients were as knowledgeable and as powerful as Beatrice seemed to think, why would he refuse to even try? "Thank you for your opinion, Beatrice," her father went on, "but we cannot waste resources looking for the Ancients when there are things we can do right now." He put both hands on the table, gazing sternly around the room. "This issue is not up for debate, council members. We must shut down the college and pull every available certified mage to help power the crystals. We don't know how much time we have, but from here on, every second is vital."

Aetrius tapped his staff against the floor. "Well put, my king," he said. "I will return to the college to prepare for the arrival of the storm mages. Let us hope most answer the call and come quickly; as you said, we don't know how much time we have."

Turning stiffly, the archmage shuffled away, his staff tapping against the marble tiles, and the guards pulled the chamber doors open for him. Gem glanced at her father and saw him briefly press a hand to his face, and her throat tightened, wishing she could say something.

"Your Majesty," Flauvius ventured as the doors swung shut. "What shall the rest of us do in this time of crisis?"

King Gallus dropped his hand. Glancing over the council, his jaw tightened, as if he were seeing them there was suddenly annoying. "Nothing for now," he said. "Return to your estates. Remember, no one outside this room is to know anything. If I wake to panic in the streets tomorrow morning, all of you will know what the inside of a jail cell looks like."

"But, sire—"

"Council is dismissed."

They were not happy. Lips thinned, backs straightened, and nostrils flared, but one by one they turned and filed out of the council chamber. Gem watched until the final member left, the door swinging shut behind them, then turned to look at her father.

He sat in his chair with his fingers laced together and pressed into his forehead. "That went about as well as expected," he grumbled, not looking up. "Still, I suppose I cannot blame them. Their entire lives are tied up in politics and kingdom affairs, commerce and industry, trade, making money. They cannot fathom what a true disaster would be like."

He glanced up, and a tired smile crossed his face as his gaze settled on his daughter. "Gemillia," he greeted her. "I am happy to see you, though this is probably not the welcome home you were expecting." He sighed again and rose, grimacing as he stretched. "I am sorry I had to call you back, daughter," he said. "But the princess and future queen should know the state of the kingdom, even the frightening parts, and you have always been pragmatic. I trust you will not mention any of what was discussed to those outside this room."

"I understand." Gem swallowed and pushed back her chair. Her hands were shaking, but she clenched her fists to hide it. Her father would not want to see any fear. He had always insisted that she act as a princess should. With wisdom and logic and sensibility, the traits of a leader and future queen. She had never known her mother; the queen had died shortly after she was born, and the king never spoke of her. Gem had heard from several people that she looked just like her mother. Perhaps that was the reason her father kept her at a distance. Perhaps remembering the queen was painful for him.

Gem knew her father was grooming her to become the queen; as heir to the throne, she knew it was expected of her. But there were times when she wished he would stop being the king, if only for a moment, and just be a father.

But today was not that day.

"If the college has to be shut down," she said, trying to keep her voice from trembling, "then the situation is worse than you and the archmage are letting on."

The king raised an eyebrow. "And what makes you say that?"

"There are hundreds of students who attend the college," Gem went on, "most of them from noble and wealthy families. They will have to be sent home, with an explanation that their families will not only accept, but also believe. Shutting down the college will have a severe impact on the kingdom as a whole. People will wonder why. Nobles will demand answers. It is not a decision that could be made lightly. So, for the college to be shut down, the situation must be very dire."

King Gallus shook his head. "Sometimes I wonder if I have taught you too well," he murmured.

"Are we really in that much danger?" Gem asked, ignoring the previous statement. Her father wouldn't meet her gaze, and she swallowed. "How long do we actually have before the crystals fail?"

"We don't know exactly," King Gallus said. "But not long. In fact . . ." He paused, as if debating whether or not to say anything, then sighed. "Aetrius believes we might start to see the crystals fail completely within a year or two."

"A year?" Gem felt sick. One year until the kingdom could literally fall out of the sky, dooming everyone who lived there. One year until the islands and every living creature on them was consumed by the Maelstrom. "Why is this happening?" she whispered. "The storm crystals have existed for centuries. Why are they failing now?"

"I wish I knew." For just a moment, the king's impenetrable stoicism seemed to waver, but then he shook his head and returned to his usual confidence. "Regardless, you will say nothing of this to anyone, Gemillia. I don't need to explain what would happen if word of this situation became public. You may discuss it with Archmage Aetrius and with me. No one else, do you understand?"

Gem nodded. Not that she would be talking to Aetrius about anything. The archmage thought she was a spoiled child whose father told her too much, but the king had always listened to her. And there was one part of the council meeting that she didn't understand.

"I read something about the Ancients today," she said, watching her father closely for his reaction. One brow arched, but that was it. He could be no more than slightly annoyed or absolutely furious with her, and she'd never know. "Father, Councilor Beatrice made a good point. If there is a chance that the Ancients could know something about the crystals, wouldn't it be worth seeking them out?"

"I see someone has been reading things she is not supposed to," King Gallus said with a wry smile. "But you don't know everything about the Ancients, or their history with the kingdom. There are complications surrounding the

Ancient Ones that only a few people are aware of. When you become queen, you will understand. But seeking help from the Ancients is out of the question."

"But if it could save the kingdom . . ."

"I said no," King Gallus said shortly. "That is my decision, and I will not be changing it. Put them out of your mind, Gemillia."

Gem knew that when her father switched to that tone of voice, there was no use in pressing him any further.

But she did not put them out of her mind.

CHAPTER
FIVE

The Salty Barrel was crowded tonight. Passing the airship docks on his way in, Remy saw several sky ships tethered to the piers. Many of their sails were in tatters, and a few had gaping holes taken out of their sides. Apparently, the spell storm from the night before had done some damage.

Remy ducked into the tavern and searched for Crusty Bart, finding him in his usual corner. Tonight, however, he was surrounded by sailors, and his usually thin, reedy voice rose above the crowd, his hands moving as he enacted a fierce battle between the sky knights and a cabal of rogue mages who had stolen a warship. This was one of his more popular stories because, although most pirates hated the sky knights and the authority they represented, this particular tale had lots of fighting and death and explosions, which pirates enjoyed. Bart's mug sat on the edge of the table, but it was still half-full, which meant Remy had a little time before Bart started asking for money to continue.

Slipping into the crowd, Remy made his way to the front.

"The leader of the mages stood atop the deck, lightning flashing from his hands as he tried to shoot down the swooping dragons. But Sir Hector soared over the railings on his fierce dragon Fury, and Fury ignored the streaking lightning as he pounced upon the rogue mage with a roar—"

"Did it eat him?" Remy asked loudly.

"I . . . What?" Blinking, Bart's hands faltered in mid swoop, and he glanced over at Remy with a frown.

"The dragon," Remy went on. "Did it eat the storm mage?"

"No, of course not," Bart exclaimed. "Dragons don't eat people. Or at least, domestic dragons don't. They're kept very well fed, so they never go hungry."

"So what do they eat?" Remy asked, stopping Bart from launching back into the tale.

"Meat," Bart said shortly. "Dragons are predators, after all. Do you think those fangs and claws are for show? They eat meat: sheep and pigs if they're part of a fancy stable. Though some of the smaller stables feed their dragons fish or poultry, if they don't have a ready supply of mutton." He snorted. "There are even stories of greedy nobles feeding their dragons rats to cut back on cost. Dragons aren't picky. They can eat almost anything, as long as it's meat."

Remy nodded, his mind already spinning. "They must eat a lot, then," he said as Bart opened his mouth to return to the story. "How often do you have to feed a dragon?"

Bart gave him an exasperated look. "It depends," he replied, and he picked up his mug, pausing to take a long sip.

Some of the sailors started to mutter, impatient with the delay in the story, and Remy hurried on. "It depends? On what?"

"Lots of things!" Bart plunked his mug back down and glared at him. "How old is the dragon?" he asked. "How often are you flying them? Adult dragons can store energy in their bodies, much like large lizards or snakes. If you feed them a large meal, they won't need to eat again for several days unless you take them flying. Flying takes a lot of energy, as does breathing fire, and the dragon will have to feed again soon after. Also, hatchling dragons eat a lot more often than adults; you have to feed a hatchling every day for it to grow."

Remy's heart sank at these words. How was he going to feed Storm every day? He barely scraped enough together to feed himself.

Bart was staring at him intently now, his rheumy eyes both exasperated and suspicious. "Here now, what is this?" he asked. "You haven't been interested in any of my tales in years, boy. Why the change of heart?"

"Oh, um . . ." Quickly, Remy racked his brain to come up with an excuse for his sudden interest in dragons, but at that moment, the doors of the tavern flew open with a bang.

Remy jumped. Everyone turned, looking up from their tankards, as a cold, rain-laced wind blew into the room. Remy glanced at the door and felt a chill trace his spine like a finger of ice.

A man stepped into the tavern, his knee-high boots knocking loudly against the wood. He was lean and tan and dressed entirely in black, the edges of his coat tattered as if torn by the wind. His long hair, unbound and wild, was a bright, shocking silver, which only meant one thing. This wasn't just a pirate; this was a rogue mage. And a rather famous one, at that.

Jhaeros, captain of the *Windshark*, the huge, armored warship Remy had seen last night, stepped into the room.

"Good evening." The mage's deep, amused voice carried into the room as he sauntered forward. Two rough-looking men, obviously bodyguards, followed him, but he was the only figure that mattered. "I hope I'm not interrupting anything."

Heart pounding, Remy melted back into the corner, watching the mage approach. Jhaeros observed the room coolly, a faint smirk on his face as he scanned the crowd. Pirates averted their gazes as he swept past. According to the stories, Jhaeros was responsible for sending dozens of sky ships plunging into the Maelstrom. The *Windshark* was fast, armored, and aggressive, but it was the mage captain himself who was the more dangerous. Sailors claimed he could blast lightning from his hands, turn the winds against you, and summon tornadoes to tear sails into rags. He prowled the edges of the Fringe like a predator, seeking any ships with weaknesses, but this was the first time Remy had seen him in the Salty Barrel.

"As you were," Captain Jhaeros said, waving a hand as he crossed the room. Pirates and sailors watched him intently, their expressions tight with fear. Behind the bar, Ferus was frozen, face pale as the rogue mage sauntered past.

Coming to a halt in front of Crusty Bart's table, Jhaeros smiled down at him. "Don't stop on my account," he told Bart. "Please, continue your fascinating tale. You *are* the one who knows everything about dragons, is that correct?"

Bart gazed up at the rogue mage. Watching him from the corner of the room, Remy was amazed to see a flash of anger cross the old man's face before it smoothed out again. "I'm a storyteller," Bart said calmly. "I tell stories about dragons, sky knights, airships, and mages. Doesn't mean I know anything about them."

"Oh, that's a shame," Jhaeros replied, still smiling. "Because I also heard a rumor that you were heavily involved with dragons once. Isn't that right, Bartello?"

Bartello? Remy frowned. He'd never heard the old man called anything but Crusty Bart. Of course, Bart had been around since before Remy was born; he had always been a gruff, antisocial old man who told stories in exchange for drink. No one had ever thought of him as anything else.

Bart's face tightened, but then he gave a raspy chuckle and shrugged. "That was a long time ago," he told Jhaeros, waving a wrinkled hand like it was no big deal. "Honestly, I don't remember much of it at all. Drink'll do that to you." He tapped the side of his head with a grin. "I can barely remember what I had for lunch yesterday."

"I'm sure." The rogue mage did not sound convinced. "Well, perhaps this will jog your memory." Turning, he gazed around the rest of the room and raised his voice. "I'm looking for a dragon," he said loudly, making Remy's stomach clench. "A small one, barely larger than a cat. The stupid creature escaped its cage last night and got caught in the storm, which blew it here. I would very much like it returned. And if you think finding and selling this dragon anywhere else will make you rich, let me assure you . . ."

He snapped his fingers, and one of his bodyguards heaved a small chest onto Bart's table with a clunk. His mug toppled and fell to the ground, smashing into pieces, but no one except Bart seemed to notice. Jhaeros pushed back the lid, revealing a glittering heap of gold coins, jewelry, and gems that caught the light and threw spots of color over the ceiling. Every eye in the room bulged at the amount of wealth suddenly on display.

"This is just a portion of what I can offer for the dragon's safe return," Jhaeros said into the stunned silence. "Whatever you think this dragon is worth, I can top it. You won't get a better deal than what I am offering, trust me." He closed the lid with a squeak, hiding the vast fortune from view. Those in the room took a collective breath as a bodyguard picked up the chest and tucked it beneath one muscular arm. "Oh, and one more thing," Jhaeros said, reaching into his long black coat with a smile. "Just in case anyone has any thoughts of taking my dragon for themselves, this is what happened to the *last* person who tried to steal from me."

He held up his hand, and a grinning skull perched on the tips of his fingers, making Remy's blood chill. "Poor lad," Jhaeros said, a mock frown on his face as he observed the skull. "He might be smiling now, but he certainly wasn't happy a few days past. He did have a very nice screaming voice, though."

Blue strands of lightning flickered between the mage's fingers, and the skull suddenly turned black before dissolving into ash in his palm. Remy bit his lip, and he shrank farther into the corner as the rest of the patrons let out shouts and cries of alarm.

Jhaeros dropped his arm, letting the ash drift to the floor, and dusted off his hands. "Well, I think we've made our point here," he told his bodyguards, then glanced up at the room. "Find my dragon," he said loudly. "Deliver it to me and become rich. Steal from me and become dead. Your choice. If you find the creature, or even see it, let me know immediately. I will be on my ship, the *Windshark*, until my dragon is safely returned." He smiled, then offered a small bow as he stepped back. "I wish you all a good day, and good hunting. I'll be waiting."

He strode from the tavern, boots thumping against the floor, his two bodyguards following him out like trained dogs, and the door creaked shut behind them.

Remy pushed himself out of the corner. His heart was pounding as the room exploded with noise and excitement. Pirates were grabbing their belongings, tossing money on the table to pay for their drinks, and rushing out the door. Everyone wanted to go searching for the dragon.

The baby dragon in Remy's shack.

I have to hide Storm!

Ducking pirates, Remy hurried across the room. Something jostled him as he passed a table, a bony elbow slamming into his chest, knocking him off his feet. He fell on his backside with a grunt, and a lanky pirate with a skull tattoo on his neck glared down at him.

"Stay out of this, rat," the pirate said, pointing a thin dagger in Remy's face. "This has nothing to do with you, so you just keep out of our way, got it? I catch you snooping around after a dragon, I'll throw your pathetic carcass into the Maelstrom."

Remy skittered backward, and the pirate immediately lost interest, preoccupied with starting the search. The tavern was already nearly empty, with pirates scrambling over each other to get to the door, jostling and shoving each other out of the way. Only Bart sat at his table, hands folded beneath his chin, watching the chaos unfold around him. His normally rheumy, cloudy gaze suddenly fixed on Remy and his eyes narrowed to dark slits. But Remy couldn't think about Crusty Bart right now; he had to get to Storm before the pirates found him.

Leaping to his feet, he dodged two more pirates, slipped out the door, and ran for home.

It took him longer than normal to get back to his hut. Word spread like wildfire through Cutthroat Wedge, and soon the streets were full of people searching for the dragon. Thankfully, Cutthroat Wedge was such a tangle of winding streets, structures piled on top of each other, and jumbled, mazelike neighborhoods, a baby dragon could be hiding anywhere within the nooks and crannies. Remy just hoped they hadn't yet searched a tiny, rickety shack above a stagnant pond.

The hut was quiet when Remy got there, no pirates or fellow thieves snooping around. "Storm," he whispered as he pushed back the cloth and slipped into the room. Brutus poked his head out of his hole, twitching his whiskers hopefully as Remy crossed the squeaky planks, but Remy ignored him. His only focus was the hammock where he had left the baby dragon sleeping soundly. "Storm," he whispered again, pulling one side of the hammock down and peering inside, "are you still there?"

There was a sleepy growl, and then bright purple eyes cracked open, peeking up at him in a grumpy manner. Remy let out a breath of relief as the baby dragon yawned, showing a flash of teeth, and then turned to gaze up at him. He gave a chirp that sounded like a question, and Remy shook his head.

"Sorry, little guy, but we have to move." He reached into the hammock and carefully lifted Storm out. The dragon didn't squirm or try to bite him, and Remy cradled him to his chest. "It's not safe here anymore; there are people looking for you right now. We have to get out of here, find a safe place for you to hide."

"I'm afraid there's not many of those around," said a voice behind him.

Remy jumped, and Storm gave a startled squeak. Whirling around, Remy saw a figure standing in the doorway of his hut, staring wide-eyed at the dragon in his arms.

"Oh, lad," Crusty Bart whispered, shaking his head. "What have you done?"

CHAPTER
SIX

Your father is going to kill you if he finds out about this.

Standing in front of the mirror in her bedroom, Gem observed the reflection of a girl dressed in black, a dark cloak draped over her shoulders, and shoved that thought aside. It was past midnight in the castle. Most of the servants and staff had gone to bed, and the guards were all at their various stations or patrolling the grounds. She knew where they would be, and she knew the paths to avoid them. Still, this wasn't going to be easy. And if she was caught . . .

Gem sighed, reached back, and drew up the hood of her cloak, hiding her face. *Stop thinking about it, Gem. Just go.*

She walked to her window and brushed aside the lacy

curtains, gazing out at the garden below. Overhead, the moon shone like a staring silver eye, making her wince. So bright. She would've preferred a cloudy night or even a storm, but she couldn't do anything about the weather. Or at least, she couldn't do anything about it *yet*. Experienced mages were known to part clouds, calm winds, or even summon storms themselves, but she was a long way away from being able to call down lighting.

Someday, she told herself. It was definitely on the list of things to learn.

Tonight, though, she had other things to discover. Like who were the Ancients, and why did no one want to talk about them? Especially if they could help save the kingdom? What would happen to the people if the islands fell? They would all die. People like Lighthouse, Headmistress Idella, and all the students at the college. It made her stomach turn just thinking about it. If her father, the council, and the archmage wouldn't give her the answers she needed, she would just have to find them herself.

Which meant going back to the library before the school was shut down and sneaking into the restricted wing without being caught. Gem didn't have a sky ship or a private carriage that would take her across town to the college, but she did have something that was just as good. If she could get to it.

She pushed open her window, slipped over the sill, and dropped noiselessly onto the grass. The castle gardens were silent in the moonlight, and the single guard patrol wouldn't pass by for another two minutes.

Darting across the lawn, Gem slipped into the shadows like a wraith and headed for another part of the castle.

The stables were luxurious, as befit the king's horses, with roomy stalls and a couple dozen stable hands to take care of their every need. Gem's own pony, a golden mare with a white mane and tail, was treated like royalty here, but Gem herself rarely went to the stables.

At least, not those stables.

There were two stables located within the castle walls. One for horses and one for dragons. On the other side of the courtyard, built into the side of the granite cliff that rose into the air, were the stables of the sky knights. They were located on opposite ends of the courtyard because even after decades of domestication, dragons were still elite predators and made horses very nervous if they were housed too close. More than two dozen caves had been drilled into the side of the mountain, and raised platforms soaring high above the ground allowed for easy take off and landing. Over thirty dragons—from even-tempered riding dragons to sleek, fast-as-the-wind racers to the fierce but hard-to-handle battle dragons—were housed within these caves. Gem knew all their names, all their quirks and temperaments, and loved every one of them. Even the "difficult" ones, like Rockhead, a battle dragon whose stubbornness was legendary. Or Breeze, a mischievous blue dragon who could somehow get out of every stall, cage, and pen you put her in. Gem herself had been called on once or twice to catch Breeze when she escaped from the stables. But since she knew the dragon couldn't resist her favorite snack of raw herring, Gem never had any trouble getting Breeze back where she belonged. Gem knew them all so well.

The dragons recognized her, too. Which was a good thing, as a few dozen dragons bellowing an alarm in the middle of the night would be a very bad thing for her plans.

Gem slipped through the gates into the stable yard, gazing warily around for movement. Most of the stable hands would be asleep at this hour, though there would be one or two roaming around, checking on the dragons all night.

She could hear dragons snoring and snuffling in their caves as she crept down the wooden walkways until she reached the stall she was looking for. The iron gate across the cave entrance was locked, but she had the spare key in her pocket. The gate swung open without a creak, and she stepped inside.

"Cloud," she whispered into the darkness. "It's me. Are you awake?"

A sleepy rumble answered her. The floor of the cave dropped away into a shallow pit filled with fine white sand.

A scaly lump was curled up in the center of the sandpit, but at her voice, two sapphire-blue eyes cracked open, blinking sleepily.

Gem smiled. "Sorry, Cloud. I know it's a weird hour, but I'm going to need you to sneak over the walls. I promise I'll give you all the dried lizard you can eat after this."

Unfurling from the sand, the white dragon raised his head on a long, elegant neck as he stood, shaking out his wings. Cloud wasn't large, not like some of the battle dragons in her father's stables. He was the size of a small horse or donkey, though his neck and tail made him three times as long. He had been "the runt" of a nest, but due to his coloration—pure white dragons were a rare thing in Gallecia—the dragon breeder had decided to "gift" the hatchling to the king. Gem had taken one look at the tiny bundle of wings and scales and instantly fallen in love.

Most people saw Cloud only as "the runt," or "the princess's dragon." Gem knew better. Cloud possessed an almost eerie intelligence, able to understand nearly everything she said. He wasn't her dragon just because he was pretty and flashy; he was her dragon because she trusted him to do things other dragons couldn't.

Like fly over the castle walls without being seen in the middle of the night.

The dragon shoved his long muzzle under Gem's hand, and she stroked his nose. "Sorry I haven't visited in a while, boy," she whispered. "I was away at magic school. But something bad is happening, and I need to get back into the college before they shut it down. Think you can help me sneak out of here without being seen?"

Cloud trilled something deep in his throat, and Gem smiled. "That's my boy. We're not even going to use a saddle this time."

Cloud's saddle sat on a bench in the tack room, custom-made to fit him perfectly while providing the most comfortable of seats for the princess. And while some dragons absolutely needed a saddle to be ridden, particularly when practicing nosedives a hundred feet in the air, Gem had secretly been riding Cloud bareback for a while now. This was not recommended, and if anyone saw her doing it, she would get a lecture on dragon safety. "Those straps, stirrups, and handles are not there for decoration," Stablemaster Martin would say. "More people die from falling off their dragons than getting blasted with dragon fire." But Gem trusted Cloud, knowing he would not spook, swerve, or do anything to throw her off his back midflight. And strapping on a dragon saddle took time. Time she didn't have right now.

Gem cracked open the stall gate and peered outside. All around her, dragons snored and grumbled in their individual sandpits, but she didn't see any stable hands wandering around. Carefully, she eased back the gate, then gestured to the dragon waiting patiently at her back.

"All clear. Let's go."

He padded forward immediately, silent as a ghost, and stopped beside her without being told to do so. Most dragons needed a lead rope or halter when being moved; Cloud never did.

They walked to the closest launch platform, and Gem swung easily onto her dragon's back. She could feel the muscles beneath his scales, the tendons shifting in his back and wings as he prepared to leap into the air. Still, Cloud waited calmly for the command to go; even when he knew he was going to fly, he wasn't twitchy with excitement or prancing in place, unable to keep still. Settling herself behind his neck, Gem patted his shoulder, then gazed at the clear night sky and took a deep breath.

No turning back now.

"Up," she whispered, and Cloud sprang skyward, wings pumping as he climbed into the air. Gem leaned forward over his neck, holding tightly with her knees as Cloud continued to climb. This part of the plan was the most dangerous; someone could easily look up and spot a pure white dragon rising into the air above the rooftops. Cloud was beautiful and rare, but he wasn't exactly made for stealth missions. Still, Gem would rather have his intelligence than use one of the other dragons, like Blackfang, who had scales the color of night but also the temperament of a sulky viper. More than one stable hand had been snapped at or even bitten by the dragon when she was in a mood, and Gem could not take that risk tonight.

Fortunately, no one shouted or sounded an alarm. The castle grounds remained dark and quiet as Gem and her dragon rose into the air and flapped over the wall, heading in the direction of the college.

CHAPTER SEVEN

Remy's heart plummeted. In his arms, Storm gave a tiny growl, baring his fangs at the person in the doorway. Bart stood there, white-faced, staring at the hatchling in Remy's arms.

"You have the dragon," Bart whispered. "The dragon Jhaeros is looking for. I thought you were acting strangely tonight, asking all those dragon-related questions. You've never shown any interest since . . . since your mother . . ."

Remy's jaw clenched. "Don't say it," he snapped. "I don't want to hear it. You don't have to remind me."

Bart shook his head, then ran dirty fingers through his shock of white hair. "Are you mad, boy?" he demanded. "It's one thing to steal a few coins from a pirate, but this is a completely different story. That is a dragon, and Jhaeros is no laughing matter. He'll skin you alive if he finds you, or worse! You have to give it back."

Storm growled again, but it turned to a startled squeak as Remy's arms tightened, crushing him to his chest. The thought of turning his dragon over to that scary, ruthless madman made him sick. "No," he said firmly. "No way. Storm came to me. I'm not giving him back."

"Storm?" Bart rubbed a hand over his eyes. "You've already named the beast, have you? Boy, you know you cannot keep a dragon. Even if Jhaeros wasn't looking for it, it obviously belongs to some noble or sky knight on one of the main islands. Just because Jhaeros clearly stole it from them doesn't make it right for you to steal it from him. It's still illegal for you to own a dragon, and everyone will know that."

"He doesn't belong to anyone," Remy said. "I checked all over for a tattoo, and he doesn't have one. Bart, Storm is a wild dragon."

"What?" Bart looked at him, aghast. "Impossible."

"Didn't you tell me just yesterday that wild dragons exist?"

"No, I told you that True Dragons . . ." Bart made an exasperated gesture. "That's irrelevant. Wild dragon or not, that doesn't mean one just happened to fall into your lap! Those kinds of things don't happen to people like us."

"Look, then." Carefully, Remy knelt, putting Storm on

the ground. The dragon growled, baring his teeth at Bart and flaring his wings. "It's okay," Remy told him, and Storm looked up with a questioning chirp. "He won't hurt you," Remy went on. "I won't let anything hurt you, I promise."

He looked up at Bart. The old man hesitated, then approached slowly, keeping his movements calm and unthreatening. Kneeling beside Storm, he offered a hand, palm up, in front of the dragon's nose. Storm's nostrils flared as he sniffed the long, grimy fingers, and Bart didn't move a muscle until the dragon turned away.

"There's a good dragon." Bart's voice was low, soothing. "See, you know I'm not going to hurt you now." The old man flicked Remy a glance, then returned his attention to Storm. "They can't really understand words," he said, still keeping his voice low and his movements unhurried. "But they do react to the tone of your voice. They can sense if you mean them harm."

"Storm understands me," Remy said.

"It might seem that way," Bart replied. Slowly, he slid his hand along the dragon's back until he reached the wing joint. "Dragons are fairly intelligent, even the small ones. But they are just animals, in the end."

Storm let out a snort and moved away from Bart's hand, sidling up to Remy and glaring at the old man. Remy grinned. "I don't think he liked that, Bart."

"Ah, I moved too quickly." Bart dropped his hand and looked up. "Why don't you show me the tattoo, then?" he told Remy. "The hatchling is too nervous to let a stranger touch it. Just carefully lift up the right wing; it should be there under the membrane."

"Come here, Storm," Remy murmured, opening his arms, and the dragon immediately crawled into his lap. Sliding his fingers under Storm's wing, he gently pulled it up, revealing the underside of the membrane to Bart.

Bart blinked. Stared at the wing for a long moment. "The tattoo must be on the wrong side," he muttered. "It happens sometimes. Turn the dragon around," he told Remy. "Let's see the other one."

"Turn around, Storm," Remy whispered, and Storm did, circling in his lap before lying down again. Remy lifted up the left wing, watching Bart's face. The old man's expression went from skeptical, to disbelieving, to amazed. Finally, he let out an explosive breath and sat back, shaking his head.

"And you're sure you've checked everywhere else?" he asked Remy. "All over, even the underside of the belly and chin?"

"Yes," Remy answered. "There is no tattoo. I told you, Bart. He doesn't belong to anyone. Storm is wild."

"A wild dragon." Bart gazed at Storm with new eyes. "I can see why Jhaeros wants it so badly now. He could sell it for a fortune. Or he could train it for himself, without having to worry about some noble or sky knight coming to look for it."

"I'm pretty sure Jhaeros killed his mother," Remy said

solemnly. "I thought . . . I think I saw a dragon fly overhead, right before Storm fell. There was a sky ship after it."

Bart frowned. "So what exactly do you think you're going to do with this dragon?" he asked. "Jhaeros is not going to stop looking for it. Where are you going to hide it? Here?" He looked around Remy's tiny shack. "How are you going to keep it safe? What are you going to feed it?"

"I don't know," Remy burst out, making Storm flinch. "I'll find a way. I just know I can't let that pirate have him." He would protect his dragon. He had to. He'd made a promise, and he wasn't going to abandon a fellow orphan. Especially to someone like Jhaeros.

Bart groaned loudly, pressing a hand to his eyes. Storm gave a soft chirp and slid out of Remy's lap. Walking up to the old man, the dragon trilled again and tapped Bart's other hand with his nose. Bart peered at the dragon between his fingers and sighed.

"I am a sentimental old fool," he muttered, before dropping his arm and rising to his feet. "Get up," he told Remy. "We don't have much time. Do you have a blanket or a towel you can wrap your dragon in?"

"Um . . ." Remy scrambled upright, frowning in confusion. "Yes? Why?"

"You can't stay here," Bart said. "You're going to be found, either by pirates looking for that dragon or by your neighbors, who will rat you out to Jhaeros in exchange for a reward. Here." He snatched the holey blanket from Remy's hammock and tossed it to him. "Wrap up your dragon, then put him under your shirt. You can hide it at my place, at least until the initial clamor dies down. Right now, the whole island will be out looking for that dragon. Let's hope things calm down in a day or two. But we need to move, boy. Hurry!"

Remy nodded, feeling a bit dazed, and glanced at his dragon. "Come on, Storm," he muttered, kneeling down with the blanket. "We'll get you to a safe spot."

He draped the cloth over the hatchling, not knowing if Storm would protest or throw it off. But other than a startled squawk when the blanket fell over him, the dragon didn't react. Remy wrapped the cloth around him as gently as he could, then picked up the bundle and tucked the whole thing beneath his shirt. His stomach bulged, making him look like he'd eaten a cartful of pork pies, but no one would immediately see a dragon when they glanced at him.

Of course, a dubious person might wonder what the suspicious-looking bulge under his shirt was. Hopefully, they could get to Bart's place without attracting too much attention.

"All right," Bart muttered as Remy turned to him, the bundle that was Storm held tightly to his body. "This is a bad idea in a thousand ways, but follow me, and try to stay out of sight."

Remy had never seen Bart's house. Before this, he was pretty certain the old man lived in the cellar of the tavern, sleeping during the day and only coming up in the evenings to tell stories for drink. Granted, there were hundreds of shacks and wooden shanties that covered the island, but Remy had lived on Cutthroat Wedge his whole life; he had never seen Bart enter or exit any kind of house, hut, or lean-to in all the years he had been there.

"This way, boy," Bart muttered, ducking into a narrow alley between two wooden buildings. Remy followed, and Bart held up a hand. "Shh! Don't move."

Remy froze, Storm held tightly against him. A few seconds later, two pirates went tromping by. Their swords were out, glimmering in the darkness, as they sloshed through the mud, peering into doorways and down narrow streets. Fortunately, the alleyway Bart had herded them into was pitch-dark. The men sloshed by with barely a glance, turned a corner, and stomped down another street.

Remy clenched his jaw, feeling Storm squirm against him. The search for the dragon had already begun. He desperately hoped Bart had a good place for them to hide, because if gold was involved, pirates were relentless.

"All right," Bart whispered, peering out of the alley. "It's clear. Follow—"

"Bart!" called a voice. "There you are!"

Bart shoved Remy back into the alley. He tripped, stumbled, and nearly fell, but managed to plant his feet in the mud and stay upright. In the blanket, Storm let out an alarmed squeak.

Ducking behind a rotting rain barrel, Remy peered out at Bart. The old man still stood at the mouth of the alley, his back hunched and a scowl twisting his face.

Another figure stepped into view, blocking the entrance. He wore a tattered hood and cloak and carried a lantern, which threw orange light over the wooden planks. A long nose poked out from beneath the cowl as a familiar whining voice drifted into the space between buildings.

"Bart! Where have you been?" came the greasy voice of Ferus the tavern owner. "I have an empty tavern with no patrons, which means no one buying drinks. I need you to start telling stories again."

"Are you daft, man?" Bart's voice had returned to its normal raspy tone. "The whole town is out searching for that pirate's dragon. No one is going to be coming to the tavern tonight."

"That's why I need you there! Maybe you could tell a little story about where to look for a dragon. Maybe you could even hint that you know how to find it. That way, people will come back and listen to *you*, which will be less bodies out searching for it, which will be good for *me*."

"I see." Bart's tone was flat. "You're just trying to get me to distract people, pull them off the search, so *you* have a better chance at finding the dragon."

"So *we* can have a better chance at finding the dragon,"

Ferus wheedled. "How 'bout it, old friend? Do this for me, and I'll even share the reward with you. Let's say a twenty-eighty split? Considering how much of my ale you've drunk over the years, that seems generous."

"Get out of my way, you slimy rat," Bart growled, sounding genuinely angry now. "I am not going to lie to people just so you have a better shot at finding this dragon." He gave a loud, disgusted snort. "All this hubbub over a creature no one has seen. How do we know Jhaeros is telling us the truth? The beast might not even exist, or if it does, it's long gone by now."

Beneath Remy's shirt, Storm squirmed, letting out a small chirp of impatience. Remy winced as the dragon started to climb up his body, digging claws into his skin through the cloth.

"Shh, Storm, it's okay." He tried shifting his arms around the dragon, but Storm's struggles only got worse as the dragon tried tossing off the blanket. "Ow! Storm, what are you doing? Stop."

"What was that?" Ferus straightened, his beady eyes sliding suspiciously toward the alley. "I thought I heard something."

Remy bit his bottom lip and slid into the mud behind the barrel, hunching over to keep Storm in his lap. The dragon's head emerged from under Remy's shirt, nostrils flaring as he poked his nose free.

A lantern beam sliced into the alley, crawling over the

walls and sliding along the ground. "There's something in there," Ferus said, his footsteps creaking closer. "Whatever it is, come out! You can't hide."

Remy looked around desperately and spotted a flash of yellow eyes watching him from a stack of crates farther down the alley. A striped stray cat, taking shelter from the rain, glared at him from within an overturned box. Remy bent over Storm and picked a clump of mud off the ground, wincing as he gazed back at the feline.

"Sorry, kitty," he mouthed, and hurled the mud ball at the crates. It struck the crate the cat was huddled in, spattering against the wood, and the feline instantly fled with a yowl.

"Gah!" At the mouth of the alley, Ferus jerked back with a curse. "Wretched, mangy cats!" he snarled as the poor feline streaked by him and vanished into the night. "Ugh, I'm wasting time here. Bart, think about what I said. If you see that dragon around, don't hesitate to tell your old friend Ferus, hmm? I'll make it worth your while."

Bart didn't answer, and a moment later, Remy heard Ferus's footsteps creaking away. With a sigh of relief, he glanced at Storm, who had settled down in his lap with his wings curled around himself. The end of his spade-tipped tail beat a rhythm on Remy's knee like an irritated cat.

"What was that about?" Remy asked him, picking up the blanket that had been dropped in the mud. "You almost got us caught."

Storm gave him an almost disdainful look, then turned his head toward the stack of crates the cat had been hiding in and let out a mournful trill. Remy frowned.

"I have no idea what you want," he told the dragon. Storm chirped sadly, put his head on Remy's knee, and appeared to sulk.

"It's probably hungry," said a voice above him, making Remy start. Bart peered down at him over the barrel, shaking his head. "Hatchling dragons burn a lot of energy because they grow so quickly," he muttered. "Typically, they're going to want to eat every time they wake up."

Remy's eyes bulged, even as his heart sank. "Really?"

"Yes. Unfortunately, we don't have time to feed it now. Even Ferus is searching for it, which doesn't surprise me, but it does mean we have to get out of the open. Wrap that dragon up again, and let's go. Before anything else happens."

"Sorry, Storm," Remy muttered, draping the cloth over the hatchling once more. He could suddenly feel the dragon's stomach growl as he picked him up, and winced. "We'll get you some food soon, but first we have to find a safe place to hide. Hang in there."

Using the maze of back alleys, they continued through Cutthroat Wedge. Twice, they had to hide, pressing into shadows and dark corners, as pirates stalked past. But Bart seemed to know the twisting corridors of Cutthroat Wedge just as well as Remy, for he always had a place for them to duck out of sight when needed. Eventually, Remy followed

Bart down a long, snaking alleyway that ended at a tall, rotting wooden fence. Bart pulled one of the planks aside, revealing a gap in the fence, and beckoned Remy forward.

"Watch your feet, lad," he warned. "That first step is a doozy."

Remy poked his head through the gap, and his stomach dropped as a blast of icy wind rushed up from the edge of the island. A few feet past the fence, the ground fell sharply away, showing nothing but open sky beyond. Remy could suddenly hear the roar of the Maelstrom far below. He jerked back from the opening, wide-eyed, as Bart gave a raspy chuckle.

"I told you."

"Are you sky-mad?" Remy gasped. Storm gave a breathless squeak against him, and he realized he was hugging the dragon as tightly as he could. Quickly, he loosened his grip while still glaring at Bart. "Are you trying to get us killed?"

"Relax, boy." Bart's lips curled in a grim smile. "As with many stories, things are not always as they first appear."

He slipped through the gap in the fence. Heart pounding, Remy peered after him and saw Bart sidle very close to The Edge, then glance back at him impatiently.

"Come on, boy. Don't just stand there with your mouth hanging open. I said I'd give you a place to hide that dragon, but you're going to have to trust me."

Trust Bart. Remy clenched his jaw. Carefully, he eased up beside the old man and looked down.

There was a stairway cut into the side of the cliff. Uneven and treacherous-looking, it formed a narrow, snaking path down to a wooden walkway that jutted from the side of the rock wall, attached with flimsy wooden braces. Far below the walkway, the Maelstrom roiled and churned, spitting flashes of purple lightning that crawled along the top of the clouds. There were no handrails for either the stairs or for the wooden path along the side of the cliff.

"Follow me," Bart instructed. "Stay as close to the rock face as you can. And, of course, try not to look down."

Storm grumbled beneath his shirt, shifting to a more comfortable position in the blanket. Carefully, Remy made his way down the steps, then onto the wooden path. The planks creaked under his bare feet, and through the gaps, the Maelstrom boiled and churned directly below. Hugging the wall, he trailed Bart along the rickety walkway, heart lurching every time a board shifted or bent beneath him. He envied Storm, tucked into a blanket and not having to see any of it.

Finally, the walkway curled around the rock and ended at a house perched precariously on the side of the cliff. The wooden shack teetered on a narrow ledge, seemingly held in place by a handful of posts bracing it against the wall. The windows were boarded up, and a ragged curtain hung over the doorframe, much like the one in Remy's house. The entire structure creaked and shivered in the wind, looking like it might snap and tumble into the Maelstrom at any moment.

"Home sweet home," Bart sighed, pushing back the curtain that was his door. Glancing at Remy, who hugged the cliff wall a few paces back, he raised a bushy eyebrow. "You coming or not, boy?"

"*This* is where you live?" Remy asked, picking his way across the final boards. "How has this thing not blown away and fallen into the Maelstrom?"

"Oh, that's easy," Bart replied, smiling as Remy ducked through the frame. Inside, a table with a single stool sat near a window, and a moldy green couch slumped against the opposite wall. A rickety ladder led up to a loft, where he could just see a bundle of old blankets that was probably where Bart slept.

"Luck," Bart went on. "Pure, laughable luck. Honestly, I'm surprised this place has lasted so long. I was sure it would've snapped and tumbled into the Maelstrom by now."

"And you still stay here?"

Bart shrugged. "I like the quiet," he muttered. "No one comes snooping around my door. No one shows up to ask stupid questions. I don't have to worry about thieves or nosy neighbors." Glancing at the bulge beneath Remy's shirt, he snorted. "You can probably put your dragon down now; it should be safe. Like I said, no one comes around here."

As if hearing the words, Storm squirmed in Remy's grip, wriggling free and dropping to the floor. The dragon yawned and stretched his wings, giving Remy a full view of the striking lightning patterns that marked them, then gazed around curiously.

"Oh," Bart went on, snapping his fingers, "and there is one more little feature about this place that makes it attractive. Come with me, kid. Bring your dragon. You'll have to carry him; he's still too small to fly."

The old man turned and began climbing the ladder into the loft. Remy went to pick up Storm, but the hatchling gave an irritated hiss and shrank back from his fingers. Remy sighed.

"Look, I'm sorry I had to stuff you in that blanket," he told the dragon. "But we had to keep you hidden or the pirates would get you." Storm still glared, irritable and unimpressed, and Remy made a gesture of exasperation. "Okay, if you don't want me picking you up, how are you planning to get up the ladder, then?"

The dragon chirped. He strode forward, sank his claws into Remy's trouser leg, and began climbing. Remy braced himself, gritting his teeth, as the hatchling scrambled up his body like a cat climbing a tree. When he reached Remy's shoulders, the dragon curled himself around his neck and gave a smug trill. Remy rolled his eyes.

"Comfortable up there?"

The dragon's garble sounded very self-satisfied. Remy sighed and started up the ladder.

The loft was small and cramped, and the pile of blankets

in the corner reeked of Ferus's cheapest ale. At one end of the platform, the ledge dropped into the room below, with no railings to stop you should you go rolling across the planks in your sleep. On the opposite side, nestled into the wall, was a simple wooden door. Remy could suddenly feel cold air coming through the cracks.

"Here you are, finally. And the dragon has made itself into a necktie—how ingenious." Bart put his hand on the knob and glared back at Remy. "Now listen to me, lad," he said, narrowing his eyes. "No one but me has ever been through this door. Do not tell anyone about this place, you hear? Not a soul. Promise me you will keep this place a secret, boy. Swear it!"

"I won't tell anyone," Remy said. "I swear."

"Hmph," Bart grumbled, sounding unconvinced. But he turned and pushed open the door. It gave a strident creak as it swung back, revealing a stone tunnel, a short passageway through the rock. Bart shot another glare back at Remy. "Remember, boy. What you see through here, not one word to anyone!"

He stepped through the door and vanished into the tunnel. With Storm clinging to his shoulders, tail curled loosely around his neck, Remy took a deep breath and followed.

CHAPTER EIGHT

The college grounds were dark as Gem and Cloud soared silently toward the outer wall, approaching from the back instead of using the much more brightly lit front entrance. There were also guards at the front gate, while the back of the college only had a gatehouse with a single watchman inside, usually asleep. Weirdly enough, very few were brave or foolish enough to sneak into a school full of the most powerful mages in the kingdom.

Gem wondered if she was being brave, or just foolish.

Cloud made no sound as he glided easily over the high stone wall, alighting in the grass with barely a rustle. Gem slid from his back and peered around warily. This was a dangerous part of her plan. She had chosen to land here because it was the most isolated part of the college; behind the first-year dorms were the gardens and greenhouses, where the college grew all kinds of mystical plants for various spells and rituals. No one came here at night, but she still felt very exposed, standing there on the lawn with a shimmering white dragon beside her. And though Cloud was necessary to her plan, particularly the escaping part, a dragon following her around the college was certainly going to be noticed.

Fortunately, she had a plan for that, too. Gem patted his shoulder and motioned Cloud to follow. They slipped quietly across the lawn, passing elegant glass buildings that glowed with hazy light, until they reached one of the gardening sheds tucked into the wall. The college was careful to present itself as a surreal, magical place, with no ties to the mundane and ordinary. Normal gardening tools like rakes, shovels, and wheelbarrows were all stored out of sight, so as not to spoil the illusion.

The shed wasn't locked, and Gem pushed back the door. The walls of the outbuilding were lined with shelves and tools, and bags of fertilizer sat in the corners, but there was enough space for a small dragon to stand without knocking anything over.

"Okay, Cloud," Gem whispered, stroking the dragon's nose when they had ducked inside. "I need you to wait here until I come back for you. Stay here, all right?"

The white dragon blinked clear blue eyes at her and cocked his head. Gem patted his neck and backed away. "Stay," she told him, holding up a hand. "Stay, Cloud."

Cloud burbled softly, but he didn't follow. With a smile, Gem turned and slipped out of the shed, ducking into the heavy shadows around the garden.

She didn't run into any trouble creeping around the first-year dorms. Due to a strict lights-out policy and curfew, none of the first-years were ever awake past midnight. The building was dark as she sidled along the wall, keeping to the shadows and being as quiet as she could.

The two dragon statues loomed, tall and imposing, at the steps to the library. As Gem crept around the dragons' platforms, voices echoed from the top of the stairs. Quickly, Gem darted behind the dragon on the left, and Headmistress Idella strode past, two librarians trailing behind her.

"Has Gregor finished sorting all the missives?" Gem heard the headmistress ask as she swept by.

"Yes, Headmistress. They will be ready to send out tomorrow."

"Good. Now I must think of something to say to over a hundred students tomorrow, telling them they all must go home for an undetermined length of time." The headmistress gave a heavy sigh. "What are the king and the archmage thinking? I cannot believe we must shut down the college for . . ."

Their voices faded away. Gem bit her lip, then took a deep breath and gazed up the steps to the library. Unlike in the first-year dorms, the lights here were still on. The Great Library was always open and the librarians, according to popular rumor, never slept. They just drifted up and down the aisles like wraiths all night, keeping an eye on every book shelved within. This would easily be the hardest and most dangerous part of her plan.

Luckily, she had come prepared.

Going through the front doors would be foolish. Instead, Gem crept around to the side of the massive building to the high arched windows set into the brick. They were locked, of course—the librarians were super paranoid about rain and moisture getting into the building—but there were ways around that. Especially if you were a mage. Practicing magic outside class hours was forbidden, but so was sneaking into the restricted section of the library late at night. If she was caught, a little forbidden magic would be the least of her worries.

Gem closed her eyes, briefly centering herself, finding the invisible threads of magic that flickered and swirled through the air. Magic came from the Maelstrom, and its energy was everywhere, even though the terrible storm itself was far, far away. She touched those threads, feeling the power flicker along the strands, tingling as they brushed her skin, and raised a hand toward the windowpane.

Levitation was one of the first forms of magic that students learned at the college: the art of making something weightless enough to hover in the air. With small items—pencils, coins, pins—it was easy to make them float and dance like butterflies on the breeze. Larger items became increasingly difficult. The heavier the object, the more magic was required and the harder one had to concentrate to keep it aloft. It didn't work on living creatures, only inanimate objects, so mages couldn't levitate themselves all over the kingdom. But most students were making pencils zoom around the classroom by the end of their first month.

Levitation magic was also closely tied to another form of magic, mage fingers, which wasn't taught until year two. Gem, however, had been practicing magic with a private tutor before she had first come to the college. She knew a few things the other first-years didn't.

A ghostly hand, seemingly made of mist, appeared on the other side of the window. Still keeping her magic tightly under control, Gem directed it to float down until it reached the lock above the windowpane. With a firm twist, the ghostly hand turned the lock, then shimmered into nothingness as Gem released the magic.

Her heart pounded as she pushed up the window and crawled through, landing silently on the carpeted floor. Now things were serious. Sneaking around the college after curfew would've gotten her into lots of trouble, but it was something students, especially the older students, did occasionally. If Gem was caught breaking into a restricted section of the library, not only could she be expelled from the college, it would reflect poorly on her father. Not to mention he would be furious with her.

No turning back now.

The floors of the Great Library were covered in thick, elegant carpet. It was intended to impress and show off the college's wealth, and it was both a blessing and a curse right now. Good because the carpet muffled Gem's own footfalls; if the floors had been hardwood or tile, her steps would've echoed loudly and drawn the librarians faster than cats to a dead fish. Bad because *she* couldn't hear *them*, and she knew from past experience just how suddenly they could descend if she made any noise at all. She would have to be very, very quiet.

Good thing I wore my soft boots. Now, where is this restricted section?

The library had three floors. The first floor held normal books, things like textbooks, encyclopedias, and tomes for research, with a few novels and works of fiction scattered through the shelves. The second floor held the books that had everything that had to do with magic, and the third one had rooms for meetings and special classes. None of them were restricted, so that meant . . . Was there a room *below* the library? A secret floor that held all the books the college didn't want students to see? But she had been all over the library, both inside and out, and had never seen an entrance to another room.

Wait, there is *a door.* Now that she thought about it, Gem remembered a simple, unmarked door that she had never seen anyone go through. Unfortunately, that door was near the front of the library, behind the head librarian's desk.

Gem winced. But she couldn't think of anywhere else that might lead to the restricted section. Taking a deep breath, she slipped into the labyrinth of aisles and began creeping her way toward the desk of Hawkeye Hagda herself.

No librarians caught her. No flock of scowling ladies swarmed her as she tiptoed down the hallways of books. Though one time she did have to freeze in place, not daring to move a muscle, when she heard a quiet cough a few aisles over. Even after the librarian had moved on, it was still several heartbeats before Gem could breathe again.

At last, peering between two textbooks, she finally saw what she was looking for. The door in question sat in a corner against the far wall, beyond the staircase that led to the second floor. Unfortunately, the mahogany desk sat next to the stairs as well. And Gem could see the curly gray hair of the head librarian poking over the top of an open book. If Gem placed even one toe out of hiding, Hawkeye Hagda would spot her for sure.

Gem ground her teeth. She had to get to that door, but not while ol' Hawkeye was guarding it. What could she do that wouldn't get her caught?

Inspiration struck. She was an aspiring mage, after all. She couldn't summon a storm or call down lightning, but she did have a few other tricks up her sleeve.

She peeked through the books and saw a likely target: a thick tome, standing upright on the top shelf a few aisles away. It was precariously balanced, very close to the edge. A gust of wind or a strong breeze would easily blow it over.

First-year students were not supposed to know wind magic. But Gem knew a lot of things she wasn't supposed to. Raising a hand, she pointed two fingers at the balanced textbook and sent a waft of air gusting toward it.

The book shivered, leaned a bit, and then toppled, hitting the floor with a heavy thud that seemed to echo through the building. At the desk, the librarian's head snapped up, a scowl crossing her features. Setting her book aside, she hopped down from her stool, walked around the desk, and strode off in the direction of the noise.

Gem darted out of hiding and hurried across the floor to the desk. Her heart raced, and she felt horribly exposed as she scurried behind the desk and sprinted to the door. Grabbing the handle, she half expected it to be locked, but it turned easily in her palm, and she almost fell through the doorway into a dark stairwell beyond.

Gem stifled a yelp, barely stopping herself from tumbling

down the steps. The stairs beneath her were made of stone, not wood, and descended into absolute darkness.

Gem closed the door behind her, then opened her hand. With a little pulse of magic, a light appeared in her palm, glowing a soft blue. It illuminated a narrow stairwell leading to a short stone hallway. Another door sat here, much heavier than the first, the word RESTRICTED painted across the wood in red. Holding the mage light in her hand, she crept down the stone steps to the door and reached for the old brass handle. This one wasn't locked, either, turning beneath her fingers with a soft click.

Slowly, Gem pushed the door open. It creaked as it swung back. She cringed, hoping the sound hadn't reached the front desk and the head librarian. Stepping through the frame, she gazed around in awe.

The mage light cast a flickering glow over rows and rows of books on dusty shelves. Some of the titles were in languages Gem didn't recognize, and some books were so old the words on their spines had faded entirely. Several times, Gem started to reach for a book with an intriguing title—*Dwarves: Are They Really Extinct?* or *Tendril, the Terror of the Maelstrom*, or *Secrets of the Elves*. Each time, she had to stop and remind herself: She wasn't here to browse. She was here to find information on the Ancient Ones.

Finally, on the third shelf she checked, one title jumped out at her. *The Mystery of the Ancients*. That seemed exactly like the information she was looking for.

Stomach twisting, Gem pulled the tome from the shelf. There were no tables or chairs in this part of the library, so she sat cross-legged in the corner with the book in her lap and the mage light hovering over her head.

She opened the leather cover to the first page and started to read.

CHAPTER NINE

"What is this place?"

Remy's voice echoed into the darkness, bouncing off the walls of the empty space he had stepped into. It was too dark to see anything, but the floor under his bare feet was stony and cold. Bart vanished into the pitch-black for a moment, and then the orange glow of an oil lantern sprang to life, illuminating the darkness.

Remy blinked as the light spread over the walls of a small cavern. It was empty except for an uneven table that rested against the far wall, one leg propped up with a rock. Yellowed papers covered the surface, and the faded image of a hand-drawn map hung on the wall. Remy assumed it was a map, but it was so marked up, with circles, Xs, and words hastily scribbled out, that it was impossible to tell what the original image had been.

"You can keep your dragon here for now," Bart said, hanging the oil lamp on a nail driven into the wall. "This cave is big enough for a full-grown dragon to live in, and no one will come snooping around after it. It should be safe."

Remy walked up to the table, gazing down at the mess of documents, scrolls, and crumpled balls of paper scattered across it. Unlike most people in Cutthroat Wedge, Remy knew how to read; his mother had taught him before she died. Though it was extremely difficult to make out anything on the papers; they were either faded or so messily scrawled the actual words were illegible.

Remy picked up a piece of paper that had been ripped in half and squinted as he tried reading the first line, though he could only make out every other word.

Ship . . . hidden . . . dragon . . . island . . . ?

"What is all this?" he wondered.

Bart looked over and grimaced. "Oh, that's right. I forgot you actually know how to read." He walked up and swept a hand over the table, gathering most of the papers to him. "It's nothing," he told Remy, snatching the torn note from the boy's hands. "An old project of mine from years ago. It's none of your concern, lad. Forget you saw it."

Remy stepped back, watching Bart gather the rest of the papers, hastily fold them in half, and tuck them into the waist of his trousers. He wondered if Bart would hide them away somewhere, because now he was curious. What had Bart been writing about dragons and hidden ships? Were these stories he'd made up, or true accounts?

Suddenly, Storm perked up, his tail tip slapping excitedly against Remy's neck. With a chirp, he leaped off his shoulders and darted toward the cave wall, pouncing on something beneath a rock. Remy watched as a bright green centipede scuttled away from the stones and crawled up the cavern walls before vanishing into a crack. Storm hissed, scrabbling at the hole the insect had vanished into with teeth and tiny claws, to no avail.

Bart grimaced. "Right, the creature is hungry. Wait here, I must have something left over from yesterday."

He vanished down the tunnel and reappeared a few minutes later with a blanket and a pair of Silas specials: barbecued rat and frog on a stick. "Oy, dragon," Bart called, holding up one of the skewers. "Here you go."

He tossed the kabobs to the ground, and Storm pounced on them immediately, tiny growls coming from his muzzle as he tore into the meat. "Also, here," Bart said, handing Remy a heel of hard brown bread. "You look like you need it. I got it this morning from Ferus, so it should be mostly good."

"Thanks," Remy muttered. His stomach growled, but he hesitated. Bart was nearly as skinny as him, and elderly on top of it all. He didn't want to take the old man's food if he didn't have anything else. "What about you?"

Bart snorted and held up a bottle. "I have all I need right here. Now . . ." He frowned and lowered his arm, watching Storm devour every piece of the rat skewer, even the tail. "Since I appear to have gone sky-mad and agreed to help hide this beast, at great cost to myself, we are going to sit down and you are going to tell me something."

He spread the blanket on the floor and lowered himself onto it with a groan. "Ah, the old knees aren't what they used to be," he muttered, gesturing for Remy to sit as well. Remy sank into a cross-legged seat on the corner, and Bart sighed. "All right, lad," he said. "So tell me what happened last night. I want to know how you actually stumbled across this dragon. From the beginning."

Remy told him. Starting with the night of the spell storm and seeing the silhouette of a dragon through the clouds, followed by Jhearos's sky ship. Hearing the boom of cannon fire that followed, and then seeing something flutter from the sky into the pool. At this point in the story, Storm crawled into his lap, curled into a ball, and tucked his head under his wings. At first, Remy thought he had gone to sleep, until a shiver racked the dragon's body and he began trilling softly. Almost like he was crying.

"Storm and I spent the night in the drainpipe after that," Remy finished, stroking the dragon's fluffy mane. "I didn't know Jhaeros was looking for him, too. I thought he was after the big dragon."

Bart shook his head. "I'm not sure where Jhaeros

managed to find a wild dragon," he murmured, "but I suppose that doesn't matter now. What matters is how we're going to keep this creature out of his clutches. And us from being skewered by his men."

Remy gazed down at the curled-up dragon. "How long until Storm gets big enough to ride?" he wanted to know.

Bart gave him an amused look. "Ah, you thought you were going to fly off this rock using that creature, eh? Well, I hate to break it to you, boy, but the earliest age a dragon can be ridden safely is about three years. They need that time for their bones, especially their wing bones, to become strong enough to carry a full-grown rider and saddle. Try to ride them sooner, and you might damage their growth."

"Three *years*?" Remy's heart sank.

"And training a dragon isn't something just anyone can do," Bart went on relentlessly. "You have to start them early, getting them used to the saddle, teaching them all the commands they need to know while flying. Training them to respond to shifts in your body weight, how to wear armor and flight gear, all those things. Professional dragon trainers study for years to learn what they know. How were you planning on teaching your dragon any of this when you don't know anything yourself?"

"I . . . don't know," Remy admitted. "I thought we would just . . . figure it out together."

"Figure it out together." Bart snorted a laugh. In Remy's lap, Storm raised his head and growled at the old man, showing his fangs. Bart ignored him. "You don't know anything about raising a dragon," he told Remy, "and you have no money to buy the food, gear, and necessities you'll need to have any hope of success. Still want to keep that dragon? You could turn it over to Jhaeros tomorrow and have enough to buy your way to anywhere you wanted with the reward."

Remy's stomach went cold, and he clenched his jaw. "No," he said, tightening his grip on the hatchling. "I'm not giving Storm to that pirate. We'll find a way to survive, and when Storm is bigger, we're going to leave this place and not look back."

"You're still set on keeping it," Bart said in disbelief. "Even though you won't be able to ride it for several years. Not to mention all the coin you could get for turning it over. Not to mention the trouble you could be in if you *don't* turn it over. You still want to keep it?"

"His name is Storm," Remy snapped. "He's not an *it*; *he's* a dragon. And even if I could never ride him, I still wouldn't hand him over to that pirate. Who knows what Jhaeros would do to him? He's staying with me. I promised I would keep him safe, and I will. If you don't want to help us, that's fine. We'll figure something out without you."

Surprisingly, Bart smiled. "Ah, there it is," the old man sighed. "That undying loyalty to one's dragon, no matter how dangerous or unreasonable. Funny how they can do that to some." He chuckled and shook his head, before giving Remy a serious look. "Sorry, lad, but I had to be sure.

Raising a dragon from a hatchling is bloody hard work *without* murderous pirates breathing down your neck looking for it. I just needed to make sure that you were truly, one hundred percent committed to what we're about to do. If you had any doubts at all, it wouldn't be worth it.

"So," he went on as Remy blinked at him in wary surprise, "first things first. We need to figure out how we're going to feed this monster." He gave Storm an affectionately exasperated look. Storm curled a lip at him. "He's going to want to eat multiple times a day for the first few months. As he gets older, that will start to lessen, but it's no small task to feed a hatchling dragon. And Cutthroat Wedge isn't exactly teeming with livestock. Or fish. Or anything but pirates, stray cats, and vermin. And I don't think a diet of rats and cat guts will be good for a hatchling in the long run. So we're going to have to get creative, *without* raising suspicion."

Remy remembered a half-full coin pouch with a rabbit stitched onto the front and frowned. He was fairly certain Bart made enough money at the tavern to buy food, but he also knew all of Bart's coin went to buying drink for himself. Besides, Storm was *his* dragon. *He* needed to figure out a way to take care of him.

"The warehouses by the docks sometimes have barrels of salted fish and meat," he said. "Sometimes they even have whole pigs. I could sneak around there and see if I can find anything."

"Aye, and those warehouses are also full of smuggled

goods and stolen loot." Bart shook his head. "And pirates are very touchy about their booty, as I keep telling you. You get caught sneaking around there, they'll string you up by the toes."

"Then I'll just have to not get caught."

"It's not worth the risk, lad," Bart told him. "Especially now. Word of Jhaeros's offer is going to spread. More and more pirates, cutthroats, treasure hunters, mercenaries, and even desperate normal folk are going to be arriving every day to look for that dragon."

"Then what are we supposed to do?" Remy asked. "How are we going to get food for Storm?"

Bart sighed. "I'll take care of it," the man assured him. Remy crossed his arms and gave him a wary look, and Bart made an exasperated gesture with one hand. "Like I said, boy, lots of people will be arriving at Cutthroat Wedge looking for a dragon. Lots of people will be desperate to find out anything they can about dragons. And I happen to be a dragon expert."

"You're going to tell them dragon stories," Remy guessed.

"I'm going to give them what they want," Bart corrected, holding up a thin finger. "Which is information about dragons. Where they live. What they eat. What their nesting rituals are. None of which will have anything to do with finding *your* dragon, but they will all be willing to pay for such valuable information." He gave a half smile and rubbed his hands together. "Interest in everything dragon related will be at an all-time high; I intend to capitalize on this opportunity."

"And you'll use what you make to buy Storm food?" Remy wanted to know. "And not throw it all away on ale?"

Bart's face darkened. "My drinking habits are none of your business, boy," he growled, bushy eyebrows drawing together. "I'll thank you to keep such opinions to yourself." He rose and stomped across the room to the door, before turning and pointing at Storm. "You and that hatchling are lucky I decided to help," he snapped. "I swore a long time ago that I wanted nothing to do with dragons; they'll only break your heart in the end. You'll see what I'm talking about in time, boy. Keep caring for that dragon, feed it, raise it, love it, give it everything, and you'll see what I mean soon enough."

Remy hugged Storm to him and didn't answer. Bart scratched the back of his neck and sighed.

"Stay here in the cave, the two of you," he said, stepping toward the exit again. "Don't go poking around in my house. If the dragon gets hungry, try to keep it occupied until I come back. If you hear anyone, which you shouldn't, lock the door to the tunnel and hide the dragon. I'll return as soon as I can."

He stepped into the tunnel. Remy listened to the footsteps moving away, heard the door creak shut behind Bart, and he was alone.

Except for Storm. Remy gazed down at the dragon, who stared back with glittering purple eyes.

Keep caring for that dragon, feed it, raise it, love it, give it everything, and you'll see what I mean soon enough.

"What do you think he meant by that?" Remy asked Storm, who blinked and twitched the end of his tail. "You don't think Bart ever had a dragon, do you? Well, even if he did, it doesn't matter. I'll still take care of you, no matter what. And then, when you do get big enough to ride, we'll both fly out of here and not look back. What do you think?"

The dragon yawned, showing rows of needle teeth. Squirming from Remy's arms, he dropped to the blanket, then began tugging and nosing it around until he had made a nest. Curling up once more, he tucked his nose under a wing and closed his eyes. Watching him, Remy wrinkled his nose.

"Hey, you know, that blanket was meant for both of us. Where am I going to sleep?"

Storm cracked open an eye, peering up at him, then closed it once more with a sniff. Shaking his head, Remy sat down, gathered the dragon, blanket and all, into his lap, and leaned back against the wall.

He wouldn't be able to ride Storm for three years. Pirates were out looking for him. Storm had to eat every day. Remy didn't really know if he could trust Bart. Problems with no solutions swirled through his head, frustrating and exhausting. But a baby dragon, his dragon, snoozed peacefully in his lap, and the blanket was warm across his legs. Eventually, he fell into a restless sleep.

CHAPTER
TEN

In a forbidden section of the Great Library, Gem closed a book that she was never supposed to see and leaned back in her chair. Her mind was spinning. Her fingers were shaking, and she felt dazed, not knowing what to think.

The Ancients . . . were dragons. True Dragons. The dragons that had existed before the Shattering of the World. The ones who were sentient and enormous and had taught magic to humans in ancient times. The Ancients were not mages or exiles or a sect of primordial wizards practicing forbidden magic. They were dragons. But that wasn't the most amazing part.

According to all the history records, True Dragons were

not extinct. No one knew where they had gone, or how they survived, but there were several instances throughout the kingdom's history when someone had seen or even met a True Dragon. Some of these accounts were from pirates who had seen a huge creature out in the Maelstrom, or a dark, winged silhouette passing beneath their ship.

The most recent incident happened barely thirty years ago, to a sky knight called Sir Bartello Axtell when he was on a mission with his dragon.

From The Mystery of the Ancients, *chapter thirteen, page 271: Encounters with the Ancient Ones*

This is the account of Sir Bartello and his "encounter" with a True Dragon, known as an Ancient, on the southern border of the kingdom. Sir Bartello was escorting a merchant ship to the town of Pyre when they were set upon by sky pirates. Sir Bartello and his dragon, Blazetalon, fought the pirates bravely, but Blazetalon was struck by cannon fire and fatally wounded. Both dragon and rider fell into the Maelstrom and were presumed lost.

Nearly ten years later, a privateer vessel found Sir Bartello on a small, uninhabited land chunk many miles from the edge of the kingdom. The island in question was unnamed, and normally surrounded by fierce storms; the privateer vessel happened to be in the area at a time of calm and saw the distress smoke in time to rescue Sir Bartello. When asked how he survived, Sir

Bartello claimed that he had been saved from the Maelstrom and put on the island by a dragon. Not his own dragon, but one who spoke to him, a True Dragon, before it vanished back into the storm.

Sir Bartello was returned to the castle, but his health, both physical and mental, had degraded too far to resume his duties as a sky knight. Those who remembered him well said he had changed, that he had grown paranoid and obsessive. He claimed that the island was a place where the True Dragons gathered, that he had seen numerous Ancients in his ten years of being stranded there. Physicians called upon to determine his mental health concluded that Sir Bartello had suffered greatly from stress, dehydration, and hallucinations while on the island, and that the loss of his own dragon, Blazetalon, caused him to produce the illusions he thought were True Dragons. He was given permanent leave from the sky knights and told to begin a normal life.

Three months after he was rescued, Sir Bartello left the capital without warning. His last known location was aboard a merchant ship called the Flying Hart that was heading toward the eastern islands. It has been recorded that the Flying Hart docked at the port of Rim, and that Bartello left the ship and entered the city. Beyond that, all traces of the sky knight known as Sir Bartello Axtell vanished, and the ex-knight's location is currently unknown.

Sir Bartello. Gem drummed her fingers against the page in thought. *It's only been thirty years since he was stranded on that island. That means there are probably some people at the castle who knew him. And if he knows anything about the Ancients or where to find them . . .*

Her heart pounded, and she breathed deeply to calm it down. She was getting ahead of herself. First, she had to return to the castle to see if anyone there remembered Sir Bartello Axtell. And if they did, maybe they knew where he had gone. The sky knight had met an Ancient; he had been to an island where the Ancients gathered. If anyone could save the kingdom's storm crystals, it would be the True Dragons. At the very least, they would know what to do to help.

She had to find the True Dragons. And for that, she had to find Sir Bartello.

The sky had lightened to navy blue by the time Gem snuck her way out of the library and across the college grounds again. A faint pink glow hovered on the horizon, and several of the lights in the dorm windows had come on. It was nearly dawn. She had spent all night in the library, but she had the knowledge she needed now. Find Sir Bartello and ask him where to find the Ancients. The True Dragons.

Her stomach gave a weird little twist. The True Dragons were real. Everyone thought they were extinct, but they still existed, somewhere, out in the Maelstrom. Dragons who could not only understand you, but could speak to you as well. Who were immortal and, according to every story, had taught humans the ways of magic in the time before the Shattering.

But if the True Dragons still existed, why hadn't they made themselves known? Why had they chosen to remain hidden and isolated in the Maelstrom? Were they deliberately keeping themselves away from humankind? Why? She would have to ask that question when she found them.

Cloud was waiting in the shed where she had left him, and she wasted no time flying back to the castle. The sun was just breaking over the horizon when she and Cloud swooped over the walls and landed in front of the dragon stables.

Empty. So far, so good—

"Your Highness!"

Gem jumped, nearly falling off Cloud as the voice boomed out behind her. She glanced back to see the tall form of Sir Cassandra, the captain of the sky knights, stride across the yard toward her. The woman's dark hair was cropped short, and she wore a sword at her hip, always ready for action. She led Tempest, her silver-gray battle dragon, on a chain lead, and the dragon's darksteel armor glinted in the predawn light.

"What do you think you are doing, Princess?" Sir Cassandra demanded, stopping Tempest a few paces from Gem and Cloud. Tempest was a heavily spiked, muscled brute of a battle dragon and could sometimes be a bully to the dragons smaller than himself. Which was nearly all of them.

Gem stifled a wince. "Just taking Cloud out for a morning flight," she said, waving a hand at the lightening sky. Hoping the sky knight captain didn't know her well enough to realize she almost never got out of bed before the sun came up.

"Out for a ride." Sir Cassandra raised a thin, skeptical eyebrow as she glanced at Cloud. "With no escorts? Dressed in a very suspicious cloak and hood?"

Gem's stomach twisted, but she forced herself not to panic. "Oh, well, I . . ." she began, then sighed heavily. "I was flying without a saddle," she confessed. "And I didn't want anyone to see me."

"Princess." Sir Cassandra's voice was disapproving, and one gauntleted hand went to her hip. "You know that is against the rules. You know how dangerous that can be, even with a mild-tempered dragon like Cloud." At her side, Tempest gave a rumble, eyeing the smaller dragon evilly, and tried stepping forward. Sir Cassandra snapped his lead in warning.

"I know," Gem said, looking at the ground. "But it was such a nice morning, and putting on the saddle takes so long." She shuffled her feet, then gave the captain a pleading look. "Don't tell Martin," she begged. "He'll lecture me about being a bad dragon owner, and then he'll tell my father, who will forbid me from riding Cloud again until I've 'shown more responsibility.'"

The knight captain sighed. "I won't tell your father, or the stable master. This time." She raised an armored finger. "*If* you promise you will not attempt such foolishness again. We cannot have the princess of Gallecia falling off her dragon because it was too inconvenient to put on a saddle. Understand?"

"Yes," Gem replied, secretly breathing a sigh of relief. "Thank you, Captain."

Sir Cassandra gave her a genuinely affectionate smile only slightly tinged with exasperation and started to lead Tempest away. Gem hesitated a moment, then took a deep breath. If she was looking for information about an ex–sky knight, the sky knight captain might be the perfect person to ask.

"Actually, Sir Cassandra . . ." Gem stepped forward. "I have a question. Would you be able to help me with something?"

"Of course, Princess." The captain paused, holding Tempest firmly as the battle dragon growled, sounding impatient. "Whatever you need."

"I heard a story at the college a few days ago," Gem went on. "Of a sky knight who fought a band of pirates by himself. Well, with his dragon, of course. But he disappeared one day, and no one knows where he went. His name was Sir

Bartello, or something like that. Didn't he used to live here, at the castle?"

"Ah, Sir Bartello." The sky knight captain shook her head sadly. "His story is quite well known among the knights of the castle. I was but a girl when Sir Bartello joined the sky knights," she said. "My grandfather was the acting captain back then. He said that Sir Bartello was one of the bravest young knights he had ever seen. I noticed him because he was also one of the most handsome." Sir Cassandra blushed slightly as she said this, then shook her head. "When he was presumed dead," she went on, "we all mourned for him. When he suddenly returned, nearly ten years later, we were all overjoyed. I had become a knight by then, and I was ecstatic at the thought that I would be serving alongside one of the castle legends."

Sir Cassandra sighed, a pained frown crossing her face. "Unfortunately, that dream would never come to pass. Bartello had returned, but he was changed. And not for the better. I heard they found him floating on an island above the Maelstrom, and that, combined with the long years of isolation, had driven him a bit sky-mad. He was convinced that he had seen True Dragons, that they had spoken to him. Poor Bartello. The Maelstrom can do that to a person, even one like him. A shame, really."

"So . . . what happened to him, after he left?" Gem went on, hoping she was not pushing her luck. "Where did he go? Where is he now?"

Sir Cassandra's lips pursed. For a moment, she hesitated, as if debating whether or not to continue the story. Finally, she sighed.

"Sir Bartello was obsessed with returning to the island," the captain went on. "Even after being stranded there, he still wanted to go back. I suppose he thought that he would be prepared to deal with what he found. He tried finding a captain and a ship that would take him back to where he thought the island was located. But that part of the sky is extremely dangerous; the storms that rage there constantly would tear a ship apart. No captain would risk the flight—at least, none here in the capital would.

"The last I heard of Bartello," Sir Cassandra finished, "he was on a ship flying out to the Fringe, to a place called Cutthroat Wedge, which is nothing but a barren rock that is a haven for smugglers and sky pirates." Her lip curled, and she gave a snort of contempt. "I guess he thought he would have a better chance of finding a captain who would undertake such a risky journey if they were all criminals and lawbreakers anyway."

The Fringe. Gem shivered, remembering what she and Lighthouse had talked about . . . had it really been just the day before? The Fringe was the outermost ring of islands farthest from the capital, the final chunks of land before the great nothing beyond. It was a wild, unlawful place where thieves lurked in every shadow and pirates roamed the skies, preying on ships and each other. Merchants avoided the

Fringe at all costs, and no honorable, law-abiding citizen went there without a retinue of armed guards. It was definitely not a place a princess should set foot in.

"And so that is the somewhat tragic story of Sir Bartello," Sir Cassandra finished. "A brave and courageous sky knight who sadly went sky-mad and vanished chasing after an illusion. I wish it had ended differently." She blinked then and gave Gem a suspicious look. "Why is it that you want to know these things?" she asked.

"Oh, um . . ." Gem thought quickly. "I'm doing a report on the sky knights of the past, and their heroic efforts to protect the kingdom," she said. "Sir Bartello's name was at the top of my list."

"I see." Sir Cassandra narrowed her eyes, but at that moment, Tempest gave an irritated snort and raked at the ground. His talons left deep gouges in the hard-packed earth, and the sky knight captain frowned. "Oh, fine, you impatient thing," she said, glancing at the battle dragon. "I've never seen a lizard so eager to get to training. Princess, if you will excuse me. I fear if we stand here much longer, Tempest will be an absolute nightmare to work with."

"Of course," Gem said, suddenly grateful for the battle dragon's impatience. "Don't let me keep you. And thank you, Sir Cassandra."

The sky knight captain gave a salute, then turned and led Tempest away. Gem watched them leave, the thick tail of the battle dragon swinging behind him, until they were lost from sight.

Back in the castle, Gem hurried down the hallways to her room, hoping not to run into anyone on her way. Her mind was spinning, and her stomach was doing somersaults at what she had learned. She needed to sit down and think, to plan what she wanted to do next. Unfortunately, she ran into the very last person she wanted to see at that moment. Rounding the final corner to her room at the end of the hall, she stopped as a tall figure turned from her doorway and spotted her.

Her father.

"Gemillia." His voice was never loud, but it made her jump all the same. "Where were you?" the king demanded, footsteps echoing as he strode down the hall. "I've had servants out searching everywhere for you since dawn."

"I . . . took Cloud out for a ride," Gem answered, hoping he would not hear the tiny pause in her voice. The king was an expert in detecting untruths, and Gem was careful never to outright lie to him. Not that she wanted to; her father trusted her, and she hated deceiving him, even now. "I'm sorry, Father. I didn't mean to worry you. I needed to clear my head after everything that happened yesterday."

The king's expression softened. "I know it was a lot," he said gently. "You handled it well, better than some of the so-called adults in the room. You acted like a true princess; I was proud."

Gem blushed. For a moment, she wondered if she should reveal where she had really been last night, and the knowledge that she had learned. She was the princess, but her father was the person who made things happen. If she told him about Sir Bartello and his encounter with the Ancients, with the True Dragons, maybe he would see wisdom in going to look for them. Even if he became angry with her for ignoring what he said yesterday, it was worth a try.

"Speaking of the council meeting," she began, choosing her words carefully. "I did a little research . . . about the Ancients. I found out what they really are." The king frowned at that, and she hurried on. "I know you said not to think about them, that we can't ask for their help, but what if we knew they could help us? What if there was someone who could show us where they were?"

But the king was already shaking his head. "No, Gemillia," he said firmly. "I know where you're going with this, and yes, I am aware that the Ancients are True Dragons." Her eyes rounded with surprise, and the king shook his head again. "I don't know where *you* got that information, but I know better than to ask questions I don't want answers to."

"But, if you knew about the True Dragons, why didn't you say anything at the meeting?"

"Not many people know the True Dragons still exist," the king told her. "The general consensus is that they went extinct hundreds of years ago, and that the few sightings today are the ravings of sky-mad pirates. The crown has its reasons to keep this information a secret."

"But if we know the True Dragons are real, why haven't we gone to look for them?"

"That is something you will understand when you become queen," the king explained. "Not before. Also, while it is true that we know the True Dragons exist, we don't know *where* they are. Only that they live somewhere out in the Maelstrom. *How* they can live in a place where nothing else can survive is one of the great mysteries of the world. No one has ever seen the home of the Ancients, if one even exists at all."

"But the kingdom is falling," Gem argued. "The islands are sinking into the Maelstrom! Millions of people could die if we don't do something."

Her father's jaw tightened. "What do you think I have been doing, Gemillia?" he asked, not angrily, but Gem could see he wasn't happy with her. "Do you think I have been doing nothing this entire time? There is no way to safely send ships into the Maelstrom to search for creatures that have been elusive and in hiding for centuries. And even if we managed to find them, there is no guarantee that they will be able, or even willing, to help us. We have had virtually no contact with the True Dragons since the Shattering of the World. We don't know what they are like now, if they are still favorable to humankind, if they still retain their sentience, or if they have changed drastically over the centuries. We know virtually nothing about the Ancients, only that they have chosen to remain hidden and isolated within the Maelstrom, so it could be that they want nothing to do with us, either.

"As such, I must make the choices I know will yield results," the king finished, "rather than chase myths and rumor in the blind hopes that they will be able to help us. So, while I am aware of the Ancients and True Dragons, I cannot waste resources pursuing them. I'm sorry, Gemillia. I know that is not what you wanted to hear, but you need to forget about the dragons. There is nothing I can do to find them."

"Yes, Father," Gem murmured, but her mind was already working. "I understand."

He gave her a faintly suspicious look, as if he knew she might be planning something even now. But then a pair of guards appeared around the corner of the hallway, bowing deeply to the king. "The *Royal Bastion* has landed, sire," one said, referring to the king's personal sky ship, an armored monstrosity that required three storm mages to move through the air. "We are ready to depart, on your orders."

Gem glanced curiously at her father, who sighed. "The archmage and I must travel to Wyndhaven to speak with Duke Nox about the storm crystal crisis," he said, referring to their closest neighboring island. "I might not return for a few days." He put a hand on her head with a smile. "Stay out of trouble, Gemillia. That is an order from the king. I'm leaving Matron Edea in charge of your schedule until I return."

"Yes, Father," Gem said. "Have a safe trip. I will see you when you come back."

He ruffled her hair in a rare show of affection, then turned and walked away with the guards. Gem waited until her father had turned the corner, listened until his footsteps had completely faded away, then hurried into her room.

Leaning back against the door, she took a deep breath. Her heart was pounding, but the path was clear now. Gem knew what she had to do. Somewhere, beyond the borders of the kingdom, were the True Dragons. The True Dragons had been around since before the Shattering. They were ancient and wise and, according to some stories, immortal. They had to know something about the failing storm crystals and how to fix them.

And if her father couldn't send anyone to search for the True Dragons, then she would go herself. She had a name. She had the island where Sir Bartello was headed last. If she could find him, he might know where to find the Ancients. It was a long shot, but at the moment, it was the only lead she had.

She had to do this. She was the princess and future queen. This was her kingdom, her people, in danger. Her father was doing everything he could, but there were things that he *couldn't* do as king. Gem wanted to help. She wanted to save her people. People like Lighthouse, and Sir Cassandra; she couldn't bear the thought of them dying in the Maelstrom. This was something she could do that her father could not.

And if she did find a way to save the kingdom, maybe then her father would be so proud, he would finally start treating her like a daughter.

Quickly, she planned out what she would need for a long flight to the outer islands. A few extra sets of clothes, a little money, and some rations from the kitchen. Not much, only what would fit in Cloud's saddlebags. She thought about taking an airship all the way to Cutthroat Wedge, but if people recognized her as the princess, there would be lots of questions, and it could get back to her father. Better that she go alone. It was a long way to the outer edges of the kingdom, but dragons had been bred to carry their riders over long distances. She knew Cloud was strong; he would be able to get her there easily.

If she didn't get them lost.

She closed her bedroom door and was about to head to the kitchens to grab the rations for her journey when she heard a cough in the hall behind her. Turning, she jumped as Lighthouse stared down at her with wide blue eyes.

"Lighthouse! You scared me. What are you doing here?"

"The college announced that they were shutting down this morning." Lighthouse gave her an accusatory look, as if she had been the cause of it. Or at least, that she had known and hadn't told him. "They had us all pack our bags, and my father came and picked me up. He was furious. Do you know what's going on?"

"Where's your father now?"

"He came here to talk to the archmage, but both the king and the archmage have left the castle. Everyone at the college is scrambling around, and no one knows what's happening. It's pretty bad. Something is really wrong, Gem. Do you know what it is?"

Gem bit her lip. She didn't want to lie to Lighthouse, but she couldn't tell him the truth. She had promised her father she wouldn't, but even more than that, she knew that Lighthouse would panic if he knew about the failing storm crystals. And then he would tell his father, who would tell the other nobles, and things would go from bad to worse. She did not want her father to come home to a rioting kingdom.

"No," she said, shaking her head. "Sorry, Lighthouse. I have no idea what's going on, either."

He narrowed his eyes, taking in her thick cloak and the pack slung over her shoulders, and her stomach clenched. He didn't believe her. "Are you leaving?" he asked. "Where are you going?"

"Lighthouse, please." She sidled around him, trying not to look at his face. "I can't tell you."

"You know something." He followed her, trailing her

down the hall. "What is it? What's going on, Gem? Tell me. Or at least take me with you."

"I can't! I'm sorry, Lighthouse, but I have to go. Don't follow me." She gave him one last guilty look, then took off running down the hallway with her cloak flapping behind her.

It's better this way. Lighthouse doesn't have a dragon. He can't come with me. And I certainly can't tell him what's going on.

Still, guilt gnawed at her as she made her way to the kitchens and then the dragon stables. She kept glancing behind her every few paces to make sure she wasn't being followed, but Lighthouse had never been very athletic. It seemed he had given up chasing her in the hall.

For the first time, a prickle of fear went through her stomach. She was really doing this: taking her dragon and flying away from the capital, away from her father and her home and everything safe and familiar, to a pirate-infested island on the edge of the kingdom. Searching for what? A delusional old sky knight who *might* know the location of the legendary True Dragons. There would be no one to help. No guards to protect her. No one to tell her where she should go next. She would be doing this alone.

I'm doing this for Father. And for the kingdom. I can't let being scared stop me.

Avoiding the stable hands and the few sky knights wandering the stables, she slipped into Cloud's stall and quickly closed the gate behind her.

The white dragon blinked at her in the dimness, cocking his head. Obviously, he was surprised to see her again so soon after last night's adventure. Gem stepped forward and hugged his neck, pressing her face into his cool scales. He gave a soft trill, and she took a deep breath to calm her roiling stomach.

"Hey, boy. Sorry, to ask this of you so soon, but we're going on another trip. A much longer one, this time. I don't . . ." She trembled a moment, closing her eyes against his mane. "I don't really know when we'll be back. But we have to do this. What do you say? You up for another adventure?"

Cloud gently bumped her arm with his nose. Gem smiled and scratched the top of his head between his horns, his favorite spot.

"All right," she whispered. "Wait here. This time, I really do have to get your saddle."

Cloud stood patiently as she put the dragon saddle on him, cinching it tight around his belly and chest. By the time she was finished, the sun had risen high overhead. The castle would be bustling with activity by now, and there would probably be some people looking for her. In her father's absence, Matron Edea would certainly want to know where she was.

It was time to go. With a deep breath, Gem pushed open the doors of the stall. But instead of leading Cloud to one of the launching platforms, she swung herself into the saddle right there. The dragon gave a questioning chirp, glancing back at her curiously, and she smiled.

"All right, boy. This is going to be a longer flight than what you're used to, but I know you're strong. We have to find a place called Cutthroat Wedge, out on the edges of the kingdom. I'm counting on you to get me there, okay?"

Cloud trilled excitedly, fluttering his wings, and Gem nodded. "Then let's go! To find the True Dragons and hopefully save the kingdom. Cloud, up!"

With a bugling cry, Cloud burst out of his stall, launching himself into the air. Gem heard cries of alarm and surprise from the stable hands as she and her dragon rose swiftly into the air. The castle fell away, and as they soared higher, Gem could see the whole city spread below her like a multicolored carpet, stretching on to the horizon.

Gripping Cloud's mane, Gem turned him east, toward the rising sun, and began her quest to find the True Dragons.

PART II

CHAPTER ELEVEN

Storm was hungry again.

It had been nearly a week since Crusty Bart had let Remy and Storm begin their stay in his cave house, and since then, it seemed the hatchling got hungrier by the day. Bart did a fairly good job of keeping them all fed. His dragon stories at the tavern were more popular than ever now, and he used the coin he made to buy meat for Storm, such as it existed on the island. Most of what he brought back was greasy sausage links, extremely salty fish, hunks of mystery meat from stews, and the occasional rat or pigeon kabob from Silas. Storm wasn't picky, wolfing down even the greasiest, most questionable of meat chunks and then curling up for a nap almost immediately. But as the days passed, the dragon's naps grew shorter, and his appetite more voracious. Until he no longer spent most of the afternoon sleeping, but instead prowled restlessly around the cave, searching for spiders and giant purple centipedes.

"Storm, come on," Remy muttered, bending down to pick up the dragon, who was at the door of the cave peering mournfully up at the doorknob. "You know you can't go outside yet. There are still all those pirates looking for you. You have to stay here."

Storm gave a trill that was half-mournful, half-indignant, and squirmed from Remy's arms, dropping to the floor. Remy sighed again. "I don't like it, either," he told the dragon. "But Bart says there are even more people out there looking for a dragon. It's not safe for us. And who knows how long Jhaeros is going to stay? We're going to have to keep hiding, at least for a little while longer. Once he gives up, things will calm down, I promise."

Storm lashed his tail against his flanks and snorted. Which told Remy that the hatchling was starving. The hungrier Storm got, the more irritable he became. He'd never actively bitten or even snapped at Remy, but he had once bared his teeth at Bart when the old man had withheld a string of sausages and told him it was for later.

The cave was constantly dark, but from the streams of red sunlight coming through the cracks in the door, Remy guessed it was still early evening. Bart usually came home late at night after a few hours of telling stories at the tavern, and that was when he usually brought home dinner. Both for humans and dragon.

Remy glanced at Storm, prowling restlessly around the cave searching for giant arachnids, and was afraid his dragon couldn't wait that long.

Sniffing around one corner of the cave, the hatchling suddenly gave an excited hiss and dove onto a pile of rocks, scrabbling furiously with his talons. Another of the massive green centipedes scurried out of the rock pile in a flurry of orange legs, and the dragon pounced at it with a growl.

The centipede dodged the hatchling's claws, scuttled across the floor, and vanished into a large hole near the bottom. With a defiant hiss, Storm went after it. Remy saw the dragon dart into the crevice and vanish into the darkness, wings and tail disappearing from sight, and his heart dropped.

"Storm!"

He lunged after the dragon, dropping to his belly to peer into the hole. He couldn't see anything but darkness, but the gap in the rocks was bigger than he'd first thought. Large enough for a hatchling, and maybe even a skinny street rat, to squeeze into.

"Storm!" he yelled again, hearing his voice echo down what might have been a tunnel through the rocks. "Get back here right now! I'm not coming after you!"

No answer. If the dragon heard him, he wasn't listening.

Remy ground his teeth. Holding his breath, hoping he

wasn't sliding face first into a nest of centipedes, he poked his head and shoulders through the hole and wriggled his way inside.

As his eyes adjusted, he found himself in a cramped burrow of stone. There was barely enough room to move, but a tunnel snaked farther into the darkness, winding around a bend and out of sight. A luminescent orange cockroach crawled along the wall in front of him, waving hair-thin antennae, and Remy clenched his jaw.

I'm going to kill that dragon, he thought, crawling forward on hands and knees. The cockroach skittered away, vanishing into a crevice, and Remy continued down the tunnel.

At first, the way was nearly pitch-black, the only light coming from the glowing cockroaches skittering along the walls. Sometimes, the passage was so tight Remy scraped his knees and the top of his head trying to squeeze through. But after a few minutes, a faint blue light began filtering through the tunnel, pushing back the darkness. Remy felt a hum in the air, a subtle energy that vibrated the rocks around him. A light appeared at the end of the passage, and he crawled steadily toward it, feeling the faint vibrations rumble through his chest.

The tunnel finally came to an end. Pulling himself out of the hole, Remy straightened, dusting off his hands as he rose. Looking around for his dragon, he found himself in yet another cave, huge stalagmites rising from the floor like teeth. Lichen and luminescent toadstools grew along the walls, and glowing patches of moss covered the stones, all lit with a bluish-white glow that pulsed through the air. The light seemed to be coming from the center of the chamber, though it was blocked by the numerous stalagmites jutting up toward the ceiling. Shielding his eyes, Remy made his way around the largest stalagmite, and his stomach dropped.

A cluster of enormous blue-and-purple crystals sat in the center of the chamber, the jagged tips spiking up until they touched the roof of the cavern. They were huge, the center crystal probably thirty feet tall and twenty feet long, nearly the size of an airship. Remy could hear the hum coming from the massive gemstones. He could feel the vibrations of energy and magic that went through the floor, making his teeth itch.

Remy's heart pounded. There was no doubt in his mind of what he had stumbled onto. The storm crystals of Cutthroat Wedge. The only things that kept the island from plummeting into the Maelstrom. Suddenly, he felt like he shouldn't be here. That if he did anything at all, tripped over something, or touched something he shouldn't, the crystals might stop working. Or even shatter. And that was a terrifying thought.

"Storm," he whispered, reluctant to even call the dragon's name in case it might affect the glowing gemstones overhead. "Where are you?"

A soft trill answered him. Scanning the floor, Remy finally spotted the hatchling. Storm stood directly in front of the crystals, his neck craned to gaze up at them. The light from the crystals made the stripes along his back and wings glow with neon luminosity.

"Storm," Remy hissed. Gritting his teeth, he picked his way carefully into the chamber, moving lightly, as if the crystals might suddenly explode and shatter in front of him. "What are you doing? Get over here."

Storm turned to gaze at him, and for a moment, the dragon looked frightened and . . . almost sad. His eyes glowed with the same purple-blue light as the crystals.

"Storm, come on." Remy reached the dragon and bent down to pick him up. As he did, the back of his hand brushed the smooth edge of the largest crystal.

A jolt went through him, like a massive static shock. Remy cried out, nearly dropping Storm, and heard the dragon yelp. Panting, he staggered away from the crystals, his heart racing in his chest. Emotions swirled through him: fear, anger, sadness, hunger. . . .

Wait. Hunger?

Blinking, Remy looked down at Storm. The hatchling peered back with large purple eyes and gave a questioning chirp.

"Are you hungry?" Remy asked him, and Storm cocked his head questioningly. "Am I feeling what you're feeling? That's not possible. Is it?"

The dragon let out a soft trill and buried his head in the crook of Remy's elbow. As he did, the swirl of strange emotions inside Remy faded away. He stared at Storm, wondering what had happened, if anything had happened at all. Maybe it was just a weird side effect from being this close to the crystals.

He wished the hatchling could talk. All he knew was he had gotten some kind of magic shock from the storm crystals, and it had made him feel strange. One thing was for certain: He didn't want to be there at any point. The crystal's vibrations could be felt through the whole cavern, and the bright, pulsing glow was starting to make his eyes hurt.

"Come on," he whispered to the dragon. "We shouldn't be here, and my head hurts. Let's get back to the cave."

Storm didn't protest and allowed Remy to carry him back to the hole, slipping into the tunnel without hesitation. But as they crawled back through the passage, the dragon let out a soft growl and stopped right in the center of the tunnel. Behind him, staring past his tail, Remy frowned.

"Storm, what are you doing?" he whispered. "Keep going."

Instead, the hatchling backed away, going between Remy's arms and legs as he retreated. Wary now, Remy crept forward until he could lie down and peek out of the tunnel into the cavern.

A man was standing in the middle of the cave, gazing around intently. A skinny, greasy little man who Remy recognized.

Ferus, owner of the Salty Barrel, rubbed his thin hands together and started walking across the floor toward them.

CHAPTER
TWELVE

They were almost there.

Gem was exhausted, and beneath her, Cloud wasn't much better. The journey to Cutthroat Wedge had been grueling. Not to mention terrifying. It had started off fine. Gem had been excited to see the kingdom spread below her like a brilliant, multicolored sea. There had been the capital city, with houses and shops lining the roads, and the docks with rows of sky ships floating along the piers. There had been marketplaces and squares and fountains bubbling with sparkling water. And then, as she moved farther from the capital, the city had given way to small farming communities, with acres of crops, silos, and red-and-white barns scattered throughout the fields. Even on the outskirts of the capital, Gem saw that space was at a premium. It surprised her a little. There were no open places, no green rolling hills, no sprawling forests. All available land was either taken up with crops, livestock, or with buildings of some kind. With few open spaces between them.

Gem was aware that it took a lot of resources to feed the kingdom. She knew the crown owned smaller islands scattered around the capital that were solely dedicated to growing food or raising livestock. But as Gem flew above the kingdom on her white dragon, it became glaringly obvious that things were very crowded, with people building on whatever space they could find. She wondered what would happen if the kingdom kept growing, and there were no more islands to build on.

Or even worse, if the islands fell out of the sky. Into the storm below.

And then, just as she had that thought, Cloud soared over the edge of the capital island, and they were flying over the Maelstrom.

Gem's stomach dropped, and her heart thudded loudly in her ears. She had seen the Maelstrom before, of course. On airships, traveling with her father from island to island, the Maelstrom was always there, seething and surging beneath the ship. But standing on the solid wood of the deck, the storm seemed farther away and unable to reach them. And if she went below deck, she couldn't see it at all. Out of sight, out of mind.

That was not the case while riding a dragon.

The Maelstrom howled below her, wind gusting up and tossing her hair and clothes, snapping at Cloud's wings. The dragon struggled to keep steady in the gale, and some of the fiercest gusts would cause him to dip or surge upward, causing Gem's stomach to lodge in her throat. The clouds were never still, always roiling, swirling, bubbling up like the contents of an angry cauldron. Strands of purple lightning flashed within the storm or crawled along the top of the clouds, turning the air sharp with crackling energy. The absolute worst moment was when the outline of the capital island finally vanished behind her, and it was nothing but her, Cloud, and the Maelstrom, as far as the eye could see.

At this point, Gem almost turned around. Almost pointed Cloud back in the direction of the capital and flew home. But she set her jaw, curled her hands into Cloud's mane, and kept flying east. Following the sun as it climbed over the storm and the horizon. She had to find the True Dragons. She wouldn't give up until she did. The fate of the whole kingdom depended on it.

Thankfully, there were many islands surrounding the capital, and she reached the port of Farcliff later that evening. Farcliff was a good-sized town—not as large as the capital, but it had a lively market and an inn, complete with dragon stables attached. Gem was happy to get a room for herself and a stall for Cloud that night. She suspected that the farther she got from the capital, the fewer accommodations she would find.

Her room was small but cozy, and though the innkeeper seemed a bit curious as to why a twelve-year-old girl was paying for a room all by herself, he didn't seem to recognize her as the princess of Gallecia. The next morning, she was up with the sunrise, saddling Cloud and flapping off as the sun climbed over the horizon.

She had left Farcliff behind and was headed for the next closest island when, below her, the Maelstrom began to surge.

Lightning flickered, and a strand of purple suddenly snaked up from the clouds, passing uncomfortably close. Gem gasped, and Cloud let out a bugle of alarm, swerving to the side. The clouds were starting to darken, swirling ominously like whirlpools, and gusts of wind began tugging at them savagely.

"Cloud!" Gem cried as the Maelstrom boiled and a huge wall of clouds began rising from its depths. "Up! Get higher!"

The white dragon responded instantly, flapping his wings and soaring higher into the air. They rose into the sky, but the storm seemed to follow, lightning streaking out and turning everything purple-white. Overhead, gray clouds were forming, blotting out the sky. Gem couldn't see anything but swirling clouds above and below, with lightning flickering between them.

A blast of wind caught Cloud, sending him swerving toward a fogbank. Gem cried out, grabbing his mane and the saddle horn in both hands, hunching low in the saddle as the dragon struggled to right himself. Lightning flashed, streaking down so close Gem felt the white-hot energy against her skin.

A shadow fell over her. She glanced up to see a huge shape descending through the storm. Long and dark, it got bigger and bigger, until the clouds parted and the hull of a massive ship appeared. With a squeak, Gem swerved Cloud out of the way, watching as the sky ship drew alongside her, sails flapping in the wind.

Heart pounding, Gem stared at the ship. It was a little smaller than many merchant vessels in the capital, and much smaller than her father's sky ship, the *Royal Bastion*. It was long and sleek, built for speed and maneuverability, and had several cannon ports along the side. But the most intriguing thing was that a pair of long, narrow sails extended out from the sides of the hull like giant wings. They moved like wings as well, seeming to propel the vessel through the air as if it were a massive dragon.

Gem gazed up at the mast, at the sails billowing in the gusts, and saw what she feared. The image of a skull and crossbones, emblazoned against a field of black, stared out from the center of the sail, making her stomach drop.

A pirate ship!

"Hey! Dragon rider!"

A voice came to Gem over the howling wind, making her start and gaze around wildly. A figure stood on the bow of the sky ship, both hands on the wheel, staring right at her. The figure wore a long purple-and-black coat that was trimmed in gold, and a curved saber hung at her side. Bright crimson hair billowed beneath a captain's hat that somehow resisted flying off in the gale.

"What are you doing way out here, dragon rider?" the pirate woman called. "Are you lost? This isn't great weather to be flying around in!" A strand of purple light sizzled overhead, making Gem flinch. The pirate woman shook her head and raised a gloved hand. "Come aboard before you both get struck by lightning. Your beast is small enough to fit in the cargo hold for now."

Despite the lightning and shrieking wind, Gem hesitated. These were pirates! Real pirates, not fictional hero pirates like the ones in Lighthouse's books. Sir Bartello himself had fought a battle with sky pirates right before he was stranded. Pirates were criminals and cutthroats, and could not be trusted.

But then a spear of lightning sizzled down, and Cloud gave a bellow of alarm as it barely missed his wing tip, leaving the smell of ozone behind it. Gem winced. Pirates or no, it was dangerous to keep flying, not just for her, but also for Cloud. The last thing she wanted was for her dragon to get hurt. She would risk facing a crew of shady, untrustworthy pirates if it meant Cloud would be safe.

"Come on, boy," she said, and turned the dragon toward the sky ship. "Let's get out of the storm, at least."

She could feel his exhaustion. The dragon was panting and his body trembled, but he wheeled around, gave his wings a flap, and soared in the direction of the vessel.

As they flew over the railings, Gem saw more people on the deck of the ship, scurrying back and forth, securing lines, and tying down ropes. The crimson-haired woman at the wheel pointed and shouted, and the sailors rushed to follow orders. Cloud soared over the deck and touched down hard, landing with a jolt that would've thrown Gem over his neck had she not been prepared for it. He was more tired than she had realized, and guilt gnawed at her as she straightened in the saddle, patting his shoulder.

"It's okay, boy. We're okay. We're safe now." Glancing up, she saw two rough-looking men stomping toward her across the deck, and her stomach clenched. "I think."

Sensing her fear, Cloud stirred. Rising to his feet, the dragon lowered his head, opened his wings, and let out a low growl that echoed over the storm. The two figures stopped instantly, and one of them dropped a hand to the curved sword at his waist.

"Jack! Soras! Stand down!"

The men jumped, then stepped aside as the crimson-haired woman strode up, a dark scowl on her lips. "What are you doing, antagonizing a dragon rider, you fools?" she snapped. "If that beast breathes flame and sets my ship on fire, I'll have both your heads. Get back to your stations and do something useful before I toss the pair of you overboard!"

"Yes, Captain!"

The pirates scattered. The woman watched them go for a moment, then turned to look at Gem and Cloud. Cloud let out another warning rumble, baring his fangs, and the woman raised a hand.

"Easy there, dragon. Don't make me ask your rider to leave; you don't want to go back into this weather." Her gaze shifted to Gem, one corner of her lip turning up. "I would ask you to keep your beast under control," she warned. "This is my ship, and I invited you aboard, but I will be extremely irritated if your dragon bites someone. Or worse, sets my ship on fire. Please calm your beast before we all do something we might regret."

"Cloud," Gem said, and quickly slid from the saddle. "Shh, it's okay," she soothed, rubbing his neck as he glanced back at her. "Everything's fine. You're a good boy; you can relax."

The dragon gave a questioning trill, but he calmed, folding his wings to his back and covering his fangs. The pirate woman nodded. "Good. Take your dragon to the cargo hold while you wait out the storm. There should be plenty of room for a smallish beast like that one." She pointed a gloved hand to the large, square hole in the center of the deck.

Gem knew from her experience on other ships that it led belowdecks to the cargo hold. "Now, if you'll excuse me," the captain went on, "I need to get back to the wheel before Tuhga steers us into a tornado, but I'll come check on you when we're through the storm. Again, please don't let the dragon set anything on fire. Is that understood?"

"Yes," Gem answered, still feeling slightly dazed at the turn of events. *Lighthouse*, she thought, *you would probably love this*. Real sky pirates, and Gem had landed smack-dab in the middle of their ship. Still, this woman was helping her, so she felt it was important to be polite. "Thank you, Captain . . . ?"

"Cutlass" was the brisk reply as the pirate woman smiled and touched a finger to her hat. "Captain Cutlass. Not my real name, of course, but it's what everyone in the Fringe calls me. Welcome aboard the *Queen's Blade*."

CHAPTER
THIRTEEN

Ferus? What's he doing here?

The owner of the Salty Barrel tavern turned in a slow circle, beady eyes peering into the cracks and shadows of the room. Remy's heart pounded, and he felt Storm press close as Ferus began a slow, unhurried walk toward the wall where the tunnel was. Remy skittered back, scraping his arms and knees on the stone floor, as the tavern owner drew close. His muddy, booted feet stopped just a few paces away from the entrance to the hole, and he tapped one foot against the floor in thought.

"Hmm, what are you hiding down here, Bart?" Ferus mused to himself. His soft, nasally voice made Remy's skin crawl. "I wonder, could it be something scaly and worth a lot of money? Have you been holding out on me?"

Remy held his breath, Storm frozen against his side. The feet paused a moment more, then took a deliberate step toward the hole. One knobby knee hit the stones as Ferus started to bend down to peer into the tunnel.

"Ferus!"

The little man jerked up as a voice boomed through the chamber. He quickly sprang to his feet as Bart strode into the cave, scowling. The old man held a greasy brown-paper package beneath his arm, tied with string. Storm squirmed hungrily, recognizing their dinner for the night, but Remy was more relieved to see Bart.

"Oh," Ferus exclaimed as he strode away from the hole. For a moment, his beady eyes glinted in annoyance, his thin mouth pressed into a tight line, but the look was gone in the next heartbeat as he smiled widely at Bart. "*There* you are, my friend. I was looking for you."

"Looking for me," Bart repeated in a dubious voice. "I just left the Salty Barrel a few minutes ago. In fact, I *told* you I was leaving for the night, and you still had customers when I left. Why are you here?"

"Ah, well . . ." Ferus scratched the back of his skinny neck, as if trying to think quickly. "I was worried about you, Bart," he wheedled. "Your dragon stories have never been so popular, but you haven't bought a drink from me in days. You're getting plenty of coin from all those pirates looking for the dragon, but you haven't purchased a single bottle since Jhaeros walked into the tavern that night. So"—he held up a dirty green bottle in one hand—"I thought I would bring you something. Sort of a thank-you, to my favorite customer."

"Hmm, the cheapest bottle of penny grog you have," Bart said flatly. "What a gift." But he reached out and grasped the neck of the bottle with his free hand, slipping it into the pocket of his long coat. "But I don't see why you couldn't have given it to me at the tavern," he went on, "instead of snooping around my house."

"So, Bart, my friend, I was wondering." Ferus completely ignored the last question. His beady eyes shifted to the parcel in Bart's other hand. "If you're not buying drink, what are you spending all that money on?"

"That's not any of your business," Bart growled.

"Isn't that a package from Jon the butcher?" Ferus's voice was curiously ruthless. "Is that meat? What are you buying at the butcher's stall that you can't get from me?"

"A link of sausage that isn't fifty percent rat," Bart said shortly. "I have to eat, too, you know." He slipped the parcel into his other pocket, hiding it from view. "Now, if you're finished here, you can leave. My throat is dry from telling stories about dragons. I need to rest."

"You wouldn't know anything about this dragon, would you?" Ferus eyed Bart's coat pocket, then gazed suspiciously around the cavern. Remy bit his lip and pretended to be a rock. "I know you said you haven't seen it, but Jhaeros stopped by again the other evening, waving bags of gold around and asking if anyone had made any progress finding his dragon. Got the crowd riled up all over again. If you have seen the creature, or know anything about its whereabouts, we could be rich men."

"Do you see a dragon around here?" Bart snapped, waving a hand at the seemingly empty cave. "Just because I have the only house attached to a cave in Cutthroat Wedge doesn't mean there's a dragon in it. If you don't recall, I want nothing to do with lizards, and even less to do with pirates. I'm certainly not going to go crawling through every hole and passage in Cutthroat Wedge searching for the scaly rat."

"You say that now," Ferus said, frowning. He lifted a thin, dirty finger and pointed it accusingly in Bart's direction. "But I remember when you first came here, Crusty Bart. I remember that weak, sick, penniless sky knight, searching for a captain to sail him into the Maelstrom. Sky-mad, he was. So ill and confused he couldn't even see straight. I took pity on you, because if I didn't help, you would've probably stumbled off the edge in a drunken stupor. You're still alive now because of me."

Bart's face went dark. "You 'helped' me by letting me pass out on the cot in the root cellar of the tavern," he snarled. "And when I was well enough to leave, you told me I owed you a debt for food and board, and if I couldn't pay, you would have me thrown in jail. I started telling stories at the tavern just to pay off what I owed you, and I never left." Bart curled his lip at Ferus, disgust clearly written on his weathered face. "I've wasted my life on this mud-covered rock," he growled. "I used to be something. I had dreams of seeing the Ancients, of discovering new lands and battling pirates, of doing something that mattered. Then I landed here, and all those hopes were buried under mud, and ale, and the stink of corruption and greed that clings to every fiber of this place." Bart gave a heavy, disgusted sigh and shook his head. "What happened to me?" he muttered, taking a step back and gazing around the cave. "What am I even doing here?"

As he watched him, Remy's eyes got huge, his mouth hanging open in shock. He couldn't believe what he'd just heard. Bart had been a *sky knight* once? He'd had a dragon of his very own? Remy felt like the world had just been turned on its head. Bart had never spoken to him of his past, or how he'd come to Cutthroat Wedge. If anyone had asked Remy about it, he would've said the old man had always been there.

Clearly, he didn't know Crusty Bart at all.

Ferus sniffed, looking like a rodent searching for crumbs. "All I did was put a roof over your head in your time of need," he said. "I was being charitable, but I couldn't do it for free, of course. I had expenses. Anyway, just think about what I said, Bart. If you do find out anything about that dragon, let me know. Why, with the money Jhaeros is offering, you could *buy* a ship to sail out of here. Let that sink in, eh?"

"Get out," Bart spat, and pointed to the door. "Leave my house, you greasy little parasite, and don't come back."

Ferus gave an oily smile, then sauntered from the cave. Remy watched as he strode across the room to the door, opened it, and paused in the frame. His beady eyes scanned the cavern once more, as if he were hoping to catch a glimpse of something that was hidden. His gaze passed over the hole where Remy was pressed to the floor with Storm trembling against his side. But then it continued on, and after a moment, the tavern owner turned and swept through the frame. The door creaked shut behind him, and Bart was left standing alone in the cave.

Bart paused for a long time, his gaze firmly fixed on the door, as if he were making certain Ferus wasn't lurking just outside, peering through a crack. When over ten seconds had passed, he whirled and glared angrily around the cave.

"Boy! Where are you?"

Wincing, Remy scrambled from the tunnel, scraping his hands and knees as he wriggled free, with Storm beside him. Seeing them, Bart relaxed, though his face was pulled into a dark scowl.

"There you are! What happened? Did Ferus see the dragon?"

Remy shook his head as Storm squeaked and bounded up to Bart, wings fluttering excitedly. "Storm found a tunnel into another part of the cavern," he explained. "I went after him, and Ferus was already in the cave when we came back."

Bart shook his head. "I regret ever telling him where I live," he muttered. "At the time, I really did think he was helping me. If I'd truly known what a greedy lamprey he was, I wouldn't have told him anything." He reached into his pocket and withdrew the lumpy parcel with a sigh.

Storm leaped for the package, snapping at it with sharp hatchling teeth, and Bart jerked his arm up. "Hey, you can hold your horses, lizard!" he scolded. "Hard as it is to believe, this isn't just for you."

"You didn't tell me you were a sky knight," Remy said as Bart walked over to the unsteady table near the wall. Storm trailed behind him, squeaking impatiently. "No wonder you know so much about dragons."

"I don't want to talk about it," Bart muttered, setting the package on the table. "It's not something I like to remember. Hey, get down!" he snapped as Storm immediately leaped onto the surface. "Impatient hatchling, I'm getting to it."

Storm chirped, thumping his tail against the corner. Bart scowled and shooed him off, causing him to squeak again in protest as he dropped to the floor. The old man sighed. "I forgot how voracious hatchlings were," he muttered. "But I've forgotten a lot of things. Those days when I was a knight . . ." He sighed again, even louder than before, and shook his head. "It was a long time ago."

"Did you have a dragon?" Remy asked. Bart shot him an exasperated look.

"Of course I did! Blazetalon, the strongest, fastest dragon

in the order. He was . . ." Bart trailed off, his eyes clouding over, and ripped the paper off the package sitting on the table. "Never you mind, boy," he went on, frowning. "I don't want to talk about it, and you have your own dragon to take care of. There . . ."

He dropped a large shank of meat to the floor, the bone still clinging to it, and Storm instantly pounced on it with a growl. "Yes, stuff your face, dragon. Hopefully that will keep you quiet for a few hours. And yes, I have something for your boy, too."

He tossed Remy a hard loaf of bread, though it was still slightly warm from the oven, and frowned. "There. My duty for the night is done. Though how I ended up spending my own coin to feed a mud rat and a lizard is beyond me."

Remy had so many questions. How did one become a sky knight? What was it like, riding a dragon to wherever you wanted? What drove Bart here, to Cutthroat Wedge, to become a nobody who told dragon stories in a greasy tavern?

But Bart didn't give him a chance to start asking. With a scowl, he reached into the pocket of his coat and withdrew the bottle of grog Ferus had given him. Hunching his shoulders, he stomped out of the cave and back through the door, slamming it shut behind him.

CHAPTER
FOURTEEN

"Hey, dragon rider! The captain has called for you."

In the dimness of the cargo hold, Gem looked up from where she was sitting against Cloud. One of the crew members stood at the bottom of the stairs, squinting as he peered at her over barrels and crates.

"Oy, girlie! Did you hear me?" he called, walking a little farther into the room. He was lanky like a scarecrow, with tan skin and hair bleached almost white from the sun. He looked like he spent all his days climbing around in the riggings. "Captain wants you," he said again, moving with an almost monkey-like gait around a barrel. "Said to leave your dragon in the hold and come meet her in her quarters. I'm here to escort you up—"

Cloud's rumbling growl caused the pirate to stop in his tracks, quickly raising both hands in front of him. "Hey, hey," he said, backpedaling around a crate. "I don't want any trouble. Tell your dragon not to bite me. I'm just following orders here."

Gem patted Cloud's neck, and the dragon's rumbles ceased. "I'll be up in just a second," Gem told the lanky pirate, who immediately bobbed his head and left, eager to be away from the growling dragon.

She pushed herself to her feet, and Cloud immediately rose as well. "No, Cloud," she told him, and the dragon cocked his head. "You have to stay here. I won't be long. Stay. Stay."

The dragon didn't move at first, obviously reluctant. But finally, he lowered himself into a sit, then lay down again. Gem smiled.

"Good boy. I'll be back soon. Don't bite anyone who comes down here, okay?"

The white dragon yawned, then tucked his nose under a wing and closed his eyes. Gem turned and made her way through the cargo hold, up the steps, and onto the deck of the ship.

Wind tugged at her as she stepped into the open, blowing her hood off. Quickly, she pulled it back up, hiding the silver streak in her hair as she gazed around. The pirate crew moved about the deck, tying down ropes, working at the sails; one skinny boy with straw-colored hair pushed a mop around the deck, intently not looking at her. Beyond the rails, the sky shone a brilliant blue, fluffy clouds scuttling across the expanse like sheep. Taking a deep breath of cold air, Gem turned and headed toward the aft of the ship. Toward a single door behind the mast that marked the entrance to the captain's quarters. Raising a hand to the battered wood, she knocked loudly.

"Enter."

Gem slipped through the door. Beyond the frame, the large captain's quarters greeted her, dark wood floors spreading to walls of shelves, all covered in various treasures and knickknacks. Gem saw a floating crimson orb under glass, next to the open jawbone of some massive fish with razor-sharp teeth. A crown sat on the head of a skeleton in the corner, an enormous ruby glittering in one hollow eye socket. A golden birdcage rested atop a barrel, and a tiny yellow creature flitted back and forth inside, cheeping.

A battered wooden desk sat in front of the back wall, glass windows showing the endless sky beyond. Two figures were seated there, the red-haired pirate woman Gem had seen before, and an older boy with bright silver hair pulled into a ponytail.

A mage? Gem's heart pounded. She hadn't thought about it, but of course there would be a storm mage aboard. They were the ones who powered the crystals that flew the ships through the air. Pulling her hood even farther up, she edged into the room.

"No, Lysander," the pirate woman was saying as Gem walked up. "This isn't negotiable. You were powering the crystal through the storm all night. I'm not going to have my only storm mage passing out in the middle of the route because he's too stubborn to know when he has to rest."

"I'm fine, Captain."

"I know you think that." The captain held up a gloved hand. "And that's why you're going to take a break. One day away from the crystal chamber isn't going to kill you. We have enough charge to coast for a few hours, and the winds are favorable today. I figure we won't need to power the crystal until tonight, at the very earliest. So you are going to spend some time belowdecks. Sleeping."

"But—"

"That's an order, Lysander."

The mage sighed. Throwing up his hands, he turned to storm out—and ran smack into Gem as he was leaving.

"Ouch!" Gem stumbled back, wincing. "Excuse me! I'm standing right here."

"What? Oh, the dragon rider." The mage boy glared at her, his eyes a stormy green under his silver hair. He did look tired, she noticed. Dark circles crouched under his eyes, which were quite bloodshot. "I hear you're the reason we had to drop altitude so quickly and get so close to the Maelstrom," he accused. "Don't you know better than to go flying during a storm? No, of course not." His lip curled in a sneer. "You're just some pampered rich noble who doesn't know anything about the real world—"

"Thank you, Lysander." The pirate woman's voice cut through the mage's rant. "That is enough. Dismissed. Oh, and if you throw a tantrum and it damages the ship even a little, it is coming out of your pay. I am tired of finding scorch marks in the cargo hold. Understand?"

"Yes, Captain." The mage gave Gem one last glare, then stalked across the room, making the door squeal as he wrenched it back.

"And don't slam my door," the captain called after him. The mage winced, stepped out of the cabin, and closed the door very gently behind him.

The captain shook her head. "Don't mind Lysander." She turned and smiled at Gem, gesturing toward one of the chairs in front of her desk. "He's always cranky when he's tired. If I didn't force him to lie down every few days, he'd stay in the crystal chamber until he withered away. Have a seat. Do you want anything?"

"Um, no thank you." Gem perched gingerly on one of the chairs, watching as the captain opened a drawer and pulled out a bottle, setting it on the desk. "I did want to thank you for letting Cloud and me land here during the storm."

"Don't mention it." The pirate captain poured herself a glass of . . . something and smiled across the desk at Gem.

"It's not often we run into a dragon rider way out here. Especially one who is so . . . prestigious?"

Gem tensed. "What do you mean?"

The pirate woman leaned back in her chair, regarding Gem thoughtfully with her glass raised. "Like I said before," she began, "my name is Captain Cutlass, and this is my ship, the *Queen's Blade*. Have you heard of it?"

"Not really," Gem admitted.

"Of course you haven't," Captain Cutlass said. "Few in the capital would. The lives of those who live on the Fringe are below the attention of most. Until they cut into their profits. Then they send the warships and the sky knights, but by that time, most pirates have already fled."

The pirate woman tipped back her glass, then set it on the desk. "The capital doesn't pay much attention to the Fringe," she went on, "but the Fringe always pays attention to the happenings in the capital. And some of us are more observant than others. For instance, most of my crew assumes that you are just a noble who got caught in the storm with your dragon. I am not about to correct those assumptions, even if *I* know there is only one person in the kingdom who owns a rare white dragon, who comes from the capital, who is also a mage." Captain Cutlass smiled at Gem and laced gloved fingers beneath her chin. "Isn't that right . . . Princess?"

Gem stiffened so quickly she nearly fell out of her chair. The pirate woman raised an eyebrow, still smiling, and

Gem's heart began to race. There was no use denying it, not when the pirate woman already knew. "How did . . . ?"

"I told you. I'm observant." She sat forward in her chair, regarding Gem intently. "As captain, it's my job to keep my ship and my crew safe. Sometimes, unfortunately, our paths cross with the sky knights, who belong to the king. I've made it a priority to know everything I can about him, and the royal family." The woman smiled again, leaned back, and put her boots on the desk. Her green eyes never left Gem's across its surface. "So, Princess Gemillia Sunwind Gallecia. I'm afraid we have a few things to discuss."

Gem clenched her fists in her lap. She knew she shouldn't have trusted a pirate. Her mind was spinning, thinking of ways to escape. If she could just reach Cloud, she could jump on his back and fly out of here.

"Relax, Princess." The pirate woman's voice was amused, as if she knew exactly what Gem was thinking. "Don't panic and do anything rash; I'm not going to kidnap you and ransom you back to your father. We're not those kinds of pirates."

"Oh." Gem was relieved to hear it, but she did not relax. "That's . . . good. I suppose."

"Though there *are* those types of pirates out there," Captain Cutlass warned. "You're very lucky you landed on my ship, instead of, say, the *Windshark* or the *Bloody Gale*. Someone like Jhaeros wouldn't hesitate to use you against the king. Which brings me to my next question. Why are you way out here in no-man's-land, instead of in the capital, where you'd be safe?" She waved an arm at the wall to her left. "You realize you were flying that dragon straight at Cutthroat Wedge, right? One of the roughest and most dangerous pirate outposts in the Fringe?"

"I know," Gem said quietly. "I'm looking for someone."

"In the Fringe?" Captain Cutlass asked incredulously.

"On Cutthroat Wedge," Gem corrected.

The pirate captain raised a very red eyebrow. "Who?"

"I would rather not say," Gem said carefully. She was grateful to Captain Cutlass for helping her during the storm, but she certainly didn't trust her. She was a pirate, and friendly or not, she was a criminal. "I'm on an important mission, for myself," Gem went on. "I need to find someone, and their last known direction had them headed to Cutthroat Wedge."

"Hmm." The captain leaned back again, stroking her chin in thought. "The daughter of the king, on a secret mission to one of the most dangerous places in the Fringe. How . . . intriguing. This could benefit both of us."

Gem frowned, instantly wary. "How?"

"If you're going to Cutthroat Wedge, you're going to need help," Captain Cutlass went on. "It's not a place to venture into alone. You're just asking to get robbed, or worse. And, of course, there's the question of your dragon."

"What about Cloud?" Gem asked.

"He's a valuable animal," the captain replied. "Anything of value on Cutthroat Wedge is in danger of being stolen. *Especially* now, thanks to Jhaeros stirring the island into a frenzy over a missing hatchling. From what I've heard, the whole island has gone sky-mad looking for it." The captain snorted, shaking her mane of red hair. "Trust me, it is *not* a good time to bring a dragon into Cutthroat Wedge.

"So this is my proposal, Princess," the pirate captain said. "My crew and I will take you to Cutthroat Wedge, and we'll accompany you while you do whatever you need to do. You'll have our protection, something that you're going to need while you're in the Fringe. Your dragon can stay here, on the ship, as long as it doesn't set the cargo hold on fire. That way, it stays safe, and you don't get a knife in your back from an overambitious thief."

"Okay." Gem crossed her arms. She could agree that having a crew of pirates watching out for her in a pirate town was not the worst of ideas. If she could trust them. "And what do you get out of this arrangement?"

"You're the princess," Captain Cutlass said, smiling. "Surely helping the princess of Gallecia carries some sort of reward. Your father is the king; I'm certain we can work something out."

"Like what?" Gem wanted to know.

"What indeed." The captain snapped her fingers. "How about this: When you return to the capital, put in a good word for me and the *Queen's Blade* with King Gallus. Let him know that this particular ship is off-limits, and the sky knights should . . . look the other way if they ever encounter it. You do that, and we'll make sure you find who you're looking for and not get your throat cut in the process." Captain Cutlass swung her boots off the desk and leaned forward with a smile. "So what do you say, Princess?" she asked. "Do we have a deal?"

Gem thought about it. She'd be putting her trust in pirates, of course, but from what the captain had said, Cutthroat Wedge was a bad place to take a dragon. If something happened to Cloud, if he was hurt or stolen, she would never forgive herself.

"Yes," she said, glancing up at the pirate captain. "We have a deal."

CHAPTER
FIFTEEN

Remy woke up to the ground shaking beneath him.

Bolting upright on the hard cavern floor, he gazed blearily around the cave. The entire room was vibrating, pebbles bouncing over the floor and dust falling from the ceiling. Storm was still curled up on the blanket they shared, unaware of the cavern trembling around them. The hatchling was pretty much dead to the world right after he'd eaten, especially a large meal. He did not seem to feel the tremors going through the ground, but Remy leaped to his feet, heart pounding, ready to snatch up Storm and bolt out the door if the ceiling started to collapse.

Faint voices sounded through the door, making his heart

lurch. He spun, bent down, and wrenched Storm from the blanket, pressing him to his chest. The hatchling did wake up then, giving an irritated chirp as he was yanked off the ground. He was a lot bigger than he had been when Remy first found him, the size of a small dog instead of a cat. Heavier, too. Considering how much he ate, it wasn't surprising.

The voices outside sounded closer. Gritting his teeth, Remy bolted for the back of the room, toward the only hiding place he knew of: the small tunnel that led to the chamber that contained the storm crystals.

"Sorry, buddy," Remy whispered, falling to his knees in front of the hole. Placing Storm down, he gave the dragon a push toward the entrance. The dragon hissed at him, still looking annoyed, and Remy winced. "Get in there—hurry! People are coming! Go!"

A shout echoed right outside the door, and Storm finally seemed to realize the danger. The hatchling vanished into the tunnel, wings and tail sliding through the hole in an eyeblink. Remy followed, but he went in backward since there was no room to turn around in the tunnel. Scraping knees and elbows against the rocky floor, he wriggled his way back, grabbing a large stone at the entrance and heaving it across the opening.

Just in time. The door that led to Bart's shack burst open, slamming against the wall and breaking into pieces. A group of five rough-looking pirates spilled into the room, swords in hand, gazing around the hidden chamber. Remy held his breath, watching them through the crack between the rocks, as the pirates stalked around the cavern. His heart pounded against the hard floor, and he could feel Storm shaking against him.

"Well, there is a cave," one of the pirates said, sounding annoyed, "but no dragon."

Another kicked a pebble and spat on the floor. "Think that little weasel at the tavern lied to us?"

"If he did, Jhaeros will string him up by his thumbs before peeling the skin from his bones." The pirate paused, gazing down at Remy's discarded blanket, then bent to snatch something next to it from the ground.

A third pirate prodded a toe at something near the wall, a piece of bone left over from one of Storm's many meals. As it clinked over the stones, the pirate frowned. "Looks like *something* has been here," he muttered. "But it's gone now. Boss isn't going to be happy."

"What am I not going to be happy with?"

A shiver went through the air, and Jhaeros himself stepped into the cavern. Remy's heart nearly stopped beating as the pirate mage sauntered into the middle of the room, gazing around with cold eyes.

"The dragon ain't here, boss." The pirate who had spoken last gave a shrug and nudged the bone again with his boot. "Looks like it might've been, at one point. But the cave is empty now."

"It cannot be far." Jhaeros continued to observe the room carefully, hard blue eyes sweeping over every corner. His boots thumped against the ground as he walked. Storm trembled and pressed his nose into Remy's side as the pirate mage drew close. "It is a hatchling. It won't be able to fly for another month at least. It is somewhere on this island, and after all this time, we should have found it. Unless *someone* has been hiding it from me. Which would be *very* annoying."

He spun, gesturing sharply, and lightning shot from his hands, slamming into the wall. Storm squeaked, and Remy bit his lip as rocks rained down from the ceiling and smoke curled into the air. Fortunately, the lightning had struck the wall opposite the tunnel, though Remy still felt the ground beneath him tremble, and pebbles fell onto his head. The smoke cleared, leaving behind a charred, blackened circle in the center of the wall and the pirates gazing around fearfully.

Jhaeros inhaled deeply, then smiled. "I think we need to pay a visit to the tavern," he stated, causing Remy's stomach to drop. "That old storyteller has obviously been hiding something from us. I think it is time to . . . put some pressure on him." Raising an arm, he clenched a fist, and lightning sparked from his fingers again, crawling over his hand. "I have been patient long enough, and my goodwill is at an end. If he won't give me my dragon, things are going to go poorly for him."

Lowering his arm, he glanced at his men, who stood rigidly around him as if afraid to move. "Well, why are you fools just standing there with your mouths open? Let's go."

"What about the cave, boss?" one of the pirates asked. "If the dragon was here before, do you think it could come back?"

Jhaeros gave an evil smile that made Remy's skin crawl. "Oh, don't worry," he crooned. "We'll make sure it doesn't have anything to come back to."

That sounded ominous. The pirates left the cavern, following the rogue mage into the hut. Remy waited until he was sure every pirate had left the room before shoving away the stone and wriggling out of the tunnel.

Storm followed, chirping wildly. Ignoring him, Remy hurried across the cavern to the remains of the shattered door. There were no pirates that he could see or hear, so he started to creep down the tunnel.

He nearly fell as a scaly body pressed close to his legs, curling a tail around his ankles. Wincing, he looked down at his dragon.

"Storm." Remy knelt and put a calming hand on the scaly head, feeling horns through the mane. Storm trilled and gazed up at him, almost in accusation. "I have to see what they're up to," he told the dragon. "Bart might be in trouble. Stay here. I promise I'll be right back."

The dragon whined but sank back and put his head on the ground, flattening himself to the floor. Remy swallowed and crept into the tunnel, making his way through the corridor until he reached the curtain hung over the entrance.

Pushing it aside, he peered into Bart's shack, and his heart plummeted.

Straight ahead, through the open front door, hovered a sky ship. It had black sails, and the ship itself had been painted to resemble a terrible, giant shark swimming through the air. But that wasn't what caused Remy's heart to freeze in terror.

Along the sides of the ship, portholes were slowly opening, the black mouths of cannons poking through. Pointing straight at Bart's house.

Oh no . . .

Remy spun, bolting back down the tunnel, as behind him the shout of *"Fire!"* rang into the air. Reaching the cave, he snatched Storm off the floor and flung himself to the side as something whizzed by in a black streak, slamming into the cavern wall.

With deafening roars, a volley of cannonballs smashed into Bart's house, snapping timbers and punching through walls. The cavern shook, rocks, pebbles, and dust raining from the ceiling. Storm howled, digging his talons into Remy's skin, but his voice was lost in the cacophony. Remy staggered to a corner and pressed himself to the wall, keeping his body hunched over Storm as stones fell around him, bouncing painfully off his back.

For a few seconds, cannons boomed, the walls shook, projectiles roared as they smashed into everything, and it felt like the world was breaking apart. But then, as suddenly as it had started, the noises ceased. The rumbles faded, the ground stopped shaking, and calm descended once more.

Remy peeked up, blinking dirt out of his eyes. Storm trembled violently against his chest, sharp claws digging through his shirt into his skin. The cavern was smaller now; rocks and boulders had been shaken loose with the cannon barrage and were scattered everywhere across the floor. Dust hung thick in the air, turning everything hazy and choking. Remy coughed, then started picking his way across the floor, avoiding the boulders and easing around the jagged stones that had fallen.

Another tremor went through the ground, but this time, it was far stronger. The earth heaved under his feet, and he lost his balance, stumbling back and dropping Storm. The dragon gave a bleat of fear as he landed, making Remy wince.

"Sorry, Storm," he panted. "Come here, I'll pick you up. . . ."

He reached for the hatchling, but the dragon suddenly let out a terrified cry and bolted away from him. Shocked, Remy watched Storm scurry across the floor, scrambling over rocks and stones toward the back of the cavern.

He bit his lip. The wall that held the tunnel to the other cavern had been blasted apart by the cannonball, and a giant crack split the rock in two. Storm frantically clawed away a mound of rubble, revealing the mouth of the tunnel, then vanished into the gap.

"Storm! Hey, wait!"

Remy hurried after the dragon, wriggling through the passage one more time. As he heaved himself from the hole into the other chamber, the cave trembled. More rocks fell, clattering to the ground, and centipedes crawled frantically over the walls. Waving away the dusty haze, Remy gazed frantically around for his dragon.

Storm stood in the middle of the room, neck craned back and staring up at the ceiling. At the cluster of crystals attached to the roof. As Remy followed the dragon's gaze, his heart dropped to his toes and stayed there.

One of the crystals was flickering, like a candle left out in a strong breeze. A terrible crack ran from where it connected to the ceiling down to the tip of one of the shards, the crack starting wide and then branching out like spiderwebs.

The storm crystal flickered again, and the island trembled in response.

Remy felt cold. His chest was tight, but he staggered across the floor and gathered Storm in his arms. The hatchling shook violently, and Remy held him close, feeling the dragon's heart racing beneath his scales.

"It's okay," he whispered into the dragon's mane. "We're okay, Storm. We're fine. It's just a crack. That doesn't mean the island is going to fall."

The ground rumbled under his feet, seeming to challenge that statement, and his stomach twisted so hard he felt sick. "Come on," he told the dragon, staggering back toward the tunnel. "We have to get out of here. There's nothing we can do."

He crawled back into the cave, then carefully picked his way to the shattered door once again. Creeping down the passage, he peered out into Bart's cabin.

There was no more cabin.

Bart's house was gone. A scorched, empty cliff face was all that was left of the house that had been perched precariously against the rocks. Only the walkway and a few beams clinging to the side of the cliff remained. The pirate ship had vanished, leaving the air outside the shack empty, but the damage had been done. The hut was completely destroyed.

Storm, peering around his legs, gave a sad chirp, and Remy clenched his fists. Bart's house was gone, but Jhaeros and the pirates were on their way to the tavern, looking for him. He had to reach Bart and warn him before the pirates got there, but he couldn't take Storm topside. Jhaeros would see him for sure.

Turning, Remy knelt and stroked the dragon's mane, making the hatchling gaze up at him questioningly. "I need you to stay here, buddy," he whispered, and Storm immediately squeaked in protest. "I have to warn Bart about the pirates, but you can't follow me up there. There's too many people looking for you. You have to stay here and wait for us. Will you do that? Please?"

Storm gave a mournful trill, gazing at Remy with sorrowful purple eyes. But he turned and crawled back into the cave. Finding an overturned chair, he curled up beneath it, pressing his wings and tail tightly to his body while staring at the door. His accusing gaze made Remy's stomach tighten, but he rose and took a step toward the door, toward the edge that dropped away into nothing.

"I'll be back soon," he told the dragon. "I promise."

Storm didn't answer, or move from his place beneath the chair. Worry and guilt raging an equal battle within, Remy turned and hurried out the door, hoping to reach Bart before Jhaeros did. Hoping he was doing the right thing in leaving his dragon behind.

CHAPTER SIXTEEN

"Well, there it is."

Gem shielded her eyes, peering over the railings at the island in the distance. At first, all she could see was a silhouette against the glare of the sun. As they drew closer, the shape turned into a floating island, but one that was so jagged and sharp she wondered how anyone lived there. The capital island was mostly flat, with rolling hills to break up the land, and so big it had mountains surrounding the city that weren't even close to The Edge. Cutthroat Wedge looked like a giant hand had reached down, grabbed the very top of a mountain, and wrenched off the tip before turning it loose to float in the air. Shanties were built on any available space, crushed together and stacked on top of each other, looking like they would topple at any moment. The wooden huts also seemed to spill down the sides of the island, crammed onto narrow ledges and connected by ladders or rickety wooden walkways. It did not look safe at all, and she wondered how many of the tiny shacks had come loose from the side of the cliff and toppled into the Maelstrom.

"It's . . . so small," she said, as politely as she could.

Beside her, the lanky pirate from that first day in the cargo hold laughed. "Yep, welcome to Cutthroat Wedge, the meanest chunk of rock in the Fringe," he cackled. His real name was Jack, Gem had learned, and he was very nice. Though the crew said he was a bit sun-addled given how much time he spent in the riggings. "The last piece of civilization before the Great Nothing beyond. Though calling it civilized is a bit of a stretch. Only ones here are desperate rat eaters, smugglers, and pirates." He snorted and flashed a toothy grin. "At least we'll feel right at home, eh! Oh," he said, holding up leathery, callused hands. "No offense to you, Miss Mary."

"It's all right, Jack," Gem replied. Mary Featherbottom was her alias, something she and the captain had come up with to hide her true identity. None of the crew knew she was really the princess; they all believed she was a noble from Wyndhaven, traveling to Cutthroat Wedge to search for a long-lost uncle.

"Miss Featherbottom," came the voice of the captain

behind her. Gem turned to see Captain Cutlass peering down at her from the aftcastle. "We'll be landing at the Cutthroat docks soon," she told her. "I suggest you check on your dragon; make certain the beast is settled before we go landside."

"Yes, Captain."

Gem hurried into the cargo hold, descending the steps and gazing around for her dragon. They had given Cloud his own corner of the hold, and though there were no real stalls, they had stacked several crates and put down straw to make a cozy spot for him to sleep. The captain had been worried about the amount of flammable materials piled around the dragon, but Gem had assured her that Cloud never breathed fire without being told to do so. To which the captain had responded that if the dragon *did* burn down her ship, she fully expected Gem's father to buy her a new one.

Cloud was curled up with his nose tucked under his tail, half-buried in straw, when Gem saw him. But as she approached, he uncurled, yawned widely, and gave a sleepy trill. She smiled.

"Hey, boy," she greeted, stroking his nose. He smelled vaguely of fish, and an empty fish bucket sat close to the makeshift stall. Jack had been feeding the dragon nonstop since his arrival in an effort to make friends, and Cloud had certainly appreciated the extra snacks. It also made him sleepy, which was a good thing, she supposed.

"I have to leave the ship with the captain for a little

while," she told the dragon, who yawned again with a blast of very fishy breath. "You stay here and be a good boy, okay? Don't try to follow me; I'll be with the crew, so I'll be all right."

The dragon burbled and gave her an affectionate shove with his nose, then settled down and put his chin on his tail. Confident that Cloud would likely go right back to sleep, Gem turned and went topside again, feeling the wind tug at her cloak as she stepped onto the deck.

Cutthroat Wedge was much closer, a jagged, looming mountain above the roiling sea of purple-and-black clouds. The Maelstrom itself was also much closer, Gem saw, a mere stone's throw away from the bottom of the island. A purple lightning strand flickered up, thread-thin fingers seeming to reach for the land, and Gem shuddered.

"Coming in on the docks, Captain," said First Mate Tuhga, a dark, muscular man with colorful tattoos running the length of his arms and back. Gem peered over the railings and saw a web of piers jutting out of the side of the island, with several sky ships already docked.

"Steady as she goes, Mr. Tuhga" was the captain's response.

"Ooh, it's crowded today," Jack mused, coming up beside Gem. "So many ships. The only other time I've seen Cutthroat Wedge so lively was when that rum smuggler died and left behind a holdful of barrels."

"It's because of Jhaeros," Captain Cutlass said, walking to

the edge of the aftcastle. Gazing at the island with her arms crossed and her hair fluttering in the wind, she frowned. "He's got the whole island in a frenzy because of his search for that dragon hatchling."

Gem gasped, immediately perking up. "A baby dragon?" she asked.

"Aye. That's why I didn't want you parading through Cutthroat Wedge on that beast of yours." The captain shook her head. "Rumors are Jhaeros discovered a wild dragon out over the Maelstrom. He shot it down, but it had a hatchling with it that escaped, and the hatchling landed somewhere in Cutthroat Wedge."

Gem put her hands over her mouth in horror. "That's terrible."

"Yes, and now Jhaeros has the entire town, and most of the pirate population in the Fringe, out looking for this hatchling. He's offered an obscene amount of gold for its return, enough that word of it has spread throughout the Fringe, and more pirates arrive every day looking for dragons." Captain Cutlass turned to look at Gem straight on. "So make sure your beast stays on this ship and out of sight," she said, pointing straight down at the deck. "Knowing pirates, they won't care that Cloud is an adult, that he already has an owner, that he is the wrong age, the wrong color, the wrong everything. They'll just see a dragon, and they'll try to take him back to Jhaeros for a reward."

Gem bit her lip, her stomach twisting. She hadn't known

any of this before she began her journey. If she had flown into Cutthroat Wedge on Cloud, as she had been planning to do, what might've happened to her dragon? She was suddenly very grateful for the storm that had blown her into the *Queen's Blade*, and that she had accepted the captain's offer.

"Hmm." Captain Cutlass continued to observe the docks as they swept in. "I don't see the *Windshark*, though," she mused, eyes narrowed as she gazed at the other ships. "You would think it would be obvious with how huge that ship is; you can't miss it."

"Maybe he left," Gem said hopefully.

"Not without his dragon," the pirate captain said grimly. "Jhaeros is a lot of things—narcissistic, egocentric, power-hungry—but one thing he is not, and that is a quitter. He doesn't give up, and he's not afraid to tear the entire island apart until he finds what he's looking f—"

A massive *boom* rocked the island, the sound of explosions and cannon fire causing everyone on the *Queen's Blade* to jump. Gem gasped, grabbing the railings, as more cannon fire rang out, echoing on the wind.

"What in the world!" Captain Cutlass strode to the edge of the deck, grabbing a rope as she leaned over the railings. "Who is attacking the island? Where is it coming from?"

A black plume of smoke began curling into the air, coming from the other side of Cutthroat Wedge. Watching it, Gem felt her stomach squeeze tight. She had never seen violence; in the capital, she was always protected, safe behind the castle walls or in the company of royal guards. The closest she had been to actual violence was seeing a guard chase a thief through the market square. Watching the billow of smoke curl over the island, the echoes of cannon fire ringing in her ears, she suddenly felt sick with genuine terror.

"Ease up, Mr. Tuhga," the captain ordered, holding up a fist. "Slow her down a little; if the island is being attacked, I want to know what is happening before we go rushing in."

"Yes, Captain."

The *Queen's Blade* slowed, flaring the wings on its side, and as it did, another vessel suddenly appeared. This one was enormous, almost as big as her father's ship, the *Royal Bastion*, back home. Despite its size, it was sleek and built for speed, though its armored hull, the numerous cannon ports along its side, and the painted, toothy face of a grinning shark made it perfectly clear: This was a vessel of war.

"The *Windshark*," Jack muttered as they watched the other ship cruise easily around the island. "Looks like Jhaeros is here, after all."

"Turn us around, Mr. Tuhga," ordered Captain Cutlass. "I don't know why Jhaeros is firing on the island, but it is not something I want to get involved with. And I especially do not want to get into a firefight with the *Windshark*. We'll return to Cutthroat Wedge in a few days, when things have calmed down a bit."

"Aye aye, Captain."

They were leaving? Now? "Wait!" Gem whirled around,

glaring up at the aftcastle. "Captain, can I speak with you privately?" she called. She wanted to protest then and there, but she knew, from dealing with her father, that questioning authority in front of that person's subordinates would only anger them and make them less likely to listen. "Please," she added as the captain's lips tightened. "It won't be long. Just hear me out."

The pirate captain gave her an impatient look, then sighed. "Stay the course, Mr. Tuhga," she said to the first mate before walking swiftly down the stairs to the deck. "In my quarters, then, Miss Featherbottom," she snapped as she passed Gem. "Make it quick."

In her quarters, the captain didn't even go to her desk, but turned to Gem as soon as the door closed, crossing her arms. "What it is, Princess?" she asked. "I assume this is important and could not wait until we are safely away from the island?"

"Yes," Gem replied. "Captain, I need to get to Cutthroat Wedge now. I can't wait even a few days. Please reconsider your decision."

"No," Captain Cutlass said immediately. "Captain Jhaeros and the *Windshark* are too dangerous to cross, especially if I don't know why I'm crossing them in the first place."

"But—"

"You want me to risk my crew and go back?" Captain Cutlass bent down to look Gem in the eye. "Tell me why you need to go to Cutthroat Wedge so badly. What are you looking for? Maybe if I understood that, Princess, I'd be more inclined to put my ship and crew in danger for you."

Gem clenched her fists. She knew she couldn't tell the pirate captain everything. Even if Captain Cutlass had kept her secret about being the princess, if Gem told her the real reason she was there—to save the islands from falling into the Maelstrom—she doubted the captain would take it well. And if Cutlass told even one member of the crew, the word would spread, and there would be panic and chaos and everything her father was afraid of.

But the captain was asking for her trust, she realized. She had to give her something.

"I . . . I have to find someone," she said at last. "An old sky knight, by the name of Sir Bartello. He left the capital years ago, and his last known location was on a ship headed to Cutthroat Wedge."

"Sir Bartello." The captain frowned thoughtfully. "There's no one by that name in Cutthroat Wedge. Unless you mean old Crusty Bart, the storyteller at the Salty Barrel." She snorted, shaking her head. "Are you telling me that crabby old windbag was once a sky knight? I find that hard to believe. Although"—she tapped her chin in thought—"it does make a certain amount of sense. All he talks about is dragons; he won't shut up about them. Still, I wouldn't have pegged that sour drunkard to have been part of the king's shining squadron of elite dragon riders." She gazed down at Gem once more. "So what is it you have to ask our old storyteller, assuming he *is* a sky knight like you claim. Or was, rather."

"That is . . . classified," Gem said, making Cutlass narrow her eyes. "But it is about dragons; I can say that much."

"I see." The captain continued to ponder. Gem held her breath and tried not to let her impatience show. "So," Cutlass said at last, "the question now becomes whether it's worth risking a confrontation with Jhaeros and the *Windshark* just to see if Crusty Bart is indeed a rogue sky knight like you say. The smart choice, the safe choice, would be to leave the island until Jhaeros is finished with whatever business he has with Cutthroat Wedge.

"Of course," the captain went on after a moment, and smiled, "if we always went with the safe choice, we wouldn't be pirates, would we?"

Gem felt a flutter of hope and gazed warily up at the pirate captain. "Does that mean . . . ?"

Brushing around Gem, the captain strode out onto the deck. "Mr. Tuhga!" she called to the first mate. "Turn this ship around. Full speed. We're going back to Cutthroat Wedge."

CHAPTER SEVENTEEN

The narrow streets of Beggar's Row were empty as Remy pushed himself through the mud and weeds, sliding between houses and through alleyways, trying to reach the tavern. Most everyone had fled into their homes, doors shut and shutters closed against the chaos happening outside. If Remy peered up past the ramshackle roofs, he could just see the last curls of smoke writhing into the sky from where the cannons had destroyed Bart's old house. The residents of Beggar's Row knew something was happening and responded as they always did: by hiding and hoping it went away.

A tremor went through the ground, causing Remy to stumble and nearly fall into the mud. Clenching his jaw, he kept going, ignoring the fear crawling in the pit of his stomach. He couldn't think about what was happening to the island, about the cracked storm crystal in the hidden cave. He had to reach the tavern and warn Bart that Jhaeros was coming for him.

Lightning flickered overhead as Remy stumbled up the hill to the Salty Barrel, and in the flash, he could see a small crowd outside the tavern. Along with something else that made his heart sink. The *Windshark* floated in the air above the tavern, casting its dark, imposing shadow over the ground and the crowd gathered outside. Including Bart.

"You know, I've been a patient man." Even with the growling thunder, the low hum of the *Windshark*, and the wind howling up from the Maelstrom, Jhaeros's voice carried over it all. The pirate mage circled Bart like a hungry dog trying to decide the best attack angle. "I haven't asked for much, just something that is mine that I would like returned to me. And I have been *more* than generous."

He shot a chilling look at the few patrons who were not his crew, and they cringed. Heart pounding, Remy glanced around, then dove into the tall grass and weeds off the edge of the path. Keeping his head low, he began creeping forward.

In the center of the ring, Bart looked unconcerned, even as Jhaeros turned on him again. "All I want is my dragon," the pirate mage told the older man. "I will ask politely, one last time, before I truly lose my patience. There is a hidden cave behind your house that clearly had something alive in it very recently. And my good friend Ferus tells me that you have been buying a lot of food lately. A lot of meat. We both know how voracious newborn hatchlings can be. So, as I am not a fool, this can only mean one thing."

Jhaeros stepped closer, towering over Bart. His cold eyes bored into him even as his mouth curled in an ominous smile. "You know where my dragon is," he said. "And you are going to tell me where to find it right now. From one gentleman to another."

"Gentleman?" Bart gave the pirate mage a look of contempt. "If you're a gentleman, then I'm a sky whale," he scoffed, and Jhaeros's face twisted in anger. "Look, pirate, let me make this as clear as I can," he said loudly. "I don't know where your dragon is. As Ferus so kindly pointed out, yes, I have a cave behind my home, because it's the only place on this entire godforsaken island where I can keep things hidden and safe from thieves. And yes, I have been buying a lot more food, because, thanks to you, I suddenly have a lot more coin to spend. This doesn't mean I've been keeping a dragon in my house; contrary to popular belief, I don't like dragons. I know a fair bit about the winged lizards, but I tell stories about them because they make me money, that's all. And I'm certainly not going to stick my neck out for some ravenous scaled vermin when I know how much trouble it is, especially if I could foist it off on you and make a fortune." His lip twisted in a humorless smirk. "So I'm afraid I *don't* know where your dragon is, but if you do end up finding it, do me a favor and take it as far from here as you can." He waved a shriveled hand at the watching crowd. "I'm getting tired of the clamor it's causing."

Hidden in the grass, Remy held his breath. Bart's argument was so convincing, *he* almost believed it himself. Maybe it was so convincing because Bart *didn't* like dragons. For just a moment, Remy wondered why Bart was even helping him and Storm if he hated dragons so much.

But Jhaeros smiled. "You're a very good liar," he told Bart, making Remy's stomach drop. "Unfortunately, there is one tiny piece of the puzzle that doesn't fit. If there has been no dragon hatchling in your house, how do you explain this?"

He held up his hand, and Remy's blood ran cold. Something glimmered between the mage's two fingers, something tiny and bright, like a shard of metal. Even from this distance, Remy knew what it was.

A dragon scale.

"Hatchlings shed constantly, don't they?" Jhaeros crooned as Bart went very still at the sight of the scale. "Little gluttons. Always eating, always getting bigger. Always losing their scales and growing new ones. I will say, you did a remarkable job of keeping that disgusting hovel clean of dragon clutter. Knowing how rapidly hatchlings lose their first set of scales, I am impressed you got rid of as many as you did. Unfortunately, you seem to have missed this one."

Bart straightened quickly. Remy didn't know what he was about to do, but one of the pirates behind him suddenly raised his sword and struck him in the back of the head with the hilt. He fell, crumpling into the grass, and Remy bit down a cry of horror.

"So . . ." Jhaeros continued, smiling as Bart pushed himself to his hands and knees. The pirate crouched down so he could look Bart in the face, his voice becoming hard and terrifying. "I will make it very simple for you, Bart. I am officially out of patience, and negotiations are over. We are now moving on to ultimatums. You have five seconds to either give me my dragon, tell me where my dragon is, or give me the name of the person hiding my dragon, *or* you can die a very painful, excruciating death." Jhaeros stood, raising a hand, and strands of lightning began sparking between his fingers. The pirates standing closest to Bart took a few nervous steps back, leaving him alone in front of Jhaeros. "So, *Sir Bartello*," the pirate mage said as the strands grew brighter in his palm, snapping in the air, "is this hatchling worth dying over? Make your decision quickly. Five . . ."

No, Remy thought, his stomach twisting like snakes inside him. *I can't stand here and watch Bart die. What can I do?*

"Four," Jhaeros went on calmly. "Three. Your time is running out, Bart. I just want my dragon. Two . . ."

Bart coughed, the harsh sound breaking the tense stillness. "All right," he rasped. "All right, fine. You want the wretched beast so badly? I'll tell you where you can find it."

Remy's heart stood still. Jhaeros lowered his arm, and Bart struggled to his feet, glaring at the pirate mage. "You can find it in the Abyss," he spat at Jhaeros, "along with your humanity, your honor, and your sense of decency as a human being. You're nothing but a bloodthirsty predator."

"I've never claimed otherwise." Jhaeros smirked and raised his hand again, the lightning between his fingers almost blinding. "That was, however, the wrong answer. Good-bye, Bartello. Say hello to my humanity if you see it in the Abyss."

"No!" Remy leaped to his feet, and several things happened all at once.

At his shout, both Bart and Jhaeros jerked their heads in his direction. For just a second, Remy saw their faces, Jhaeros looking surprised and Bart staring at him in alarm. Then there was a ripple of movement in the grass, a flash of silver and blue as, with an explosion of scales and bared teeth, Storm leaped into the air and clamped his jaws around Jhaeros's wrist.

Jhaeros let out a shout, stumbling back with the dragon clinging to his arm. Storm growled, flapping his wings and clawing at the mage as the rest of the pirates stared in shock and confusion.

"Storm!" Without thinking, Remy rushed forward. He didn't know what he could do to fight Jhaeros and a whole group of pirates. He just knew that he had to get to his dragon before it was too late.

Jhaeros raised his arm, eyes gleaming at the sight of Storm. He started to grab the dragon; then Bart threw himself forward, tackling the pirate around the waist, and all three of them tumbled into the mud.

"Storm, get out of here!" Bart shouted, and the dragon cringed. "Don't worry about me! Go with the boy, and don't come out again until it's safe. Go!"

Storm turned and fled as Jhaeros gave a roar of outrage and sat up, shoving Bart off him and into the mud. "Get that dragon!" he bellowed at his men, who immediately sprang forward after him.

"Storm!" Remy cried as the dragon raced toward him, a horde of pirates on his tail. "This way! Hurry!"

Storm put on a burst of speed and leaped into Remy's arms, talons sinking into his shirt. Remy dodged the pirate that lunged at him and dove through another's legs, which caused the pirate to overbalance and fall into the mud. Springing to his feet, Storm clutched tightly in one arm, he started to run.

"I don't think so!" Jhaeros's shout made Remy glance back, which was a mistake. The mage stood, wind snapping at his hair and clothes, and threw out an arm.

A blast of wind shrieked down from nowhere. It picked Remy off his feet, flinging him backward and slamming him to the ground. He rolled several paces through the mud, the world spinning around him, before he came to a dizzying stop.

Beneath him, the ground still felt like a swaying ship, but he raised his head, clenching his jaw to keep from puking, and looked around for Storm. The hatchling lay on his side several feet away, unmoving at first, which sent a spear of ice through Remy's stomach. But then his wings fluttered and he raised his head blearily, just as two pirates stomped up, grabbed the hatchling by the tail, and dropped him into a burlap sack.

No! Storm! Remy scrambled upright and lunged after the pirates. "Let him go!" he yelled, grabbing for the bag. But one of the pirates turned with a scowl, and Remy didn't see the fist coming until it caught him across the face, knocking him back. Stars exploded behind his eyes as he collapsed back into the mud, and the world went blurry for a few seconds.

"Got the dragon, boss," he heard the pirates saying, watching as they walked back to Jhaeros with a squirming burlap bag. Remy tried getting up, to stagger after them, but his limbs weren't cooperating, and every time he moved his head he nearly vomited. Jhaeros smiled a slow, evil smile and took the bag, watching it writhe and hiss angrily.

"Excellent. Now we can finally leave this piss-pot island and get on with the real mission." A high-pitched snarl came from the bag, followed by the sound of flapping wings, and Jhaeros chuckled. "You're a bit feistier now," he told the squirming dragon. "Not that it will help you for long. Still, I suspect you're going to be difficult to handle on the ship."

His cruel eyes slid to Bart, sitting on the ground with two pirates standing over him, and his smile widened. "Well, Bart, congratulations," he said. "Since the dragon obviously likes you, you get to come along and take care of the beast until I'm ready for it." He snapped his fingers, and the two pirates behind Bart grabbed his arms and hauled him to his feet. Bart didn't resist, standing there with his head bowed and his shoulders slumped, and Jhaeros gave a triumphant laugh.

"We got what we came for," he announced. "Let's go."

The pirates turned away, walking toward the looming airship hovering overhead, Jhaeros carrying the squirming bag and two pirates following Bart with their swords drawn. Panicked, Remy tried surging to his feet to follow, but the darkness crawling along the edge of his vision finally rushed in, and the world went black.

CHAPTER EIGHTEEN

"The *Windshark* is coming!"

The shout echoed over the decks. Gem peered over the railings to see the massive bulk of the warship rise into the air then swoop toward them on the wind. For a moment, panic stabbed through her. Was the *Windshark* going to attack? She knew airships, and though the *Queen's Blade* was fast and agile and could probably fly circles around the larger ship, the *Windshark* definitely had it outgunned. The captain had been right to be concerned. If they got into a firefight with the warship, it would blow them to pieces.

"Steady as she goes, Mr. Tuhga," Captain Cutlass told

the first mate. "No need to panic quite yet. But watch the cannon ports; if they open up, then we're in trouble."

"She's coming in starboard," called a sailor from the riggings.

Gem held her breath as the huge warship floated by, casting the smaller vessel in its shadow. Pirates from both ships stared at each other over the rails, but it seemed to Gem that the *Windshark* crew was meaner and even more dangerous-looking than the pirates of the *Queen's Blade*. They leered or gave the crew mocking salutes as they went by; one of them even drew a thumb across his throat while grinning at Captain Cutlass. She ignored him, but Gem shrank back against the railings and pulled her hood up as far as it would go.

And then, as the *Windshark* continued to pull alongside them, Gem saw a figure standing atop the aftcastle, much like Captain Cutlass was doing on the *Queen's Blade*. A man in a tattered black coat, his pure white hair snapping behind him in the wind.

A chill went through her, and she gasped. "Is that the captain?" she asked Jack, who was still standing next to her at the railings.

The lanky man gave a solemn bob of his head. "Aye, that's Jhaeros, captain of the *Windshark*."

"I didn't realize he was a mage."

"Oh yes. That's what makes him so dangerous. Well, that and the huge armored warship he got from who knows where. But yes, Jhaeros is a mage, and a pretty nasty one if all the stories about him are true."

Gem watched Captain Jhaeros and the *Windshark* pull away and continue across the Maelstrom. "I wonder whether there really was a dragon on Cutthroat Wedge," she murmured.

"Well, we'll be stopping by in a few minutes," Jack said, peering at the approaching island. "I'm sure someone will tell you if you ask."

I intend to, Gem thought. *There are a lot of questions that need asking, actually.*

A few minutes later, the ship docked at one of several sky piers near a row of rusty-looking old warehouses. As a sailor began securing the vessel to the posts, Captain Cutlass walked onto the deck and gazed around at the crew.

"I'm going landside with Miss Featherbottom," she announced. "Jack, you're with us. Mr. Tuhga, you're in charge until we return."

"Yes, Captain," both answered at the same time.

"Oh, and someone get Lysander up here. I want him with us as well." The captain pointed a finger at another sailor. "Fetch our mage. Tell him this is an order from the captain; I'm not giving him a choice."

The sailor didn't look happy at the command, as if he feared getting yelled at, or shot with lightning, but nodded. "Yes, Captain."

A few minutes later, a trapdoor to the lower decks opened

and the young man Gem had seen the other day stepped onto the deck, frowning. In the sunlight, he looked even younger than before, only a few years older than Gem. He was busy pulling his hair into a ponytail as he walked across the deck, but as he passed Gem, she spotted a few bright yellow strands mixed in with the silver. He glanced at her as he passed, but since she had pulled her hood all the way up to hide her hair, he didn't seem to notice that there was another mage on board. And from his sour, bored expression, she doubted he would care if he did notice.

"Good of you to join us, Lysander," Captain Cutlass said as the scowling young mage stopped in front of her. "It's so nice to see your smiling, cheerful face above deck for once. Perhaps next time you could obey your captain's order with a little more haste." She turned and raised a hand toward the dock. "Now, if everyone is ready, let's go. I don't want to stay on Cutthroat Wedge any longer than I have to."

"Captain, with all due respect, why do I have to go landside?" Lysander's green gaze flickered to the hunk of rock that was Cutthroat Wedge, and his lip curled in blatant disgust. "I know nothing about this place, other than that it's a smuggling haven for pirates. I'd be much more useful belowdecks in the crystal chamber. Why am I a part of this party?"

"Because it is an order from your captain," Cutlass said in a tone that Gem had heard often from her father. His *because I am the king, and I said so* voice. "And it is literally part of your job," the captain went on, striding across the deck toward the gangplank. Gem and the others struggled to keep pace with her. "When captains go landside, they either have their first officer or ship mage with them. Or both. It's not going to kill you to get out and actually talk to people now and again."

"It might," Lysander muttered as they reached the plank that led from the ship to the end of the dock.

"Well, you're not allowed to die," Captain Cutlass said in a cheerful, completely serious tone. "Because then I would have to find another storm mage that isn't a college-bred imbecile, and that would just be a headache. So no dying. That's an order."

Gem frowned. "I'm sorry. College-bred imbecile?" she repeated. "What do you mean by that?"

Lysander snorted. "She means that the so-called mages that come out of that college are weak, simpering idiots who believe whatever the council tells them." He stuck his nose in the air, his voice turning nasal and stuffy. "You need a proper education to learn magic," he wheezed. "If you don't go to the college, you're a danger to yourself and everyone around you. Magic can only be taught by college mages, and you must obey all the stupid rules and restrictions they preach or you're not fit to attend."

Gem bristled. "I know several college mages," she said stiffly. "The rules are there for a reason. Magic *is* dangerous, and we . . . I mean, the students have to learn control before they can use it properly."

"Really." The young mage gave her an unfriendly smile. "I learned how to control storm lightning the first year I discovered I was magic-touched," he said. "How long does the college make students wait? Two years? Three?"

"Four." Gem blinked at him. "Wait, are you saying that anyone with magic affinity can wield storm lightning?"

"Well, I certainly didn't go to college." Lysander shook his head. "I learned on my own. I'm better than any mage who got 'the proper education.'" He curled his lip at the words. "You don't need a college education to use magic. The college teaches structure and control, but magic is wild, untamed, unpredictable. Anyone with the talent can use it. You just have to be careful it doesn't tear you apart."

"But if anyone with the talent can learn magic on their own, why are there only college mages in the capital?" Gem wondered. "The only noncertified mages I've heard of are pirates or smugglers."

"Because those are the only ships who will give us a job," Lysander snapped. "Because there's a law regarding mages in the capital. You *have* to be college certified to be a storm mage on any merchant or capital ship. They won't take you otherwise." He made a disgusted gesture with one arm, curling a lip. "Never mind that the college is so insanely expensive, only the nobles can afford to send their special, magic-touched children there. The rest of us dirty commoners are out of luck."

He glanced at Captain Cutlass with a twisted smile.

"Fortunately, there are captains who don't care if you have a 'proper' magic education or not. They just need a storm mage to power their crystals and fly the ship. Even if they do force them to go landside and talk to useless people when they'd rather be in the crystal chamber alone."

"And I'm very grateful for it," the captain said. "However, we are on an important escort mission for Miss Featherbottom." She nodded in Gem's direction. "And people with ill intent think twice about attacking a party if there's a mage present. So sadly, Lysander, you don't get to hide from the world today. You're with us all afternoon, so smile and bear it."

Lysander rolled his eyes. "I'll bear it," he muttered, casting a sour look at Gem. "But I'm not going to smile."

A blast of wind caught them as they stepped off the ship onto the docks, making the sails flap and yanking Gem's hood halfway off. Quickly, she pulled it up again, hoping nobody saw the streak of white in her hair. Thankfully, Lysander's and Jack's attention seemed to be on the squat, run-down building atop a hill where the *Windshark* had been hovering just a few minutes ago.

As they started up the path, Gem tried to concentrate on why she was there, but it was hard. Her mind spun, thinking of what Lysander had said about magic. He wasn't a college-educated mage, yet he could wield storm lightning. No one had taught him; he had learned on his own. He was young, but the captain tolerated, even respected, him as a competent mage. Even if his social skills were severely lacking.

She wondered if *she* could learn magic faster.

"There's quite the crowd," Jack muttered, shading his eyes against the glare of the sun through the clouds. Gem followed his gaze and saw a large group of people in the muddy front yard, staring after the departing *Windshark*. "I guess Jhaeros found what he was looking for and left."

"That's good for us," Captain Cutlass said as they started walking toward the building atop the hill. "I didn't want to deal with his narcissism right now. And Cutthroat Wedge isn't my favorite place, either. As soon as we find the person Miss Featherbottom is looking for, we can leave."

"So who *are* you looking for, anyway?" Lysander asked, pinning Gem with a narrowed green gaze. "Cutthroat Wedge isn't a place nobles spend time in. Everyone here is either a pirate, a criminal, or just scraping by. Who are you here to find?"

Gem felt Captain Cutlass's eyes on her and swallowed. "His name is Sir Bartello," she said, and saw Lysander's brows arch at the name. "He was once a sky knight in the king's army, many years ago."

"A sky knight?" the mage repeated. "Here? Mingling with the pirates and lowlifes? That's unlikely." He snorted.

"I would try looking in the capital, or on an island that's not so . . . dirty. He's not going to be here. Flighty, airheaded nobles, wasting our time—"

"Lysander," the captain said calmly as Gem set her jaw, "Miss Featherbottom came to me for help, and I agreed to help her. Please refrain from being too much of yourself around important clients. Shockingly, they don't find your complete lack of manners charming."

"Like I care what some pampered noble thinks of me," Lysander muttered. But he didn't say anything more as they climbed the hill to join the crowd of people up top. Gem looked up and saw an old wooden sign creaking above the door. It was barely legible, but read THE SALTY BARREL in faded letters.

"Since Jhaeros is gone," a man was saying as they approached, "does that mean no one gets the reward? Did someone else get the reward?"

"It isn't fair," another whined. "I've been looking for that beast everywhere. I haven't slept or bathed in a week. I *needed* that reward!"

Gem started forward, but Captain Cutlass put a hand on her arm, stopping her. "Hold on there," she warned. "These types aren't going to take a child seriously. Let me do the talking. I speak their language, and that language is pirate."

The captain strode up with Gem and the others behind her. "Gentlemen," she said. "If I could have a moment of your time. We're looking for someone, and we heard he was here."

The men eyed her, their mouths twisting into ugly leers, but then they seemed to notice the captain's hat, the mage behind her, and the sword at her waist. Their grins faded, and the color drained from their faces when they seemed to recognize her. "Aye, Captain, if you're here looking for Jhaeros, you're too late," one of them grumbled. "He's already gone, with his dragon and my reward."

"*Your* reward?" scoffed the other. "It should've been mine."

"So you can drink yourself into a stupor and fall off the edge of the island?" The first man snorted. "Bloody waste that would've been."

"I am not looking for Jhaeros," Captain Cutlass interrupted. "Any fool with eyes could see the *Windshark* leaving just a few minutes ago. I'm looking for Bart. Is the old crab still at the tavern telling stories?"

"Crusty Bart?" the first man said, and laughed. "You're still too late, Captain. Jhaeros grabbed the dragon, and he took Bart as well." He stretched out an arm toward the sky. "Both of them are on the *Windshark* right now, sailing away, out of anyone's reach."

No. Gem felt her heart plummet. Sir Bartello *was* here. But somehow, he was involved with Jhaeros, and now both were on board that monstrous pirate ship.

"They took him?" Captain Cutlass demanded, frowning at the men. "Why? Jhaeros isn't into kidnapping, as far as I know. He's more likely to kill everyone on board a ship and then sink it into the Maelstroem. Why did he take Bart?"

The men shrugged. "Dunno. Said he needed someone to 'take care of the dragon.' That's all we heard."

"I see." Captain Cutlass sighed and took a step back. "That's unfortunate. I kind of liked the old geezer." She turned with a shrug. "Well, there's nothing we can do about it now. Back to the ship, men. We'll prepare to cast off in an hour—"

"Wait." Gem quickly put herself in the captain's path. "Captain, we have to go after them."

The captain stared at her for a long moment, then gave a rather brittle smile and turned to Jack and Lysander, who were waiting off to the side. "Excuse me a moment, boys. I need a private word with Miss Featherbottom."

Cutlass took Gem's sleeve and pulled her around the side of the tavern.

"All right, look, Princess," she said in a quieter voice. "I was willing to fly you here, to Cutthroat Wedge, one of the most dangerous pirate outposts in the Fringe, because I trusted myself and my crew to keep you safe. I was willing to do you a favor, because you are the princess and it seemed like a good idea not to let the king's daughter go gallivanting into danger without any idea of what she was getting into."

"Because you're hoping for a reward when this is over," Gem said.

"I thought that was obvious," Cutlass responded. "And I'm trusting that you will remember what we did for you when you do return to your father. However"—she raised one gloved finger—"I did *not* agree to go chasing after one of the most infamous sky pirates in the Fringe. You saw the size of the *Windshark*. That ship has destroyed countless vessels, and Jhaeros is not someone you want as an enemy." The captain straightened, giving Gem a firm look. "So I'm afraid I'm going to have to refuse, Princess. I'm not going after the *Windshark*. I have my own ship and my crew to think about, and this isn't our fight. We'll be returning to the inner islands after this; you're welcome to join us. We'll be happy to drop you off at whatever town you please, and from there, you can easily find your way home."

Gem clenched her fists. "No," she said, making Cutlass arch a crimson eyebrow. "I can't. I can't go home. I have to find Bart. He's the only one who might know where the True Dragons are."

Both of the captain's eyebrows now arched into her hair. "True Dragons. That's what this is about?" she asked. "The True Dragons are a myth, old sailor stories. No one has seen a True Dragon for hundreds of years."

"Bart has," Gem said. "He might know where the True Dragons are. That's why I need to talk to him."

"Why?"

Gem bit her lip. "I can't tell you that."

Cutlass shrugged and started to walk around her. "Well, then I suppose you're going to have to fly home alone."

"Wait!" Gem held up her hands, making the captain

pause. "If . . . if you help me," she began, hating the fact that she had to negotiate even more, "if we can get to Bart and rescue him from Jhaeros, then I . . . I'll make sure my father rewards you with anything you want when we return to the capital."

Captain Cutlass blinked. "Anything?" she asked softly.

"I mean . . . within reason," Gem stammered. "I'm sure he wouldn't be able to give you the whole island or every ship in the city. But . . . yes, whatever you want, I'll see that you get it. That is a promise."

"Hmm." The captain crossed her arms, thinking. "I will admit, that is a very tempting proposal," she mused. "If we're talking about wants, I can think of a lot. But you still have to be alive to enjoy them. Besides, we don't even know where the *Windshark* is going."

"I know where they're going," said a voice behind them.

CHAPTER
NINETEEN

Remy's head ached.

His whole body hurt, really. He'd woken up with his face pressed into cold mud, the back of his skull throbbing and a dull pain radiating below his eye. But that was nothing compared to the sudden hollowness in the pit of his stomach, telling him both Storm and Bart were gone. That Jhaeros had taken them both, and he'd been left alone. Again.

Remy clenched his fist, feeling mud squelch between his fingers. The loss of his dragon felt almost physical, like someone had reached into his center and ripped out something vital, and now there was a huge, gaping hole inside. For a few seconds, he'd just lain there in the mud, trying not to vomit, as his head throbbed and his thoughts spun wildly. There was only one thing on his mind now: how he was going to get Storm back.

Storm. Closing his eyes, he thought of his dragon, searching for that strange feeling that had awakened when he'd touched the storm crystals. *Where are you?*

For a moment, there was nothing. Remy felt nothing but cold mud beneath his hands, the frost-laced wind against his face. But then a surge of fear and anger bloomed inside him, making him gasp. Opening his eyes, he gazed out over the horizon. He could suddenly *feel* Storm, faint and far away. He knew which direction his dragon was going.

Abruptly, he became aware of voices, speaking quietly a few yards behind him.

"True Dragons," one of them said. A woman's voice, low and cynical. "The True Dragons are a myth, old sailor stories. No one has seen a True Dragon for hundreds of years."

"Bart has," replied the other. Also female, though younger. "He might know where the True Dragons are. That's why I need to talk to him."

They're looking for Bart. Remy's stomach churned. Clenching his jaw, he pushed himself upright, still listening as the voices discussed rewards and going after Jhaeros. The world swayed as he got to his feet, but he ignored the nausea and turned slowly, looking around for the speakers.

A woman stood several paces away, speaking to a smaller figure in a cloak and hood, a cowl drawn up to cover their face. The woman's long red hair and dark purple coat rippled behind her in the wind, and a shiver crawled up Remy's back as he recognized her. She rarely came to Cutthroat Wedge, but Captain Cutlass was somewhat of a legend, too. At least among the sailors who frequented the tavern. Her ship, the *Queen's Blade*, was one of the fastest in the Fringe and, according to the stories, had escaped many impossible situations. Whether this was due to the quality of the ship or the prowess of the captain and her crew was a source of debate among the sailors, but there was no denying that Cutlass was another dangerous pirate who you didn't want to cross.

Remy set his jaw. This was for his dragon. He was going to get Storm back, but he couldn't fly to the *Windshark* on his own. He needed to track Jhaeros, and a sky ship or a dragon was the only way. This time, he wasn't going to be left behind.

Taking a deep breath, he raked back his hair, raised his chin, and strode up to the captain, just as she was telling the girl that they didn't know where the *Windshark* was going.

Perfect timing.

"I know where they're going," Remy announced.

Both the captain and the hooded figure turned, and he saw the face of the second figure for the first time. Beneath the hood was a girl around his own age, her blue eyes narrowed in suspicion as she stared at him.

"Who are you?" she demanded.

Remy ignored her. The girl wasn't important. The girl

couldn't help him get his dragon back. The one he had to convince was Cutlass.

"My name is Remy," he told the captain, meeting her amused green gaze. "I live here. I was here when Jhaeros took Stor . . . took the dragon and Bart. I can tell you where they went."

"Hmm, one of Cutthroat Wedge's many street rats," Captain Cutlass remarked, not unkindly. She reached into a coat pocket and withdrew a small leather pouch. "I suppose you want to be paid for this information. . . ."

"No," Remy interrupted, making the girl scowl and the captain arch a brow at him. "I don't want money," he said as his heart began a loud thud in his chest. "I want to come with you. Take me along, and I'll show you where they went."

"What?" the girl exclaimed. "Take you with us? Why? We're going after Jhaeros and the *Windshark*. It's going to be dangerous. Why would you want to come along?"

"Because," Remy said, clenching his fists, "he took my dragon, and I'm going to get him back."

Both stared at him a moment. He could feel the disbelief radiating from the girl in waves. "*Your* dragon?" she said at last. Her gaze flickered over him, at his muddy rags and unkempt hair. "Where did *you* get a dragon?" she wondered, and it sounded like an accusation. "Did you steal it from someone?"

"I didn't steal him," Remy said. "I found him. His name is Storm, and he's a wild dragon."

"You found a wild dragon." The girl's voice was dubious. "Did you check for a tattoo? All dragons have them, under their right wing. It will show who the dragon belongs to."

Remy's temper flared. "Yes, I checked for a tattoo," he snapped. "He didn't have one anywhere. I'm telling you, he's a wild dragon. Jhaeros killed his mother during a spell storm. He shot her down, and Storm ended up with me."

"Ah," said Captain Cutlass slowly, as if she had just figured something out. "So *you're* the reason Jhaeros had every pirate crew in the Fringe scrambling over each other looking for his lost hatchling. There are people who would pay anything to have a dragon, especially a baby. And if the creature is wild, they wouldn't have to worry about ownership tattoos or where it came from." She gave Remy an appraising look. "You'll be taking away an extremely valuable resource. Jhaeros isn't going to be happy if someone tries to steal his dragon again."

"I don't care!" Remy burst out. "I don't care what it takes or what I have to do, I just know that I need to get Storm back. And Bart, too. He was taken because he was helping me. I can't leave them with Jhaeros." He set his jaw, glaring at the pirate and the girl. "I know where the *Windshark* is going," he went on. "I . . . I have a connection. With Storm. I can feel where he is, and how close or far away he's gotten."

The girl's eyebrows arched, her expression dubious, and he stifled the urge to wince. "I know it sounds impossible."

"You're right," the girl said. "It does sound impossible. I've never heard of anyone having that kind of bond with their dragon, and I've lived around dragons my whole life." She crossed her arms, regarding him with suspicion. "Are you sure you're not just looking for a way off Cutthroat Wedge, and you'll say anything to get aboard a ship?"

"No!" Remy protested. "I swear, I can feel where Storm is right now. He's . . ." He paused, turning slowly, searching for the feeling again. "Storm is . . . that way," he said, pointing off into the distance. "I'm sure of it."

"'That way' is not a direction," the captain said. "Are you saying the *Windshark* has gone north, or is moving in a northerly direction?"

"I . . . I don't know," Remy said again. "I can just feel him, and he's . . . that way. But that's why I have to come with you." He could feel himself wilting under the twin disbelieving stares and clenched his jaw. He would *not* lose Storm, or Bart. Both were counting on him. "You need me," he told the captain. "I'm the only one who can track the *Windshark*. If you want to find it, I have to come along with you."

"So sure of that, are you?" Captain Cutlass gave a faint, unamused smile. "I think you're both forgetting something important," she said. "I haven't actually agreed to do this. Don't glare at me, Miss Featherbottom," she added as the girl spun on her, bristling. "Knowing where they went is all well and good, but chasing down Jhaeros is still akin to suicide. The *Windshark* is bigger, better armored, and much more heavily armed than the *Blade*. They'll shoot us out of the sky before we can even put a dent in their hull."

"We don't have to fight them," said the girl. "We just need to get Sir Bartello and the dragon out, right? I can fly over with Cloud, sneak aboard and rescue them, and get out the same way. They won't even have to know you're there."

"You have a dragon?" Remy asked. The girl gave him a scornful look but nodded.

"That seems very risky," the captain mused. "I'm not certain I like the idea of you infiltrating an enemy vessel alone."

"She won't be alone," Remy said. "I'll go with her."

"Excuse me?" The girl frowned at him. "I don't think so."

"It's my dragon," Remy shot back. "We're going to need to move fast, and I'll be able to find him a lot quicker on a big ship. I know how to move silently and keep out of sight. Besides, what if they're in the brig or locked up somewhere? Do you know how to pick a lock?"

The girl's eyes narrowed. "I suppose having a professional thief around when we're trying to steal something would make sense," she muttered.

The captain sighed again, closing her eyes and pinching the bridge of her nose. "I'm already regretting this," she muttered. Dropping her arm, she gave Remy a dubious look. "What's your name again, boy?"

"It's Remy."

"We'll be getting ready to cast off in a few minutes," Captain Cutlass told him. "If you have anything you need, I would fetch it now. We're likely not coming back to Cutthroat Wedge for a while. If ever."

Quickly, Remy thought back to his tiny shack on Beggar's Row, wondering if there was anything he wanted to save. He had no mementos of his mom, nothing to remember her by. There was no one he needed to say good-bye to. Brutus the rat would be fine without him. In fact, no one in Cutthroat Wedge would notice, or care, if Remy vanished off the face of the island and was never seen again.

"I'm fine," he told the captain with a shrug. "I don't have anything. Storm and Bart are the only ones I care about."

Captain Cutlass nodded, but the girl gave him a strange look. As if she didn't understand the concept of having nothing. Remy bit back a snort. She probably didn't. She was a rich, pampered noble, he could tell. She had probably never been hungry, cold, or filthy in her entire life.

"All right, then." The captain looked to the skies, narrowing her eyes as if tracking their quarry through the clouds. "I guess there's nothing left to do here. Let's go. I'll explain to the crew what's happening, and then I suppose we're all going after the *Windshark*." She shook her head and looked at them both. "Chasing down Jhaeros because a pair of kids want me to," she muttered, before striding back toward the tavern. "To rescue a dragon hatchling and an old man. This had better be worth it."

PART
III

CHAPTER
TWENTY

"You can't be serious, Captain."

Gem's lips tightened, but she kept her opinion to herself, watching the pirate mage, Lysander, give Captain Cutlass an incredulous look. They were in the captain's private quarters, standing around a beat-up table with Lysander, Jack, First Mate Tuhga, and the new boy, Remy. A map and a pair of tiny model ships sat on the table—or rather, the ships hovered over the table, held up by the crystal chips embedded in the bottoms of their hulls.

Irritation prickled at Gem. They were supposed to be formulating some sort of plan for what to do once they caught up to the *Windshark*, but the mage obviously did not approve of the rescue mission and let them know it, loudly and persistently.

"Go after Jhaeros? Confront the *Windshark*? The ship that's destroyed more vessels than any other ship in the Fringe?" Lysander shook his head, gesturing wildly with one hand. "That's foolish. Do you know how many cannons the *Windshark* can bring to bear? Even if I pour everything I have into the crystal, I won't be able to keep Jhaeros from blowing us out of the sky."

"Then it's a good thing we aren't planning on fighting the *Windshark*." The captain's voice was calm, as if she was used to dealing with the mage's emotional behavior. "Which you would have known had you been quiet for two seconds longer."

"But—"

"I said we were chasing down the *Windshark*," Captain Cutlass went on. "I didn't say we were going to engage it in battle. I know we are outgunned, and attacking Jhaeros's ship head-on is a fool's mission. Hopefully, if all goes to plan, the *Queen's Blade* will keep well out of any danger.

"This is a rescue mission," she went on, gazing around the table. "We are going to rescue a man named Sir Bartello, whom Jhaeros kidnapped from Cutthroat Wedge. Also, a baby dragon that apparently belongs to this boy here." She nodded at Remy. "We are going to fly in under cover of darkness, and when we are close enough, the boy and Miss

Featherbottom will take her dragon the rest of the way to the *Windshark*."

"Just the two kids?" Jack asked. "Aboard an entire ship filled with pirates? Not that I'm volunteering, but shouldn't someone go with them?"

Gem immediately shook her head. "Cloud can't carry that many people," she said. "He's strong, but we'll be pushing the limits of what he can handle once we have Sir Bartello and the hatchling. Another person will be too heavy. We're just going to sneak in, free Sir Bartello and Remy's dragon, and leave. No one will know we're there."

Lysander blew out a loud breath. "That's a terrible plan," he stated. "Ship quarters are tight and crowded, and neither of you knows how to fight. What if you're discovered? We'd just end up having to rescue you as well."

"Hopefully, they won't be discovered," Captain Cutlass broke in before Gem could say anything. "Because if they are captured, I am not going in after them."

Gem blinked at the captain, who gave her an unapologetic smile. "There is no way we can rescue you from Jhaeros should you fail," she said matter-of-factly. "We don't have a dragon, nor do we have the firepower to charge in after you. I'm afraid you will be on your own. So you will need to get this right the first time."

"Oh," Gem said, feeling suddenly breathless.

"Luckily," added the captain, "we can help make that

more likely. We might not be able to take the *Windshark* in a one-on-one fight, but we can harry and harass so all their attention is on us and not the two stowaways creeping through the ship. The *Queen's Blade* is faster and more agile than the *Windshark*, so with the element of surprise, we should be able to pelt them with a few cannonballs, drop some fire barrels on them from above, and get to safety before they can launch a full attack."

"So we *are* planning on assaulting the *Windshark*," Lysander burst out. "Which brings me back to my original argument, in which I think this is a horrible idea."

"The rescue team needs a distraction," Captain Cutlass said firmly. "We will provide that distraction, but that does not mean we're going to play fair. At no point in this conversation did I say we were going to battle the *Windshark* head-to-head. We'll do what the *Queen's Blade* does best: use our speed to keep out of reach and pelt them with cannon fire when we can."

"Oh," muttered Lysander. "More storm crystal acrobatics for me, then. Fabulous."

"However," the captain went on, turning to Gem, "that means that once we start the distraction, we'll be on a timetable. The two of you will have a limited time to find Bartello and the dragon and get out again. We can only harass the *Windshark* for so long before it shoots us out of the sky. Once the chaos starts, you'll have to move fast. Can you do this?"

Before Gem could answer, the boy suddenly raised his

head. "How are we going to get aboard the *Windshark*?" he asked. "I know we're flying over with a dragon, but there's going to be guards and watches. How will we keep them from seeing us?"

Gem hadn't really thought of that. Her midnight infiltration of the college library was the only sneaky thing she had ever done. It had worked because she was already so familiar with the library, but the boy probably knew more about breaking into places. She hadn't even thought about guards on a pirate ship.

Fortunately, Remy wasn't the only criminally minded person at the table. The captain smiled and picked up one of the tiny ship models.

"You know what a crow's nest is, don't you, boy?" she asked, and the street boy nodded.

"The basket at the very top of the mast," he replied. "It's used to keep watch for storms or other ships."

"That is correct. Well, many ships also have something called a bilge hole," the captain went on, tapping the bottom of the model. "It's much like the crow's nest, only this one is located below the ship hull, and its purpose is to keep an eye on the Maelstrom to see how close it's getting. Or, in the case of a pirate or warship, to watch for attacks from below. But if we're providing a distraction, the bilge hole should be empty. You should be able to get into the ship from the bilge hole platform and leave the same way. The bilge hole will likely lead into the cargo hold, or very close. If your Sir

Bartello is on the ship, he'll probably be in the brig, which will also be on the lowest deck. So," she said with a clap, "now that you know the ship layout, you know what you're doing, right?" She looked at Gem. "You have a plan?"

Gem nodded. "Find Sir Bartello and the dragon and get out in the confusion. Shouldn't be too difficult." Her stomach clenched as she said this. The thought of sneaking into an enemy ship filled with dangerous pirates was terrifying. If they were seen . . . She pushed that thought away. They would just have to not be seen.

"Everyone else understand the mission?" the captain continued, gazing around the table. They all muttered an affirmative, even Lysander, though he didn't look happy about it. "Good. I'll let the crew know what's going on. Any questions?"

"Just one, Captain." Mr. Tuhga raised his head, looking serious. "How are we going to find the *Windshark* without knowing where Jhaeros is headed?" he asked. "He could be anywhere in the Fringe right now."

"Well, that's going to be up to this boy here," Captain Cutlass said, glancing at the street kid. "He claims to have a connection with the stolen dragon, that he can *feel* where the dragon is, and which direction he's headed."

The disbelief and skepticism around the table was palpable. It was a testament to the crew's faith in their captain that no one immediately said how bizarre that plan sounded.

Not even Lysander, though he raised an extremely dubious eyebrow in Remy's direction.

"So what is going to happen," the captain went on, looking at Remy, "is that the boy is going to check in with the navigator every hour to make sure we are still going the right way. Do you hear that, boy?" she asked. "Every hour, even through the night. So if you are asleep belowdecks, someone is going to wake you and bring you to the helm to point the ship in the right direction. Is that understood?"

He nodded. "I understand. I want to find Storm. I'll stay up all night if I have to."

"Probably no need to go that far. Jack," the captain said, glancing at the lanky man half nodding off against the bookshelf. "I'm putting you in charge of the kid. Show him where he'll be sleeping, and what he'll be doing while he's aboard the ship."

"Sure thing, Captain." Jack pushed himself off the way and tapped Remy's arm. "You're with me, then, boy."

"And for goodness' sake, get him some better clothes," Cutlass added. "My quarters are going to smell like mud for a week. The rest of you are dismissed. Oh, and Miss Featherbottom," she said as the mage and the first mate turned away. "A word, if you don't mind."

Gem watched the rest of the crew file out of the room, then turned to the captain.

Beckoning to Gem, Cutlass strode over to her desk and

seated herself in the chair, putting her boots on the surface again. She picked up a decanter on the corner, poured herself a glass of amber liquid, and tossed it back before gazing up at Gem.

"You know this is going to be very dangerous," she said, twirling the cup in her fingers. "We're about as far from the reach of the capital as anyone can get, and there are no guards or sky knights to help us out here. Jhaeros is a terrifying person to have as an enemy. If you're caught, there's no telling what he'll do with the princess of Gallecia. You're taking an enormous risk boarding his ship. I just want you to be aware of that."

"I am," Gem replied.

"And you still want to do this."

"Yes," Gem said firmly. "I must speak with Sir Bartello. I can't reveal why, but it's safe to say that the fate of the kingdom depends on it."

"Well, it sounds very important," Cutlass said sarcastically. The captain didn't seem terribly impressed with Gem's statement. She poured herself another glass from the decanter, but instead of drinking, she gazed at the sparkling liquid within, seemingly deep in thought. "What do you think of that boy?" she wondered out loud. "You have a dragon. You said you've been surrounded by them your whole life. Are you sure you've never heard of this connection with a dragon before?"

Gem pursed her lips. "No," she said. "I never have. I'm

not sure something like that even exists." If it did, she was certain she and Cloud would already have one. "Do you think he's lying?" Gem asked. "Just to get on the *Queen's Blade* and off Cutthroat Wedge?"

"Hmm, no. I don't think the boy is lying." Cutlass's green eyes flicked to Gem. "I've seen my share of thieves and con artists, and I know when someone is trying to pull the wool over my eyes. The boy is not doing that. He definitely *believes* he has a connection to this dragon; whether or not that is actually true remains to be seen. But I don't see another way of tracking Jhaeros and the *Windshark* through open sky, do you?"

"No," Gem muttered. "I don't."

"Well, I suppose we're going to have to trust him, then," Cutlass said, and casually downed her drink. "And hope that he knows where the *Windshark* is actually going." Gem clenched her jaw, and the captain raised a brow at her. "If you're worried about it, you could always go talk to the boy," she suggested. "You both have dragons; you know more about them than most people."

"Talk to him." Gem wrinkled her nose. "He's a thief."

"And we are all pirates," Cutlass countered. "I think the ship has sailed on that one, Princess."

She swung her boots off the desk and rose, turning to place the decanter and glass back on a shelf. "Whatever your beliefs, Princess," she said over her shoulder, "remember: You and that boy will be sneaking aboard the *Windshark* together. I'm putting my ship and my crew on the line for this, so I suggest you figure out how to work with him, thief or not, or this entire mission is going to fail."

Gem set her jaw and walked out of the captain's office. A blast of wind tossed her cloak, nearly pushing her hood back, as she stepped onto the deck. Gazing around, she saw Remy standing at the helm with Jack and First Mate Tuhga. The boy was facing the horizon, the wind blowing at his rags and unkempt hair. One arm lifted, and a grimy finger pointed into the distance. With a single nod, the first mate grabbed the wheel and spun it to the left. Gem felt the *Queen's Blade* shift, very slightly, as it changed direction and flew toward the sinking sun.

Her eyes narrowed. They were putting their trust in a thief, in an unknown street kid from a pirate town. Who claimed to have such a strong connection to a dragon, he could feel him across the of miles of empty sky between them.

She would see about that.

Raising her chin, she started across the deck toward them.

CHAPTER
TWENTY-ONE

"That way."

Remy tried not to wince, to sound confident as he pointed a finger toward the setting sun. "*'That way' is not a direction*," the captain had said, but he didn't know how to convey direction any other way. Beside him, the lanky pirate, Jack, regarded him with a tongue in his cheek, then turned to the first mate, standing at the wheel.

"Three points latitude, Tuhga," he said, and the other man nodded once. He spun the wheel, and the *Queen's Blade* turned, angling toward the setting sun.

"You sure about that direction, kid?" Jack asked as they settled into the new course. "You know there's nothing out that way, right? Not islands, not ports. Nothing but sky. You sure that's the way the *Windshark* went?"

Remy closed his eyes, searching for that feeling, and bobbed his head. "Yeah, I'm sure. Storm is that way."

Jack shrugged but then straightened quickly, gazing at something over Remy's shoulder. "Lass." He nodded as Remy turned to face the girl. She ignored the pirates, her dark blue glare solely for him.

"Excuse me," she said in a stiff tone of voice. "I need to talk to you."

Remy gave a wary frown. "Why?"

"Just come with me."

He looked at Jack, who shrugged. "Better see what the lass wants, boy," he told him with a smile that said he wasn't going to intervene. "Just remember the captain wants you back here in an hour to make sure we're still sailin' straight." He grinned. "Hopefully your talk won't take that long."

Remy followed the girl across the deck to the rear of the ship, which was called the stern, according to the patrons at the Salty Barrel. Having grown up around pirates and sailors, Remy knew all the different places on a ship, even if he'd never been on one before.

"Your name is Remy, correct?"

He looked at the girl. She stood there with her arms crossed, watching him with a narrowed gaze, as if he might steal her purse if she took her eyes off him. It didn't bother Remy; he'd seen that look nearly every day of his life.

"Yeah," he answered with a shrug. "It is. You never told me your name, though."

"Mary Featherbottom," she said immediately. "But that's not important. Tell me about this dragon of yours."

Remy frowned. She still didn't believe him. "What do you want to know?" he asked.

"You said you can feel where your dragon is, that you know which direction he's going." The girl made it sound like an accusation. Remy nodded, and her lips tightened. "And this is your first dragon?" she went on. "You've never encountered one before?"

He snorted. "You saw Cutthroat Wedge," he scoffed. "Where would I get a dragon that wasn't wild? The sky knights and rich nobles don't exactly travel that far out in the Fringe."

"So you've never even seen a dragon before Storm."

"Up close? No."

She stared at him a moment longer, then turned away. "Follow me. I want to show you something."

With a sigh, he followed her again. This time down the steps into the cargo hold. Crates, barrels, and sacks were piled throughout, turning the space into a giant maze. The air smelled faintly of dust and tar, tickling his nose and making him want to sneeze.

The girl raised her head and gave a soft whistle, and from deeper in the shadows of the hold, something big rumbled an answer.

"What is that?" he whispered.

"You said you like dragons." Mary took a step back, watching him intensely. "Well, meet Cloud."

An enormous pale creature slid around a stack of barrels and came right at him. Remy's heart leaped up and lodged in his throat, a moment before he realized it was a dragon. An adult dragon, many times larger than Storm. Its scales were pure white, its horns tinged with blue, and a pair of glowing sapphire eyes peered down at him from a narrow, reptilian head.

Remy sucked in a breath. The dragon paused a few feet away. Not close, but close enough that it could reach out and bite him if it wanted. Or blast him with fire from where it stood. It loomed over him, wings partially open, head tilted as if deciding whether or not he was a threat. Remy looked up and saw no alarm, anger, or aggression in the dragon's gaze. Just surprise and a wary curiosity.

"Hey," he breathed, and the dragon cocked his head the other way. It wasn't like Storm, Remy realized. Storm was impatient, headstrong, stubborn, and very opinionated for a hatchling. This dragon was much more even-tempered, almost docile. Remembering what he had seen Bart do when he first met Storm, Remy raised a hand, palm up, and eased forward a step.

The dragon's nostrils flared. Stretching its neck out, it sniffed the proffered fingers a few times, then seemed to lose interest in Remy entirely. Stepping around him, the dragon went to the girl, trilling happily and shoving its nose under her arm. She looked annoyed for a moment, then scratched the scaly head with a sigh. Remy grinned.

"Did I pass your dragon test?" he asked. "Were you hoping it was going to eat me?"

"Cloud is a *he*," Mary said stiffly. "And no, I just wanted to see what he would do. Remember, we're both going to be riding him when we go to rescue Bart. If he didn't like you, that would be a problem."

"He's a really pretty dragon," Remy offered, and he meant it. Not that he'd seen many, but there was no argument that the white dragon *was* nice to look at. Personally, he thought Storm's silver lightning bolt stripes over his dark blue scales were more striking, but he wasn't going to mention that.

Mary glared at him a moment more, then sighed. "He was the runt of the nest," she admitted. "Apparently, he was too small to be a battle dragon, so his stable gifted him to me. He never had the battle dragon temperament, either. They're supposed to be aggressive and stubborn, even to their partners, but he's never been anything but sweet."

"Huh." Remy crossed his arms, thinking of his own dragon. "Maybe Storm has some battle dragon blood in him somewhere," he muttered. "He's stubborn enough for it."

Thinking of his dragon made his stomach churn, and he bit his lip to keep the emotions in check. He would see Storm again. He wouldn't stop until he found him.

"I've had Cloud since I was six," Mary went on, stroking

her dragon's nose. "We sort of grew up together. He knows all my secrets, and I consider him my best friend." She raised her head, staring at Remy again with a somber look. "But I've never had any sort of bond where I can just feel where he is," she said. "I've never heard of anyone having that sort of connection with their dragon, not even the sky knights, whose lives depend on their partner. If what you're saying is true, why do *you* have one, with a wild dragon hatchling? How is that even possible?"

"I don't know," Remy said, making her lips tighten. "Not exactly. But . . ." He sighed and ran a hand through his hair. "It probably has something to do with Cutthroat Wedge's storm crystals," he admitted.

Mary went very still at that. "What do you mean?" she whispered.

"Storm and I found this cave with these massive bluish-purple crystals," Remy went on. "They were huge; they had to be the island's storm crystals. When I touched one, I felt this jolt, like I had been magically shocked. And, for a second, I thought I could feel . . . what Storm was feeling."

Mary was gazing at him with wide eyes, her expression slightly dazed. Remy shrugged. "Just for a few seconds, though," he added. "It faded right after, and I thought I had imagined it. Until Jhaeros came and took Storm away."

"The storm crystals," Mary whispered. She seemed to have forgotten all about the dragons. "Did you notice anything strange about them?" she went on. "Like, were they cracked, or damaged in any way?"

"Not at that time," Remy said. "Though they did crack when Jhaeros shot Bart's house to pieces with cannon fire."

Mary's face went ashen. She looked like she was ready to faint, but before Remy could ask what was wrong, a shout came from above.

"Oy, kid! Boy, are you down there?"

Remy looked back, seeing Jack's lanky silhouette at the top of the steps. "I'm here," he called back.

"Get up here!" the pirate ordered. "Right now. There's a storm coming, and based on your directions, we're sailing right for it."

CHAPTER
TWENTY-TWO

A massive wall of black clouds loomed across the sky as Gem scrambled onto the upper deck with Remy behind her. A blast of cold wind snapped at her cloak, and she tugged her hood down to make sure it wouldn't blow off.

The captain was standing at the helm with Jack and the first mate. She gave both Gem and Remy stern looks as they approached, then gazed back at the swirling wall of clouds in the distance. Purple lightning flickered in its depths, and Gem's stomach went cold.

"That is a spell storm coming," Captain Cutlass said, sounding far calmer than Gem would've thought. "It would, of course, be preferable to go around, or even hug the edges.

Going straight through it is something I would like to avoid, but that depends on what our compass says." Here she looked directly at Remy. "So, boy, where are the *Windshark* and your dragon now?"

Remy swallowed. Stepping to the helm, he closed his eyes for a moment, facing the wind. His arm lifted, and he pointed a finger at the sky.

Directly into the storm.

"That's what I thought," Cutlass groaned. "Mr. Tuhga," she snapped, turning to the first mate. "Prepare the ship for the storm. I want everyone attached to safety lines in five minutes. Jack, get those sails furled."

"Aye, Captain!"

"Take the boy with you. He can help with the sails." The captain turned to Remy. "Boy, are you afraid of heights?"

Remy shook his head, and the captain nodded. "Go with Jack, then. He'll show you what you have to do. Jack, get a safety line on the kid before you take him up there."

"Aye!" Jack swatted Remy on the shoulder. "Come on, lad. You're with me. Safety line first, then up the sails we go. Can't have 'em open during the storm; the wind'll rip 'em to pieces."

"Miss Featherbottom." The captain turned to Gem as Jack and Remy scuttled off. "I suggest you go belowdecks for this," she said. "Things are going to get very rough once we hit that storm."

"I want to help," Gem said as a flicker of lightning arced over the approaching clouds. "What can I do?"

"Unless you can part the clouds or direct the lightning not to hit the ship or any of the crew, I'm afraid there's not a lot you can help with," the captain said. "Don't worry, though. The *Queen's Blade* has been through a couple spell storms. They're nasty, but if we keep a cool head, we'll have a chance of coming through without too much damage. We don't have all those lightning rods on the mast and hull for nothing."

Almost as if on cue, purple lightning flashed from the clouds overhead, striking the top of the mast. Or rather, the thin copper rod affixed to the very top. Sparks exploded from the rod, lighting up the sky for a moment, and Cutlass gave a grim smile.

"I'm afraid I'm going to have to insist you go downstairs, Miss Featherbottom," the captain said in a tone that brooked no argument. "I am not about to have the king's daughter flying off into the storm because she ignored safety protocols. Please, get belowdecks. I will tell you when it is safe to come out."

Gem set her jaw. On deck, Remy stood near the mainmast, tying a long coil of rope around his waist with Jack. That was the difference between thieves and princesses, she guessed. The commoner was put to work, while the princess was told to get to safety. But this was Cutlass's ship, and Gem had agreed to follow the rules. "Fine," she said, taking a step back. "As you wish, Captain. I'll be down in the hold with Cloud if anyone . . ."

A strange noise rose into the air over the howl of the wind. A low-pitched, almost musical hum. It was faint at first, then grew louder and louder, until Gem could feel it vibrating in her ears. As it grew, she thought she could hear words within the music, though she couldn't make out anything clearly.

But around her, the crew of the *Queen's Blade* were acting strange. A few moments before, they were scrambling over the deck: tying down lies, securing sails, battening down the hatches, and preparing for the storm. Now they stood motionless, faces turned to the wind, seemingly transfixed by the music.

The captain let out a vehement curse. "Sky sirens!" she snarled. Whirling on the first mate, she struck him across the cheek, hard enough that Gem heard the hollow slap through the fabric of the captain's gloves. "Mr. Tuhga, snap out of it!" she ordered as the first mate jerked up, the haze clearing from his eyes. "Shove some cotton in your ears and steer this ship! I will not have us drifting into the Maelstrom because of some lice-ridden harpies!"

A flutter overhead made Gem look up. Shapes were descending from the sky, half a dozen of them silhouetted against the roiling clouds. Lightning flickered, illuminating the terrible creatures that were half woman, half bird. Their torsos and heads were human, their faces those of leering crones with sharp, pointed teeth. But their arms were sweeping, feathery wings, and their bottom halves were scaly bird feet and talons. They dropped from the air, still singing that eerie, wailing song, and landed on the shoulders of several crew members. None of the pirates reacted, still in that strange trance. For just a moment, Gem wondered why she and Cutlass weren't affected. They *were* the only women aboard the *Queen's Blade*. Maybe, like in the ancient legends of old, the siren songs only affected males.

"Oh, I don't think so!" Cutlass reached down and drew her sword, the curved blade gleaming as she pulled it free. "You want to help, Princess?" she snapped, leaping off the helm onto the deck. "Stop those hags from flying off with the crew!"

She raced toward a bird woman as it started rising into the air, a crew member clutched in its talons. Her sword flashed, and the monster gave an alarmed shriek, dropping the pirate to the deck.

Gem looked down and saw Remy being lifted into the air by one of the sirens. With a gasp, she sprinted toward them, hoping she would get to him in time. The bird woman swiftly pulled him out of reach, but the end of the safety line Remy had tied around himself trailed across the deck.

Gem grabbed the rope and pulled. The siren screeched, flapping its wings harder, and for a few seconds, Gem found herself in the middle of a deadly tug-of-war, trying to keep the siren from flying off with Remy. Planting her feet, Gem leaned back and yanked as hard as she could.

With a hiss, the siren let go. Gem fell backward, hitting

her elbows against the hard wooden planks as the resistance was suddenly gone. Remy dropped to the deck with a thump, and Gem heard the breath leave his lungs in a rush.

The siren, or harpy, or whatever it was, landed in front of Gem with an angry, piercing shriek, flaring its wings as it glared at her. Its beady eyes glittered with malice as it opened its mouth, baring sharp yellow teeth, and took a step forward.

A streak of lightning split the skies overhead, turning everything purple-white. Gem felt the energy of the storm all around her, swirling and chaotic.

You don't need a college education to use magic, Lysander had sneered. *The college teaches structure and control, but magic is wild, untamed, unpredictable. Anyone with the talent can use it.*

The siren hissed again, her clawed foot snagging Gem's leg as she stepped close. With a yell, Gem threw out her hand, willing the energy of the storm to become a bolt of lightning that would fry the enemy in front of her.

Nothing happened. Gem felt a flicker of power at her fingertips, but no lightning came streaking from her hands at her call. The harpy flinched back at the sudden motion, but when nothing happened, it smiled evilly and stepped forward again, teeth bared and wings spread to attack.

A blast of fire shot between them, searingly bright, and the harpy screeched. Gem turned, gasping, as Cloud bounded onto the deck and charged the bird woman with a roar. The siren, seeing an actual dragon coming toward her, immediately took off, flapping frantically into the air. Cloud lunged to Gem's side, growling, wings spread as he glared around for enemies.

"Cloud." Gem hugged the dragon's neck. "Good boy," she panted. "Now help the others."

The dragon bugled a challenge and leaped forward. His fire breath streaked into the air, and the sirens gave shrieks of alarm as the dragon rampaged around the deck. The eerie song ceased, replaced with squawks and ugly hisses. Crew members who had been dropped shook themselves and gazed around, dazed and confused.

"Excellent!" The captain's voice rang over the deck as she smacked away a talon with her sword and kicked the thing in the chest with her boot. It screeched in pain and tumbled backward, and the captain stalked after it. "Whatever you're telling your dragon to do, Miss Featherbottom, keep it up. Drive these interlopers off my ship!"

With guttural, raucous cries, the flock scattered. Apparently, the arrival of an elite predator was enough for them. Wings flapping, they retreated into the air, becoming black specks against the roiling sky, and vanished into the clouds.

"Gentlemen!" The captain gave the crew no time to recover; she strode across the deck, her voice rising over the wind. "Everyone, back to their stations! That storm is still coming, and we are not losing this ship tonight. I don't care if you don't know what just happened; talk about it when we're clear of the storm. Move!"

The crew scrambled to obey. Safety lines were re-tightened, sails were furled, and ropes were fastened as the pirates rushed to beat the storm.

"Cloud?" Gem dodged a pirate speeding by and looked around for her dragon. He hadn't returned to her once the sirens had been driven off, and with all the people rushing around the deck, it was hard to see him. "Cloud, where are you?"

She spotted him then, and her heart skipped a beat. The dragon stood near the back of the ship, his neck outstretched and his muzzle nosing a body lying motionless on the deck.

Remy.

CHAPTER
TWENTY-THREE

Remy felt like he was floating.

For a few seconds, everything was dark. He didn't know where he was. He didn't know if he was dreaming. The last thing he remembered was being aboard the *Queen's Blade*. There had been . . . a song. A beautiful song that was somehow calling to him. Then everything had gone black.

But then an image sputtered to life, flickering like a candle flame in the wind. He was inside a room that somehow reminded him of the captain's quarters. The floor was carpeted; there were shelves on the walls and a desk in the corner. As his vision cleared, he saw iron bars surrounding him and suddenly realized he was in a cage.

Across the room, the door opened, and Jhaeros stepped inside. Remy gave a start; the pirate mage looked much bigger now. Actually, everything looked big. Or . . . was he the one who was little? The size of a small dog . . .

Storm, Remy thought as he suddenly understood. These visions weren't random; they came from his dragon, from what Storm was seeing or feeling at that moment. Remy was aboard the *Windshark*, and Jhaeros was standing in front of a cage that held Remy's dragon.

A low chuckle broke through Remy's thoughts. He looked up and saw Jhaeros gazing down at him, the face on the other side of the bars filling his vision.

"You know where you are, don't you, dragon?" Jhaeros asked, and Remy felt Storm shrink back from the looming pirate mage. "Don't worry, this is just like fishing; you put a line and bait out and hope something bites it. Let's hope your big brothers will sense you wriggling on the line and come up to see what's happening."

Storm hissed defiantly, baring his fangs at the mage, and Jhaeros laughed. "You're rather small to be making such big threats, dragon," he told him. "If I had the time, or the patience, to wait a few years, maybe you would be worth my while. But the amount of magic I could get from that tiny body is irrelevant. So we're going to call on something bigger."

Call on something bigger? Did he mean an adult wild dragon?

Jhaeros stepped back, no longer smiling. "A pity your mother decided to sacrifice herself to save you," he growled. "Such a waste of power. If I'd only known what I was dealing with sooner; she could've provided enough magic to fuel all my dreams. . . ."

Storm gave a furious snarl and threw himself at the cage bars, snapping and clawing. Remy shivered at the anger in the tiny dragon's body, but Jhaeros gave another chuckle and shook his head.

"I suppose that's one advantage of you being so small," he said, and bent his face close to the bars again, smirking. "You can't breathe fire yet. How sad for you." Storm hissed at him, raking the bars with his tiny claws, and Jhaeros smiled. "But look at it this way. If you were even a little bigger, I wouldn't be using you for bait, little True Dragon." He raised a hand, lightning sparking between his fingers. "I'd suck that magic energy right out of you and use it to overthrow the kingdom!"

Storm gave a squawk and leaped back. Stunned, Remy could only stare at the pirate mage, his mind reeling. Storm *wasn't* a wild dragon; he was a *True Dragon*.

Suddenly, a lot of things made sense.

Jhaeros stood, the lightning in his hand dying away, and regarded the dragon with a terrible, hungry expression. "No matter. We've almost reached the Vortex." He raised a hand, spreading his fingers toward the ceiling. "You can feel it, can't you?" he murmured. "All that energy, all that raw, unfiltered magic, swirling in one place. Right there for the taking. They said I was sky-mad to go hunting for an adult True Dragon, but at the Vortex, I'll be strong enough to bring one down. I will tear it open and take all that power and magic for myself. And once I get the power of an adult True Dragon, I'll be unstoppable." He slapped a fist against Storm's cage, making both Remy and Storm jump, and grinned evilly through the bars. "Once we reach the Vortex, I'm going to need you to call for your big brothers. Scream, cry, throw a tantrum, whatever you need to make them hear you. If you don't, *I* might have to provide a bit of incentive." Jhaeros chuckled, making Remy's stomach clench in fear. "So, little True Dragon, be ready to scream when we get there!"

Remy gasped and opened his eyes.

"Easy, kid," said Captain Cutlass's voice. Gazing around, Remy saw he was no longer outside on deck; he was lying on a cot in the captain's quarters. A bony man he'd not seen before was standing over him, peering into his face with a magnifying glass. Captain Cutlass gazed down at him over the man's shoulder, and Mary hovered worriedly at his side.

"Aha," the man said, turning to the captain with a triumphant smile. Raising the magnifying glass, he announced: "I have concluded that the boy is, in fact, awake. No need for leeches or amputation. Probably."

"Thank you, Mr. Scalpel," Captain Cutlass said flatly. "You can go now."

"Are you sure?" The man gazed down at Remy in obvious disappointment. "The boy still seems a bit out of it. Perhaps we should apply a leech or two, just in case."

Remy cringed, and the captain shook her head. "No, I'm fairly certain he's fine now," Cutlass said, to Remy's relief. "You can go back to your station. But I'll be sure to call you if he needs an arm sawed off."

"Don't get my hopes up, Captain," the man said. But he reached down, picked a saw up off the floor, and trudged out of the room.

The captain watched him leave, then shook her head and looked down at Remy. "You all right, boy?" she asked as Mary pressed forward, her face anxious. "You passed out after the siren attack, and we brought you here. You were muttering and twitching in your sleep, but we couldn't wake you up. What happened?"

"I . . . I saw Storm," Remy said. "And Jhaeros. It was like I was there, in the *Windshark*, seeing what Storm was seeing."

Cutlass raised a brow. "More strange dragon shenanigans," she mused. "I take it this is not normal, Miss Featherbottom?"

Mary shook her head. "You were seeing through Storm's eyes?" she asked in disbelief. Her lips thinned, as if she were fighting the urge to say that was impossible. "What did you see?" she finally asked. "Could you hear Jhaeros, too?"

Remy nodded. "Jhaeros is taking Storm to a place where the magic energies gather in one spot," he told the others. "I think it's supposed to enhance his power or something. He plans to use Storm as bait, to try to draw out a True Dragon."

Mary gasped. "A True Dragon," she repeated. "Why is Jhaeros looking for a True Dragon?"

"He wants to take the dragon's power," Remy said. "He said he would drain the dragon of its magic and use it to overthrow the kingdom."

"What?" Mary stiffened at that, looking almost angry. "How?" she demanded. "How does he expect to overthrow the king? No one would listen to him; he's a pirate. How does he think he's going to get past the entire squadron of elite sky knights?"

"I don't know," Remy said, wondering why the girl was so upset about this. "It's just what I heard."

"Well, isn't that ambitious," Cutlass mused. "So Jhaeros plans to use the hatchling to lure a True Dragon to him, and then he'll drain the magic from the True Dragon, probably by killing it, to make himself more powerful. I wasn't even aware a mage could do that, but then again, I don't know a lot about mages or how magic works. There is one thing I'm confused about, though. There are a lot of normal dragons flying around the kingdom. Why does Jhaeros think the True Dragons would care what happens to this one hatchling?"

"Because," Remy explained, "Storm is a True Dragon, too."

He felt dazed. Remy knew Storm understood everything he said, even though Bart claimed dragons couldn't really follow human speech. He had suspected Storm must be different somehow. But a True Dragon? The creatures that were said to be nothing but myth and legend? The powerful, immortal dragons that taught humans the ways of magic before the world fell apart? It felt weird to think of Storm that way.

"I see," Cutlass said after a moment. "Well, this is all very exciting, or disturbing, depending on how you look at it. But in your . . . communicating with your dragon," she went on, gazing at Remy, "did you happen to hear where Jhaeros is headed? I know you can *feel* your way to your dragon, but it would be helpful to have a destination in mind. Did Jhaeros give you anything like that?"

Remy nodded. "He said they had almost reached a place called the Vortex."

"The Vortex." The captain narrowed her eyes. "I've heard of vortexes," she said. "They're places out in the Maelstrom where the magical energies swirl and gather into one giant, chaotic pool, but they usually dissipate and break up after a while. There *are* stories of permanent whirlpools that have formed out in the Maelstrom, and the largest one has been responsible for wrecking dozens of ships, so most pirates avoid that section of sky. There's a huge ship graveyard around it, wrecks circling the Vortex like barrels caught in a whirlpool." She sighed. "So, naturally, that's exactly where Jhaeros is headed."

Three days aboard the *Queen's Blade* passed in a hazy blur. Time for Remy was measured in the space between trips to the helm to make sure they were going in the right direction. His visits to the helm didn't take long, but Captain Cutlass was methodical; every hour, someone would shout for "the compass" to go to the wheel. At night, they gave him a break, waking him up every *three* hours to stumble to the helm and point the way to the *Windshark*.

He didn't see the girl much; she was either shut away in her room, in the captain's quarters with Cutlass, or down in the hold with her dragon. He noticed that, except for the captain, none of the pirates really spoke to her. Since she was a girl, and a noble on top of that, they probably didn't know how to act around her. With him, there was no hesitation; as a thief, a commoner, and a street rat from a pirate town, he was practically one of their own. Jack especially took Remy under his skinny wing and showed him the ropes of living on a ship: how to climb the riggings, furl the sails, and properly tie a knot. But whenever Mary Featherbottom walked onto the deck, the sailors either politely ignored her or discreetly made themselves scarce. He wondered if she ever got lonely.

One evening, he found her in the hold with Cloud, brushing the dragon's silky mane. Unlike Storm's, which was spiky and stood straight up in places, Cloud's mane was soft and so smooth you could run your fingers through it without hitting any snags or tangles. He'd heard Mary complain once about the lack of scale oil on the ship, and he wondered how much the nobles pampered their dragons. If Cloud slept on a silk bed in a stall made of marble and gold in the capital, it wouldn't surprise him.

"Hey," he said, raising a hand to both girl and dragon. Mary smiled at him over her shoulder, and Cloud gave a welcoming trill. Walking over to the dragon, he scratched Cloud between the horns, and the dragon shoved his nose into his chest.

"There." Mary stepped back, observing Cloud appraisingly. "No more tangles or nasty bits of straw caught in your mane. I wish there was even one bottle of dragon oil lying around, though; your scales are starting to look a bit yellow."

Remy rolled his eyes. "Must be nice," he told the dragon. "No one ever offers to brush my hair when there's straw caught in it."

"Because they would probably get bitten by the rats who live there," Mary responded flatly.

Remy laughed. "Hey, leave my rats alone," he told the girl, who smiled. "They keep the birds from nesting in it."

She shook her head. Picking up a rag, she walked over to a crate that had a saddle draped atop it. At least, Remy thought it was a saddle. There were no horses on Cutthroat Wedge, and the only pack animals were donkeys that pulled carts, so he had never really seen an actual saddle before. But the thing on the crate was made of leather, had a place for someone to sit, and had several straps coming off it, so he could make a reasonable assumption.

"Is that a dragon saddle?" he asked as Mary ran the cloth over the leather, wiping down the straps.

She nodded. "I know it's a little small," she admitted, though Remy didn't know anything about dragon saddles, tack, or gear. "But Cloud isn't a big dragon. I just hope three people will be able to ride on him when the time comes. He's strong enough to carry the weight; that's not what I'm worried about. It just might be a little uncomfortable on the flight back."

A cold chill crept through Remy's stomach. Mary sounded calm and pragmatic, but soon they would be sneaking onto a pirate ship to try to rescue an old sky knight and a dragon hatchling. It was going to be super dangerous, and if they were caught . . .

He clenched his jaw. They wouldn't be caught. Too much was at stake. He was going to rescue Storm and Bart, and then maybe Captain Cutlass would let them join her crew. The life of a pirate didn't sound terrible—better than what he had on Cutthroat Wedge, anyway. He certainly couldn't go back. Jhaeros would be looking for them.

Glancing at Mary, he wondered what she would do after they found Bart. Probably return to the capital after she got what she needed.

He frowned. Now that he thought about it, he had no idea why she wanted to talk to Bart. It had to be pretty important for a noble to hire a pirate ship and its crew to chase after the most dangerous pirate in the Fringe and rescue Bart. What did the old man know that would make her risk so much?

"All right." Mary gave the saddle a final swipe with the cloth. "Dragon brushed, saddle wiped down. Not that it matters, but at least we'll be sort of clean when we fly over to the *Windshark*. That's something, right?"

"Hey, you never told me." Remy faced her head-on. "Why is it you want to talk to Bart so badly?" he asked. "I know he was a sky knight, but that was a long time ago. There are plenty of knights in the capital if you want advice from one of them. Why him?"

Mary went very still. Her voice, when it came out, was flat. "He has information I need," she said evasively.

Remy narrowed his eyes. "That doesn't tell me anything," he said. "What secret does Bart have that you need so badly? You're a noble, and he's a washed-up knight; you wouldn't have come all this way if it wasn't important." When Mary hesitated, he said, "I know I'm just a thief, but I can keep a secret. Who's going to believe me, anyway?"

"Remy . . ." Mary sighed. "I want to tell you, but . . ."

"But you don't trust me." Remy crossed his arms. "Even after everything. Because I'm a thief, and a street kid."

"No, that's not true—"

"It's fine." He shrugged, even managing to give a twisted little smile, as if it were no big deal. "I get it. I probably wouldn't understand, anyway. . . ."

"Stop," Mary said. "You *don't* understand. This is something I haven't shared with anyone, not even the captain." She gestured to the ceiling, where footsteps could be heard thumping above their heads. "Even Cutlass doesn't know why I want to talk to Bart."

Okay, he could accept that. She had her secrets, just as he had his. Maybe she was embarrassed. Maybe Bart was a long-lost uncle or something, and she didn't want anyone to know she was related to him. But still, they would be going on a really dangerous mission soon. If he couldn't trust her, or vice versa, that would make things even harder.

He turned and hopped up to sit on a barrel, swinging his legs against the wooden sides. "So is there something you've told the captain that you haven't told me?" he wondered.

Mary closed her eyes. "Yes," she admitted, and sighed heavily. "All right," she said, opening her eyes to glare at him. "Fine. But if I tell you this, you have to swear that you won't share it with anyone. Nobody here knows this about me except the captain. So if any of the crew find out, I'll know who told them."

Remy nodded. "I promise," he said. "I won't tell anyone. Thief's honor." She gave him a dubious look, as if doubting that thieves had any honor, and he hurried on. "So what's this big secret?" he pressed.

Mary took a breath. "Mary Featherbottom . . . isn't my real name."

"Oh." Disappointment bloomed. That was it? Traveling under an alias was not so uncommon, especially for nobles who went "slumming" in the Fringe. He was hoping her secret would be a little more . . . interesting. Looking down, he picked at a splinter in the wood, then flicked it away. "What's your real name, then?" he asked.

"Princess Gemillia Sunwind Gallecia the fourteenth."

Remy fell off the barrel. Cloud gave an alarmed squawk as he hit the floor. For a second, he just sat there, his mouth gaping open. "You're . . . the princess?" he stammered at last. "The princess of Gallecia. The king's daughter?"

She nodded. "But you can't tell anyone," she reminded him. "You promised. Only the captain knows who I am. You can't tell any of the crew. If word got out that the princess was traveling alone through the Fringe, people might come after us, and that would be bad for the mission. Not to mention, it would just be a hassle if they kept trying to either kidnap or 'rescue' me." She used finger quotation marks for the "rescue" part, rolling her eyes. "It's easier if no one knows who I am. So promise that you won't tell."

"Yes, Your... uh..." How did one address the princess of Gallecia? Could he get in trouble for not speaking to her properly? "Yes, Your Highness," he rasped.

She sighed again. "See. That's what I don't want to happen," she groaned. "Just call me Gem, unless we're around the crew. And don't treat me any different than you have been, okay?"

"Yes, Your—"

She glared at him, and he stopped. "Uh, yeah. Gem. Sure."

Cloud stepped forward, shoving his nose at Remy to see if he was okay, making worried burbling sounds. He gave the dragon a reassuring pat before scrambling to his feet. "But, if you're the princess," he began, "why are you here? Alone? Why aren't you traveling around with guards and knights and people to protect you?"

Gem winced. "My father... wouldn't approve of what I'm doing," she said, sounding faintly uncomfortable. "He probably has people out looking for me now. I left the castle on my own to go looking for Sir Bartello." For a moment, her eyes clouded, as if thinking about home was distressing; then she shook her head with a sigh. "I'm not supposed to be here," she admitted, "but I couldn't sit back and do nothing."

"Bart must be really important, then," Remy said, still

feeling dazed with what he had learned. "For the princess herself to be looking for him."

"He is." Gem paused again, as if debating how much to reveal. "The information he carries . . . is integral to helping the kingdom. That's why we have to find him. That's why I'm here."

Remy had about a million questions he wanted to ask, but a thump sounded overhead, and a moment later, a voice boomed into the hold. "If you kids are down here, you need to get up to the deck right now," Jack's voice called, making them both start. "Captain has called for you both!"

As Remy and Gem made their way up the stairs, Remy began to hear a muffled roar. It was faint at first, barely noticeable, but once they reached the deck, the sound vibrated the planks under his feet and made his teeth itch. As they walked across the deck toward the aftcastle, he noticed the *Queen's Blade* had stopped moving. It hovered in the sky, suspended in place, though the sails overhead were still unfurled. Remy wondered if the captain had ordered the stop, or if something else had happened to bring them to a halt.

The captain and the first mate were standing by the wheel, gazing out over the horizon. Both pirates looked grim. The captain's arms were crossed, the wind tugging at her hair and coat as she looked down. Walking up the steps to the helm, Gem gasped, her eyes going wide as she stared over the railings. "What in the world . . ." she whispered.

Remy peered out over the helm, and his heart lodged in his throat.

Words couldn't really describe what he was seeing. Far in the distance, stretching hundreds of yards end to end, was an enormous, gaping . . . hole. A whirlpool of clouds, wind, and lightning that swirled and shrieked and roared as it dropped away into nothing. The muffled roar filled his ears, and lightning crawled along the edges of the swirling clouds, making his eyes water. Wrecked ships circled the whirlpool, drifting aimlessly through space, tattered sails fluttering in the wind. Most were nothing but destroyed hulls and shattered masts, but a few still looked eerily intact. They rose and fell, careening around the edge of the Vortex, caught in an endless pull. As Remy watched, a ship that looked like it had been snapped in two collided with another, and though he couldn't hear the impact, both vessels broke apart in a spray of wood and debris. The back of one ship tumbled away and dropped into the whirlpool while the other half, suddenly free of the extra weight, rose into the air, trailing boards and shattered planks, to sail around the edges once more.

"The Vortex," Captain Cutlass whispered. "We're here."

CHAPTER
TWENTY-FOUR

The *Windshark* floated like a great black whale over a swirling, flickering vortex of clouds and mystical lightning, its grinning hull lit up in the flashing lights. Despite its size, the ship looked tiny against the monstrous whirlpool beneath. Strands of purple lightning sizzled up from the center of the Vortex, blasting objects apart, or sometimes twisting them into something else entirely. The *Windshark* hovered over the Vortex, out of reach of most of the lightning, but occasionally a purple strand would flash up from the center, striking the big ship's metal lightning rods in a burst of sparks.

Gem shivered and handed the spyglass she was holding back to the captain, who put it to her own eye again. "Well,

Jhaeros is certainly either very brave or very foolhardy," the pirate captain said. "That close to the Vortex, it's a wonder the ship hasn't been struck, either by lightning or the random debris flying around."

A wrecked sky ship drifted between them, torn sails flapping, blocking the view of the *Windshark* for a few seconds. Gem shivered again. She found the ship graveyard eerie, with its carcasses of dead vessels floating aimlessly around the Vortex, but according to the captain, it was a blessing in disguise. The *Windshark* was huge, threatening, and very noticeable, but the *Queen's Blade* was much smaller and could easily blend in with the rest of the ships. As long as they didn't get too close, the *Queen's Blade* could just be another wreck drifting among the detritus.

"Flying over there is certainly going to be a challenge," the captain murmured, lowering her arm. "Are you certain you and your beastie will be able to handle it?"

"Cloud will be fine," Gem said. "He's strong. He'll be able to make it."

"That's not what I'm worried about." Captain Cutlass closed the spyglass with a snap and slipped it into her coat pocket. "I'm no dragon expert, but I'm guessing that a pure white dragon who practically glows in the dark was not bred or trained for stealth missions."

Gem grimaced. Cloud was many wonderful things, but subtle was not one of them. Still, she would rather have him than any of the sneakier dragons in her father's stable. Even

Shadow, the female dragon who was as dark as Cloud was bright. Shadow could move as silently as a wraith, but she was also ill-tempered and very unpredictable. Gem much preferred Cloud's calm reliability, even if he wasn't the stealthiest dragon around.

"Mr. Tuhga," the captain said, turning to the first mate at the wheel. "Take us into the clouds. Sundown is about two hours away," she told Gem. "If I were you, I would get everything you need for the mission ready now. Dark will be here before you know it."

Gem heaved Cloud's saddle onto his back and buckled down the straps, making sure they were extra tight. The dragon stood quietly, though the tip of his tail thumped against the floor, and his wings fluttered. He knew he was going to be flying tonight. Looking over the saddle, Gem tried to picture, again, how three people were going to be riding her dragon. The saddle was just big enough for two, so she and Remy would have no problem, but Bart would have to sit behind it, at the base of Cloud's tail. Also, there were no extra straps or harnesses to keep either of them from tumbling off the dragon's back; they would just have to hold on tight and hope Cloud didn't have to make any evasive maneuvers.

Remy appeared, making no noise as he slipped into the dragon's corner. He had changed into darker clothes—black trousers and a dark red shirt—and looked very much like a pirate as he walked up. "Ready?" he asked.

Gem nodded. After they'd seen the *Windshark* and the *Vortex*, the captain had pulled them all into her quarters to go over the plan once again and make sure everyone knew what they were doing. It was risky, and there was a lot that relied on chance or pure blind luck, but it was the best they could come up with.

She hoped they would succeed. She hoped they would survive. Everyone in the kingdom was counting on them, even if they didn't know it.

"Are you nervous?" she asked Remy. He shrugged.

"Avoiding pirates, sneaking around, and trying not to get caught? It's what I do. Though I've never flown a dragon before." He scratched the back of his head, and she could see he *was* nervous, though he was trying not to show it. "What about you?"

Before she could answer, Jack walked around a crate stack, nodding to them as he came into view. "Sun's down," he told them, causing Gem's stomach to twist like a wrung dishrag. "Captain says it's time."

Up on deck, the wind had picked up, blowing in cold sheets across the planks. The dragon raised his head, nostrils flaring as he sniffed the air, and his wings fluttered against his sides. At least *he* was excited.

Gem could feel the intense magic in the air. It wasn't like the magic back home, or in any other place she had been.

She could always feel the energy; generally the closer you got to the Maelstrom, without ground or structures or land in the way, the easier it became. But the ripples of magic were subtle, like a breeze through your hair, or a faint smell on the wind.

This was nothing like that. This was a violent, chaotic swirl of power and energy that snapped and sizzled and made her skin vibrate. It came from the Vortex, from the concentration of Maelstrom magic swirling through the air, and it was absolutely terrifying.

Captain Cutlass stood on the aftcastle with her arms crossed, the wind whipping at her hair and still somehow not managing to sweep the hat off her head. Behind her, First Mate Tuhga worked the wheel, keeping the ship steady through the gusting wind. The captain regarded the dragon with an appraising eye, then glanced at Gem. "We're a few hundred yards from the *Windshark*," she told her. "Are you ready?"

"Yes," Gem replied, though her heart thumped in her ears and her palms were sweaty despite the cold.

"And you know what the plan is?"

"Fly to a safe spot to observe the *Windshark* and wait for your signal," Gem replied. "When the *Queen's Blade* attacks, enter the ship through the bilge hole, rescue Bart and the dragon, and get out again."

The captain gave a single nod. "Sounds easy," she said with a faint smile. "Good luck."

Gem turned to Cloud and swung herself into the saddle, feeling the dragon's muscles shifting beneath her as she settled onto the leather seat. As usual, though, he didn't squirm impatiently or dance around in excitement. Out of all of them, he was probably the calmest. She could feel her own heart racing against her ribs like a terrified rabbit's.

Remy paused, gazing up at the dragon with a faint frown on his face. "Um, so how do I get on?" he asked, and Gem stifled a wince for not realizing before. "Pretend I've never been on a dragon and have no idea how to do this."

"Oh, sorry," Gem said, and tapped Cloud's shoulder. "Cloud, lie down."

The dragon huffed but immediately sank down until his belly touched the deck. "You'll have to sit behind me," Gem told Remy. "The saddle is big enough, but there's no straps to keep you from falling off, so you'll just have to hold on to me."

He still hesitated, eyeing the saddle as if realizing just how close he and the dragon were going to be. "Are you sure?"

She rolled her eyes. "Just get up here. Do you want to rescue your dragon or not?"

His eyes hardened. Setting his jaw, he stepped forward, swung a leg over Cloud's back, and slid into the saddle behind Gem. As Cloud rose smoothly to his feet, she felt Remy shift his weight, trying to find his balance, and tried not to grimace. He was about to get the jolt of his life.

"Good luck," Captain Cutlass said. "We'll back you up

as best we can. Oh, and by the way, Lysander told me to tell you that if he dies keeping the ship from being blown apart, his ghost will haunt you for the rest of your life."

Gem grimaced. "Well, give him my apologies for making his life difficult," she said, rolling her eyes. "And I'm sorry he hates me so much."

"Who said I hated you?"

Gem glanced up, blinking as the mage climbed the stairs to the aftcastle, the wind tugging at his silver ponytail. Shock rippled through her; the only times she had seen Lysander above deck were under extreme protest.

"Lysander." The captain sounded as surprised as Gem felt, crimson brows raised as the mage stepped forward. "Aren't you supposed to be belowdecks with the crystal? Not that I'm complaining; normally I have to drag you out of the crystal chamber kicking and screaming, but you've picked a surprising time to be sociable."

Ignoring the captain, Lysander met Gem's stare. "I know you're a mage," he said, making Gem's stomach clench. "Don't act surprised; it's not hard to recognize a fellow magic user, even if they think they're being clever. I think you're insane, going aboard the *Windshark* to rescue an old sky knight, and I'm going to have to pull some complicated aerial stunts to keep this ship flying because of them, but"—his jaw tightened in irritation—"you've got guts. So just as a reminder"—he pointed a finger at the howling maw of the Vortex—"the Maelstrom gives us our power, but the Vortex heightens all magical energy. That means Jhaeros is going to be at his strongest and most dangerous, but then, so are you. You don't need a stuffy professor to learn how to use magic. Remember that."

"I will," Gem said, still amazed that the sulky, unfriendly storm mage of the *Queen's Blade* was talking to her. "Thank you, Lysander."

"And for the record, I don't hate you." He crossed his arms. "But I don't much like you, either. I still think this is the most ridiculous mission I've ever been a part of. But if keeping *you* alive means keeping *us* alive, I'll do what I have to do. Even if it means talking to a spoiled noble mage child who doesn't know the first thing about real magic."

Cutlass chuckled, shaking her mane of crimson hair. "Oh, there he is. Thank goodness; for a second I was worried." Still smiling, she turned to Gem. "We'll rendezvous at the southern edge of the Vortex," she said, "provided Jhaeros hasn't blasted us out of the sky. If you're not there when we're forced to flee, we'll have to leave without you."

"Thank you for all your help, Captain," Gem said.

"Oh, don't thank me yet," Captain Cutlass said, her smile turning grim. "Nothing has been decided. Wait till you're back and safely aboard the *Queen's Blade* before you say anything, and then we can talk about how you and your father can thank me."

Gem decided not to think about that right now. That was Future Gem's problem, provided she came out of this alive. One thing at a time. "Cloud," she went on, and she felt the bunching of dragon muscles beneath her. The pale wings unfurled, and the dragon sank into a crouch, already anticipating what was coming next. "Up!"

Cloud leaped skyward. Behind her, Remy gave a breathless yelp, and his grip around her waist squeezed tight. Cloud's powerful wing muscles pumped, sending them higher with each downward flap as they soared over the railings of the *Queen's Blade* and toward the looming hulk of the *Windshark* beyond.

CHAPTER
TWENTY-FIVE

Ever since he was a toddler, Remy had dreamed of being on a dragon.

From the days when his mom would tell him bedtime stories of great knights on dragons to the evenings at the tavern when Bart's tales still captured his imagination, all he'd wanted was to ride a dragon.

Actually flying on dragon's back was more than exciting; it was absolutely terrifying. But it was also, the most exhilarating thing he'd ever done.

Muscles shifted beneath him. He felt the beat of powerful wings as Cloud rose higher and the deck of the ship dropped away beneath them. Then they were away from the

Queen's Blade and in open sky, and there was nothing but the narrow back of a dragon between him and the vast emptiness beyond.

"Remy." In front of him, Gem's voice came out a bit strained. "You're squeezing too hard," she rasped. "I can't breathe."

"Oh!" Remy gasped, loosening his grip a little. Even that made him feel like he could tumble off Cloud's back at any second. "Sorry. Guess I'm not used to this."

Gem sucked in a breath and then leaned forward in the saddle, bending over Cloud's neck. "Do what I do," she instructed. "Lean forward and grip with your legs. Don't just sit there like a sack of grain; a rider has to feel what their dragon is doing. Shift your weight. Move with the dragon. Try to become a single creature."

It sounded like she was reciting something from a class, but Remy tried to do what she said. Squeezing his knees together, he pressed forward and tried to feel Cloud's movements beneath him. He felt a little more secure, but not enough to let go of the girl in front of him. Especially when Cloud gave an alarmed squawk and veered sharply to the right, dodging a wooden crate that fell toward them out of nowhere.

"Aagh!" Remy yelled, squeezing his knees so hard he felt Cloud's heartbeat through his legs. "What was that?"

"It came from that ship up there," Gem panted, pointing briefly with a finger. She, too, seemed startled by the sudden change in direction. Remy looked over her shoulder and saw the floating hulk of a ship drifting above them. Or rather, half a ship, shedding planks and other debris as it spun lazily through the air. The beams and wooden planks did not hover in space like the rest of the ship, but dropped straight toward the Vortex. A rain of wood began falling from the sky, and Gem gasped.

"Cloud, go!"

The dragon shot forward. Remy bit back a yelp and locked his arms around Gem's waist as Cloud began swerving to the left and right to avoid the planks dropping around them. A wooden bucket grazed the boy as it fell, bouncing off his knee, and he bit back a yell of pain.

Swooping up, they dodged the last piece of falling ship, and Remy could suddenly see the hulking black mass of the *Windshark* ahead of them. It hovered above the center of the Vortex, its grinning hull lit up by the flashing lights and black sails flapping in the wind. Shipwrecks and chunks of vessels drifted around it, slowly rising and falling with the pull of the Vortex, but the *Windshark* was a rock in the center of the chaotic sea.

At the sight of the massive ship, fear curled in Remy's stomach, along with a fierce determination. *I'm coming, Storm. Just hang in there.*

"Come on," he told Gem as impatience rose up to join the resolve. "There's Jhaeros's ship. Get closer."

Gem frowned back at him. "That's not the plan," she

said. "We have to find a place to wait for the signal. If we get too close, they'll spot us, even in this debris field."

"Well, we can't keep flying in circles." Remy gazed around and saw another ship drifting slowly toward them, tattered sails snapping in the wind. Unlike most of the vessels circling the Vortex, this one's upper deck looked mostly intact. Groaning and creaking, it floated eerily through the sky, the figurehead of a white stag angled toward the sky. Remy tapped Gem on the shoulder and pointed. "There. Can Cloud land on that ship?"

"He should be able to. Let's go, Cloud."

The dragon's wings flapped, and they rose swiftly toward the drifting boat. Swooping up the side of the hull, Cloud glided over the dilapidated railings and touched down lightly on the deck. All around them, the entire ship groaned, planks creaking and shuddering, sails flapping in the wind. For a moment, Remy wondered what had happened to the sailors. Had they all been lost to the Maelstrom? Or had something even more bizarre happened? The ship struck by mysterious lightning, its crew turning into winged snakes and flying away? He would never know.

"Okay," Gem whispered. She seemed worried for some reason. Maybe the eerie, creaking ghost ship was making her nervous. "From here, we should be able to see the signal."

But minutes passed in silence, and no signal came. The Vortex howled below them, a constant roar that made Remy's ears throb. The wrecks drifted around the edges, rising and falling and breaking apart, but Cutlass and the *Queen's Blade* were nowhere to be seen.

Remy shifted impatiently in the saddle. The *Windshark* floated tantalizingly in the distance, taunting him with its leering smile. "Come on," he muttered. "Where are they?"

"They'll be here," Gem said. "Just be patient."

Remy clenched his jaw. He was normally a patient person. He had to be patient when waiting for the perfect moment to swipe something, for someone to leave a room, for pirates to stop looking for him, or just for something to happen. Remy knew how to be patient.

But his dragon was in trouble. And he knew pirates. He had grown up around them; he knew how they thought, what they were capable of. Captain Cutlass and the crew of the *Queen's Blade* might have good intentions, but they were still pirates at heart. And no pirates he knew of would ever put themselves at risk to help him. The only person who had ever helped him after his mother died was Bart, and Remy was failing him, too.

"We should try to sneak aboard," Remy whispered. "There are other ways to get in. We could probably crawl through one of the gunports."

Gem frowned at him over her shoulder. "No. We wait for the captain's signal."

Remy scrubbed a hand through his hair. "Let's hope she hasn't turned her ship around and left us here," he muttered.

"The captain wouldn't do that. We had a deal."

"You don't know much about pirates, do you?" Gem glared at him, and he raised his hands to show he wasn't trying to pick a fight. "I'm just saying. It doesn't matter if they've made a deal, or a promise, or any kind of bargain. Pirates only care about gold and saving their own skin."

Gem's voice was flat as she stared back at him. "You could say that about thieves, too."

He started to answer when, across the Vortex, there was a streak of light that didn't come from lightning. It shot straight into the sky, a ball of blue-white luminance trailing a tail behind it, then exploded like a firework against the darkness.

Gem gasped. "That's the signal!" she cried just as the *Queen's Blade* soared between two drifting hulls and fired a barrage of cannons at the *Windshark*.

Even with the wind and roar of the Vortex, Remy heard the explosions as columns of smoke billowed into the air from Jhaeros's ship. The *Queen's Blade* wheeled away, turning to circle the other ship, and Remy could imagine the chaos taking place on the *Windshark* with the sudden attack.

"They've launched the distraction," Gem gasped. "This is our chance. Cloud," she cried, and Remy quickly grabbed her waist as the dragon crouched. "Up!"

The dragon sprang off the deck. A gust of wind caught him as he did, lifting them into the air, and they soared away toward the *Windshark*.

Remy's pulse pounded, his stomach doing somersaults as

they glided over the Vortex. The roar sounded in his ears, and vicious blasts of wind tugged at them, trying to suck them down into the swirling clouds.

As they approached the *Windshark*, he saw pirates scrambling around on deck, frantically trying to respond to the sudden attack. Along the side of the hull, gunports were being opened, the dull black mouths of cannons starting to poke through.

"Get below the ship," he told Gem. "We have to go in from underneath."

She nodded, and a moment later, Cloud abruptly dropped from the sky, so quickly Remy's stomach shot up and lodged itself in his throat. As they swooped toward the bottom of the ship, he saw a basket dangling beneath the hull, with a ladder leading up to a small, square trapdoor in the wood.

"There's the bilge hole," he said. "Let's go."

Overhead, there was a roar as the *Queen's Blade* launched a second round of cannon fire into the *Windshark* from her starboard side. The huge ship shuddered, its hull smoking from the attack, but Remy didn't see any cannons pass through. Its armored hide seemed to be preventing any real damage from the opposing ship. His blood chilled. They had to find Storm and Bart quickly, before the *Windshark* could recover and launch its own counterattack.

Thankfully, there was no one in the bilge hole, and Gem maneuvered Cloud as close as she could to the platform. Which wasn't as close as Remy would've liked; there was still a good three or four feet from the dragon to the edge of the basket. It wasn't a long jump; he'd made much harder leaps before, but not from a platform that was constantly bobbing up and down, wind tugging viciously at his clothes.

"Can't you get him any closer?" he asked.

"Dragons don't hover well," Gem called back. "If I move him much closer, he'll clip his wing on the basket. You're going to have to jump."

Jump. Remy looked at the edge of the basket, remembering the time he had to leap onto a floating rock over the Maelstrom to escape pirates. *This is the same thing*, he told himself. *Just don't look down.*

Swinging his leg over the saddle, he waited until Cloud's bobbing was at its highest, then jumped.

For a second, he didn't think he'd timed it right, and the Vortex roared beneath him as he flew through the air. But then he hit the edge of the basket, bruising his chest as he clung desperately to the rim. Kicking and clawing, he heaved himself over the edge and fell into the basket.

Gem also swung her leg over the saddle, standing up in the stirrup as she contemplated the leap before her. She jumped and, like Remy, did not look down as she sailed through the air and hit the side of the basket. Grabbing her arms, Remy pulled her over the edge and into the space with him.

For a few moments, they sat there, gasping, waiting for their hearts to return to normal. Gem moved first. Climbing to her feet, she gazed at Cloud, still beating his wings as he hovered as close as he could to the basket.

"Good boy," she told him, but at that moment, the ship overhead gave a shudder and started to move. Heart pounding, Remy scrambled to his feet, feeling energy ripple through the hull as the huge warship stirred like a beast waking up.

"Gem, come on." Putting a hand on the ladder rungs, he looked back at her. "We have to move. The *Windshark* is going to start fighting back. Hurry."

"Cloud!" she cried as the dragon gave a squawk, trying to move with the ship. "Stay here!" she told him. "Stay close, but fly below the ship and keep out of sight. We'll be right back, okay?"

The dragon's bellow didn't sound like anything to Remy, but Gem nodded and turned to him. "Okay, let's go."

Pushing back the trapdoor, they climbed through the hole and into the bowels of the *Windshark*.

CHAPTER
TWENTY-SIX

They were inside.

Gem took a deep, steadying breath as she gazed around, trying to decide where to go next. The interior of the *Windshark* was much like the inside of the *Queen's Blade*, dim and cramped, with low ceilings and narrow corridors. Barrels and crates lined the walls, and clutter like netting, lanterns, ropes, buckets, and other debris sat on shelves or in forgotten piles in the corner.

"I think we're in the hold," Remy whispered, looking around as well. "The cannon deck is probably above us. The brig should be close."

As if in response, a deafening boom echoed somewhere

overhead, the sound of several cannons firing at once. The ceiling shook, dust raining down on them from above, and Gem's ears rang with the noise.

"Come on, then," she whispered, moving between piles of crates and stacks of barrels. "We don't have a lot of time."

Carefully, they crept across the room. Above them, footsteps pounded back and forth, pirates rushing to load cannons for a second counterattack. Gem hoped Captain Cutlass and the crew of the *Queen's Blade* were all right. Nothing she and Remy were doing would matter if their ship was blown out of the sky. Plus, she was starting to sort of like the pirate captain.

A simple wooden door at the back of the room led to a narrow hallway when it was opened. A second door with a small, barred window stood at the end of the hall, yellow lantern light spilling through the cracks. The smell of mold, wet straw, rust, and filth suddenly wafted into the corridor, making Gem wrinkle her nose.

"Ew, that's definitely the brig," she muttered. "It smells awful."

"It does?" Remy looked confused for a moment. "It doesn't smell any different than the Salty Barrel," he said.

Anything Gem said in response to that would have been rude, so she didn't reply.

The door was unlocked and creaked when they pushed it open. Through the frame was a small, dark room, lit with a single hanging lantern. A pair of cells sat along the wall, thick, rusty iron bars spanning floor to ceiling. A cage dangled from a chain on the opposite wall, and shackles hung from the wall, rattling as the ship trembled.

"Sir Bartello?" Stumbling across the room, Gem peered into the first cell. The floor was covered in moldy straw, and a bucket sat in the corner, thankfully empty. At first, she thought the cell was empty, too, but then she noticed a lump of bundled rags in the corner, a pair of feet poking from beneath the covers.

"Sir Bart?" Her heart clenched. For a moment, she thought that this was a dead body. No living person could sleep through the ruckus and noise from the two battling ships. But then the lump in the corner stirred. It sat up, and a head emerged from the rags, the face of a thin, white-haired old man staring at her through the bars.

"Who are you?" he croaked.

Relief and uncertainty filled her. Relief that he was alive, but . . . *this* was Sir Bartello, the fabled sky knight of old? A skinny, unkempt, bleary-eyed old man? Would he even remember where the True Dragons were? Would he even remember his name?

"Bart." Remy lunged to the cell, gripping the bars tightly as the prisoner blinked, staring at them with glassy eyes. "Bart, it's me. Are you all right?"

"Remy?" The old man gave his head a shake, as if he couldn't believe his eyes. His vision seemed to clear, the haze of confusion vanishing in a blink. "What are you doing here, boy?" he rasped, sounding almost angry. "Have you lost your mind? You need to get out of here, now."

"Not without you and Storm."

"We're here to rescue you, Sir Bartello," Gem added as Remy reached into his shirt and pulled out a pick and what looked like a simple hairpin. Crouching at the door, he inserted both into the keyhole, eyes narrowed in concentration as he manipulated the lock. Another time, Gem would have found it fascinating.

"Rescue me. Why?" The old man snorted. "The dragon, I can understand. I'm not even shocked that this one"—he waved a thin hand at Remy, still crouched over the keyhole—"found a way aboard, looking for his beast. I get that bond. I hate it, but I understand."

Gem was surprised at the bitterness in his voice. "Why?" she asked.

The old man gazed at her with tired eyes. "You have one, too, I see," he said, sounding resigned. "And yes, at first, it's the greatest thing, this shared understanding with the most magnificent of creatures. But what happens when you lose them? What if they're stolen, or kidnapped?" He glanced at Remy, still working the door to the cell, and a sad, sympathetic look crossed his face. "That bond can consume you. It is so strong, it can drive you to attempt foolish, desperate things, all to save your dragon. And then, when you lose them for good"—a haunted expression crossed Bart's face, the shadow of an old grief hovering in his eyes—"it can destroy you," he whispered. "It's the most painful thing in the world. That's why I didn't want the boy to get attached so quickly. I knew Jhaeros would find the dragon eventually; he's not the type of man to give up. And when he did, I didn't want Remy hurt or killed trying to protect him. I didn't want him chasing Jhaeros to the ends of the earth, trying to get his dragon back." He sighed, glancing once more at the front of the cell, and shook his head. "This is exactly what I was afraid of."

There was a faint click from the lock, and Remy grinned. "Got it," he whispered triumphantly, pulling the door open. It seemed that he hadn't heard a word that Bart had said, for he gestured the old man forward while glancing over his shoulder. "Come on, Bart," he said, sounding impatient. "Let's go. We still have to get Storm."

"Hold on, boy." Bart's voice was a warning. "The dragon isn't here, and if you go rushing off, you're just going to get yourself killed."

"We don't have a lot of time, Sir Bartello," Gem said. "The captain and the *Queen's Blade* are providing us with a distraction, but they can't keep it up much longer. Where is the dragon?"

Bart sighed. "Jhaeros's quarters," he said, making Gem's heart sink. "He's up top, in the captain's personal chambers."

CHAPTER
TWENTY-SEVEN

"In Jhaeros's room," Gem whispered. "Oh no. How are we going to get him out?"

Remy took a deep breath. "You're not," he told her. "I am."

He had already guessed where Storm was being kept, even before they found Bart. He remembered the dream; the cage in the room with the bookshelves and the wooden desk near the wall. Of course, it had to be Jhaeros's personal quarters; he wouldn't keep such a valuable creature locked away in the brig. Remy hadn't mentioned it before because Gem was there to rescue Bart, not Storm. If she knew the dragon was all the way in the captain's quarters, she might've been reluctant to even attempt the mission. Besides, it wasn't fair to ask her and Bart to put themselves in danger for Storm. Remy had made the promise; he had to rescue Storm by himself.

And Remy could feel his dragon, like a compass needle pointing unerringly north. Storm was close. He just had to get to him.

Gem immediately stiffened, opening her mouth to protest. Remy hurried on before she could speak. "I know how to sneak around without being seen," he said. "I've done this all my life. With all the noise and chaos from the attack, no one will even notice me. I can hide and stay out of sight; I can't say that if there's three of us."

Gem shook her head. "I don't like the idea of us splitting up," she argued. "What if you get into trouble?"

"If I do, you won't be able to help me, anyway," Remy said. "There are too many pirates. Look, just stay here with Bart. If I'm not back in ten minutes, go back to the *Queen's Blade* without me. You didn't come here for Storm, anyway."

"That doesn't mean I'm going to leave you behind with Jhaeros," Gem cried.

"Boy," Bart said firmly, "the girl is right. You can't do this on your own." He pointed a withered finger at the roof as Remy gave him a look of betrayal. "There are two more decks between us and the captain's quarters, and they're full of pirates moving back and forth. This is a cramped ship; you won't be able to hide from everyone."

"But—"

"However," Bart went on, giving Remy a thoughtful frown, "you might be able to hide in plain sight. Come with me."

They followed him through the brig and back into the hold, stumbling a bit as the ship pitched and shuddered. Cannon fire boomed, and shouting could be heard overhead as feet pounded back and forth, making dust rain down on them from above.

In the cargo hold, Bart paused, gazing around the piles of burlap sacks, crates, barrels, and boxes stacked everywhere. "This'll work," he muttered, snatching something from the corner and turning to Remy. "Do you know what a powder monkey is, boy?" he asked.

Remy nodded. Living at a pirate haven, he was aware of what went on aboard a ship. "Powder monkeys are the boys who fetch the gunpowder from the storage room and bring it to the cannons for reloading," he told Bart, who nodded.

"Correct. And a ship like this likely has a half dozen of 'em, running back and forth." Raising his hand, he plunked a threadbare old cap on Remy's head. It was too big for him, and he had to push it back out of his eyes, but Bart seemed pleased by this. "So you see where I'm going with this, don't you?" he asked. "You are going to play the part of a humble powder monkey. Hopefully in all the chaos and mayhem, no one will look twice at you, but if anyone asks, you're on your way to get more gunpowder for the cannons, you hear?"

Remy nodded. "Yeah. I got it."

"Good. Do you see that?" Bart pointed to a ladder on the other side of the hold. "That should take you straight up to the first gun deck. From there, you'll have to find your way to the captain's quarters on your own. It shouldn't be hard, though. Just keep going up until you hit the main deck. The biggest problem will be getting back with a dragon in your arms. No one on a ship gives the powder monkeys the time of day, but they're going to take notice if you're carrying around a giant winged lizard."

"Wait," Gem said, grabbing his sleeve. "He might not have to. Does this ship have a captain's walk?"

The captain's walk was a balcony attached to the captain's quarters at the rear of the ship. Remy straightened as he realized where she was going with this. "I believe it does," Bart said slowly. "I don't know how that will help us, though. It's not like we could get to it on our own."

"That would be true," Gem said, "if we didn't have a dragon." She turned back to Remy. "If you can make it to Jhaeros's quarters," she said, "Cloud, Sir Bartello, and I can meet you on the captain's walk. From there, we can fly back to the *Queen's Blade* with everyone."

Remy nodded. "I think that's the best chance we have." Pulling the cap low over his eyes, he backed away. "All right, then," he said. "I'm going to get Storm. If I'm not at the captain's walk in ten minutes, go back to the *Queen's Blade* without me."

The princess of Gallecia bit her lip, looking worried but

trying not to show it. Taking a quick breath, she composed herself and gave him a brave smile. "Be careful, Remy," she whispered.

"I will."

"Boy," Bart said, and Remy turned around. He glanced back and met the gaze of his oldest friend, who looked both proud and angry at the same time. "Trust your dragon," Bart said after a moment. "That's the secret to being a sky knight. No matter what happens, no matter what goes wrong, always trust your dragon. If you do, they'll never fail you."

A roar sounded overhead, the deafening boom of several cannons firing at once. Remy winced as the echoes died away. They didn't have a lot of time. Hurrying to the ladder, he gazed up at the hatch overhead, listening to the sound of thudding feet and men shouting at each other as they rushed back and forth. At least Bart was safe. If anything happened, the old man would escape the ship with Gem and Cloud. Now there was just one more thing to do.

Hang on, Storm. I'm coming.

Taking a deep breath, he started to climb. Pushing up the trapdoor, he hopped through the hatch to a scene of utter chaos.

The deck he emerged onto was narrow and cramped, with low ceilings and square gunports lining both sides of the walls. The air was hazy with smoke, and the smell burned his nose and made his eyes water. Long black cannons marched down either aisle, and figures scurried between them, pirates and a few boys his age or younger. As Remy watched, a pirate would grab a cartridge of gunpowder from a powder monkey and shove it into the mouth of the cannon. A wad of cloth followed, with another pirate using a long staff to jam it down the barrel, and then the deadly black ball was heaved into the opening.

Looking down the deck, Remy spotted another ladder on the other side of the room. It was close. He just had to cross a crowded floor of pirates, guns, and cannon fire to reach it.

Tugging down his cap, he stepped forward, and someone slammed into him from behind, jostling him forward. He caught himself, heart racing as he looked around, wondering if anyone had seen him. But the pirates were all too busy with the guns to notice the collision.

"Watch it!" The boy who ran into him didn't even stop to look back as he stumbled. Clutching the gunpowder bag in both arms, he handed the cartridge to the nearest pirate, who yelled at him, then instantly scurried off to get more.

Remy clenched his jaw. Bart had been right; there was no way to sneak through this mess unseen. Pulling his cap even lower, he ducked his head and stepped into the room.

Bodies jostled him, pirates snarling or shouting curses as they moved around the cannons. Remy caught an elbow to the ribs, followed by a hard shove and a yell to get out of the way. Dodging pirates, he stumbled through the room, keeping his head low and his eyes on the stairs.

"Boy!" Something grabbed his shirt, yanking him around. Remy's stomach twisted as he stared into the angry face of a pirate, a vivid scar running down one eye.

"Where's our powder, rat?" the pirate snarled with a blast of hot, fetid breath. "I've been waiting to load this gun since the first volley!"

"Sorry, sir!" Remy gasped, ducking his head. "I just gave mine away. I was going to get more!"

Another shudder rocked the ship, and somewhere overhead there was a deafening crash, as if something large and round had finally smashed through the outer hull. The pirate gave a curse and shoved Remy to the floor.

"Useless brat! Go fetch another! Hurry, before I cut out your worthless eyes!"

"Yes, sir!"

Remy scurried away, hoping the pirate wouldn't see him going in the wrong direction, but the man was already turning back to the cannon. Men were cursing, orders were being shouted, bodies were scrambling over and around each other. Remy dodged a leg, ducked beneath an arm, and finally reached the ladder on the other side of the gun deck. Without hesitation or waiting to see if anyone was watching, he scrambled up the rungs, emerging onto another section of the ship.

This was another gun deck, but even more chaotic than the last one. Pirates were scrambling back and forth, and Remy could see a hole in the wall where a cannonball had hit just right, punching through to the other side. Cannons had been overturned, the floor was full of smoke, but despite that, the pirates were still loading the remaining guns with steely determination. Looking down the aisle, Remy felt his stomach twist as he realized how much firepower the *Windshark* actually had. The *Queen's Blade* was fast and agile, and Cutlass was a wily captain, but if their smaller ship took a direct hit from this many guns, they would be blown to pieces. No wonder she had been so hesitant to engage Jhaeros and the *Windshark*.

Glancing out the hole in the wall, he saw the distant form of the *Queen's Blade* wheel around, coming in for another pass. As it swept forward, the line of pirates down the row of cannons raised their linstocks, sticks holding a burning length of rope, over the cannon fuses.

"Fire!"

The sticks plunged down, igniting fuses, and the cannons boomed as they fired all at once. Smoke filled the air, and the cannons rolled backward several feet, sending a deadly barrage of iron at the *Queen's Blade*.

Remy clenched his fists, but at the last second, the smaller vessel rose sharply into the air, as if yanked by invisible strings. Most of the barrage missed it, but a few cannonballs still struck the bottom of the hull, smashing through wood and sending debris plummeting into the Vortex below.

"Reload!" roared the commander, and the pirates hurried to obey. On the other side of the room, the stairs to the upper deck beckoned. One final obstacle before Remy reached the main deck and the captain's quarters. With a last quick breath, he ducked his head, hunched his shoulders, and sprinted forward.

He had reached the stairs and was almost to the top step when he nearly ran into a body coming down the staircase. Quickly, he moved aside to let the pirate pass, but a meaty hand suddenly clamped down on the back of his neck, stopping him.

"Where do you think you're going, rat?" The pirate dragged him backward. "No one needs you up there; you're supposed to be getting the . . . Wait a second."

Remy's cap was suddenly knocked off, falling to the floor. "I don't recognize you," the pirate growled. "Where did we pick you up, rat?"

His mouth dry with terror, Remy started to answer when a shout of alarm rang out from the main deck. "Incoming!" someone screamed. Remy looked up and saw the *Queen's Blade* swoop overhead. As it passed, several dark shapes suddenly dropped from the ship. "Fire barrels!" someone shrieked. "Captain—"

There was a roar, and a tornado sprang up out of nowhere, seeming to rise directly out of the deck planks. It caught most of the barrels and sent them spinning away, flying in all directions to plunge into the Vortex. Remy felt his blood turn to ice. He looked across the deck to the forecastle and saw Jhaeros himself standing on the edge, hands raised and magic swirling around him. His eyes glowed with power, his coat and white hair snapping behind him in the gale, and he looked truly terrifying. The tornado howled, spinning the barrels in all directions, but one barrel hit the sails, bounced off, and fell back toward the deck.

There was a flare, and a wave of heat blasted Remy in the face as the barrel exploded against the deck, sending a bloom of fire into the air. The pirate holding him gave a yell and reeled back, nearly falling down the steps. Remy instantly bolted up the stairs onto the main deck—and found himself in the center of organized chaos. Tongues of fire snapped, eating at the deck and railings of the *Windshark*, and pirates rushed to put out the flames. Men scrambled back and forth, some in the riggings, some on swivel guns mounted to the railings, some loading even more cannons on the main deck. Wind shrieked in Remy's ears, and the roar of the Vortex echoed even above the cacophony of cannon fire and battling ships.

Remy glanced at the forecastle and saw Jhaeros shouting orders to his crew as the *Queen's Blade* circled overhead. For just a moment, the pirate mage looked down, and his gaze locked with Remy's. A frown crossed his face, but then the *Queen's Blade* passed very close, casting him in its shadow. Glancing back at the enemy ship, the pirate mage bared his teeth and raised an arm, and a streak of lightning flashed from his open palm, slamming into the hull of the *Queen's Blade*. For a moment, everyone's attention was focused solely on Jhaeros or the other vessel, and Remy bolted for the door of the captain's quarters.

No one stopped him, though he did have to dodge several bodies and leap over a section of burning wood before he came to the door in the aftcastle. The captain's private chambers. Praying that it wasn't locked, Remy reached for the handle.

It wasn't locked. The brass handle turned easily in his palm, and he slipped through the frame with barely a squeak. Beyond the door, the room was cloaked in shadow, thick curtains drawn across a row of windows on the back wall. This room was much larger than Captain Cutlass's private quarters, with a plush red carpet and shelves stacked floor to ceiling. But the most prominent feature in the room was an enormous curved horn hanging from the ceiling. It was longer than Remy was tall, and bigger than any horn, tooth, or talon he had ever seen before. There was no doubt in his mind; this must be the horn of a True Dragon.

"Storm," he whispered, easing into the room. "I'm here. Where are you?"

A weak trill answered him. A wooden desk sat near the far wall, an iron birdcage sitting beside it, draped with a blanket. Remy hurried over, stripped off the blanket, and met the purple eyes of his dragon peering at him through the bars.

Relief shot through him. Storm was all right. The dragon looked scared, and he barely had room to turn around in a cage meant for a parrot, but he was alive. He squeaked at Remy, pressing himself against the side of the cage, clawing frantically at the bars. Remy winced as the birdcage rattled loudly and put a hand against the side.

"Shh, Storm, take it easy. They'll hear us."

The hatchling immediately calmed, gazing up at Remy imploringly. Remy frowned, examining the iron lock on the door, and shook his head.

"I don't suppose the key would be lying around anywhere," he muttered. A quick scan of the cabin told him he was correct; there was no golden key sitting in plain sight to make his life easier. "Hang on, then, Storm," he said, kneeling down and pulling out his lock picks. "This shouldn't take me too long."

Carefully, Remy inserted the picks into place, biting his lip in concentration as he began working the lock. After a few moments, Storm gave an impatient trill, thumping his tail against the bars. Remy winced as the whole cage rattled.

"This takes time, you know," he muttered without looking up. "It's a delicate process; I can't just snap my fingers and . . . Aha." The lock clicked, and Remy grinned triumphantly. "Got it."

He swung back the door, and Storm leaped into his arms. Remy clutched the hatchling tight, feeling its heart race against his. Fragments of emotion flickered through his head: relief, fear, sadness, anger toward the pirate mage who brought him here. Remy wasn't sure if these emotions were his or Storm's, but there was no time to wonder about that now. They still had to get back to the *Queen's Blade*, and out of range of the *Windshark*, before they were truly safe.

"All right." Remy set his dragon on the floor and turned to look at the balcony doors. With any luck, Gem and Bart would be waiting for them on Cloud. "It's been a day. Let's get you out of here."

With a deafening noise, the cabin door crashed open. Storm gave a squawk of fear and alarm as Jhaeros stepped into the room, cold blue eyes narrowed in rage.

"I thought I recognized you," the mage crooned, smiling evilly at Remy. "The street rat from Cutthroat Wedge. Where do you think you're going with my dragon?"

Storm let out a high-pitched snarl and leaped in front of Remy, flaring his wings and baring tiny fangs at the pirate mage looming in the doorway.

Jhaeros laughed. "Don't worry, beast. I'll get to you in a moment." He shook his head and gazed at Remy again. "So this is why we're being attacked, eh? I figured it had to be the dragon; no one would be so foolish to engage the *Windshark* one-on-one otherwise. But I'm afraid your little mission ends right here, boy. That dragon isn't going anywhere."

"Storm, run!" Remy cried, and he bolted for the balcony doors, hoping to beat the pirate mage to the captain's walk. They still had a chance. If Gem and Cloud were waiting as they'd promised, he and Storm could still get away.

"Get back here!" There was a blast of wind, and the

balcony doors burst open, glass shattering as the vicious gust came through. The wind slammed into Remy, plucking him off his feet and hurling him back into the cabin. He hit the ground and rolled into a cabinet, feeling the world spin around him. Dazed, he looked up to see Jhaeros step forward, drawing his sword as he did. He was still smiling.

"You are nothing," Jhaeros said as that deadly curved blade rose, angling toward Remy's heart. "A mud rat. A nobody. You are unworthy to have a dragon. And when I kill you, no one will even notice you're gone."

He drew back his sword, and Storm leaped forward with a screech, his jaws gaping wide. Blue light glowed from his mouth a second before a streak of lightning flashed through the air, striking the pirate mage in the chest. Jhaeros was hurled away, smashing into a bookshelf, tomes and crystals falling around him. Remy leaped to his feet, scooped Storm up, and ran for the balcony.

Behind him, he heard Jhaeros lunge upright with a bellow of rage. Remy burst through the swinging balcony doors and gazed around wildly, looking for the white dragon. But the captain's walk and the skies were empty. Gem and Cloud were nowhere to be seen.

"Nowhere to run now, rat." Jhaeros pushed through the doors. His eyes glowed ominously, watching as Remy scurried back as far as he could, Storm hissing and snarling in his arms. They hit the railings, and Remy could only watch as the pirate mage stepped closer, smiling again. "Your ship is crippled, your allies have failed, and soon you will join them as I hurl you all into the Vortex."

"Remy!"

A shadow fell over him, and Cloud swooped down from overhead, soaring alongside the balcony. Gem reached out a hand, her eyes wide with fear. "Jump!"

"No!" roared Jhaeros, throwing out an arm. As Remy scrambled onto the railing, a streak of lightning smashed into the wood where he'd been standing moments before. Storm let out a shriek as the balcony and railing beneath Remy crumbled, and they both plummeted toward the Maelstrom.

CHAPTER
TWENTY-EIGHT

"Remy! Storm!"

Gem gave a gasp of horror, watching Remy and his dragon fall away into the Vortex. Behind her, Bart let out a strangled cry, thin fingers reaching out to the figures tumbling into the great beyond. "Cloud!" she cried. "Go after them!"

The white dragon bellowed and started to dive, but Jhaeros let out a howl of rage, and a blast of wind shot up from below, catching the dragon in midair. It shot them upward, and another gust slammed into them from the side. Unable to fight the winds, they were flung through the air, the world careening around them. Cloud struck the deck of the ship, and Gem was flung from the saddle, rolling across the planks until she came to a dizzying stop near the mast.

Gasping, she looked up, the world still swaying around her. A few feet away, Sir Bartello was being hauled to his feet by a pair of pirates. Farther on, Cloud lay in a heap against the side of the ship, one wing crumpled beneath him. Pirates swarmed him, throwing lines over his body, looping ropes around his jaw, tying him down. Gem's stomach clenched, and she staggered to her feet.

"Get away from my dragon!" she cried, but something grabbed her from behind, lifting her off her feet. She kicked and struggled, feeling her heel strike the pirate in the leg. He grunted, grabbed her arm, and twisted it painfully behind her back, making her gasp in pain.

"Enough!"

Jhaeros strode across the deck, white hair streaming behind him, his coat snapping in the wind. His eyes glowed feverishly bright as he stopped in the middle of the deck, observing the situation.

The pirate holding Gem dragged her forward and pushed her at Jhaeros. Panting, Gem raised her head and glared at the pirate mage, her hood thrown back and her own hair blowing loose in the wind. Jhaeros regarded her silently for a moment, then smiled a cold, cruel smile.

"Well, well. Fate does work in strange ways, doesn't it?"

Gem looked around desperately. The pirates had Cloud pinned down near the railings. Two more stood over a kneeling Sir Bartello, their swords drawn and pointed at his back. Overhead, the *Queen's Blade* drifted past, trailing smoke from its hull, one of its wing sails torn and hanging limply. No one was left to help her; Gem was on her own.

"You've cost me the power of a True Dragon," Jhaeros said, taking a step forward. "But it seems I haven't lost everything quite yet." His smile widened, eyes glittering with malice. "Isn't that right . . . Princess?"

Her heart sank even further. Kneeling between two pirates, Sir Bartello raised his head, his face slack with amazement and disbelief. "Princess," he repeated. "Princess Gemillia. Why would you come here? You've given Jhaeros all the power he needs to use against the king."

Ignoring him, Gem glared up at Jhaeros. "Whatever you're planning, it won't work," she warned him. "If you do anything to me, my father won't stop until he's hunted you down."

"I don't fear the king," Jhaeros said with a shrug. "Gallus is many miles away in the capital. He won't be able to help you now." He raised an arm, flickering strands crawling up his clenched fist. "Once I gain the power of a True Dragon, your father's kingdom will fall before me, and I will be the one to rule it all. And now that I have his precious daughter, Gallus will do nothing as I march into his capital and seize it from the inside." The pirate mage gave a ghastly smile, looking like a grinning skull in the flickering light. "I've lost a dragon but gained a princess. I suppose that's a fair enough trade."

Gem thought of Remy, falling away into the Maelstrom, and her eyes burned. Anger, grief, and desperation flared, and magic rose up like a whirlwind. She could feel it, swirling within her like a storm, and clenched her fists at her sides.

You don't need a college education to use magic, Lysander had sneered. *The college teaches structure and control, but magic is wild, untamed, unpredictable. Anyone with the talent can use it. You just have to be careful it doesn't tear you apart.*

"Captain." One of the pirates next to Cloud gave a grunt as the dragon tried to get up, fighting the men and the ropes holding him down. "What do we do with the beast?" he asked, clenching his jaw as the dragon growled and struggled. His tail lashed, hitting a pirate in the stomach and doubling him over before another grabbed the swinging tail and pinned it down.

Jhaeros curled a lip. "I don't need a normal dragon," he said contemptuously. "Get rid of it. Throw the old man overboard, too. His usefulness has ended."

"No!" Gem shrieked, and threw out an arm. A flare of power lanced through her, like electricity beneath her skin, and lightning streaked from her fingers. Jhaeros instinctively raised a hand, and the lightning slammed into his palm. Grimacing, he took a step back, teeth clenched in concentration as the lightning crackled around him. The ring of pirates let out cries of alarm, staring at their leader in shock. Gem watched in stunned silence, eyes wide, her thoughts racing frantically.

I . . . I did it! I called down lightning from the Maelstrom. Lysander was right; you don't have to be an elder mage to use storm magic.

With a shout, Jhaeros flung both arms out to the side, and the strands sizzling around him dispersed. Panting, he straightened, his hair floating wildly around him, and gazed at Gem in both surprise and grudging respect.

"Well, Princess. I believe I've underestimated you." He smiled, and his eyes flashed an ominous blue-white. "Congratulations. It won't happen again."

He raised an arm. Gem braced herself, but what hit her wasn't lightning. It was wind, lifting her off her feet and hurling her back across the deck. She hit the planks hard, the breath driven from her lungs in a painful expulsion. Trying to gasp in air, she scrambled back on her elbows, watching as Jhaeros strode forward, smiling lazily.

"You have raw talent, I'll give you that," he said, gesturing with one hand. A surge of wind lifted Gem a few feet in the air, then dropped her to the deck. She landed with a gasp of pain. "But it still takes power. Power and control, to fully manipulate the elements. Without power, you are weak. Without control, the magic itself will flare out of hand. The True Dragons were the only ones who could fully integrate and control the magic, because they were magical creatures themselves. Once I have the power of a True Dragon, nothing in the world will be able to stop me. I will rule this land as the strongest creature alive. And you are going to help me get there."

Gem scooted back until she hit the railing of the ship. Her head hurt, and she couldn't seem to draw in enough air. But she glared at Jhaeros and defiantly raised her chin. "I'll never help you," she spat.

"I'm afraid you don't have a choice, Princess." Jhaeros smiled. "Your ship is crippled, your knight is a pathetic old man, and your luck has run out. There are no dragons around to save you."

He raised his arm, and a shadow fell over them both. Gasping, Gem looked back as, with the sound of beating wings, a blue-and-silver dragon rose over the side of the *Windshark*, glaring down with blazing purple eyes.

CHAPTER
TWENTY-NINE

Remy had thought he was dead.

The wind shrieked in his ears, stinging his eyes and tearing at his clothes as he fell. Around him, he caught flashes of debris tumbling with him: chunks of wood, broken planks, pieces of ships, all spinning lazily toward the huge swirling mass below. The Vortex howled, lightning flashing in its depths, a gaping maw ready to swallow him whole. For a moment, Remy wondered how it would end; would he be disintegrated by lightning, be turned into something horrific and monstrous, or just keep falling until he hit whatever lay beneath the Maelstrom?

If there *was* anything beneath the Maelstrom. No one knew what lay below the storm. Maybe he would just keep falling forever.

Storm. I'm so sorry. Twisting in midair, Remy searched for his dragon. Storm had wings, of course, but he was still too young to fly. He would fall as well, and there was nothing Remy could do to stop it.

He saw him then, several feet overhead. The hatchling was tumbling through the air, spinning head over tail, a speck of brightness against the void of the Vortex. Remy saw him try to flap his wings, to fly as he must've known he was meant to do. But he continued to plummet, and around him, strands of purple flickered ominously through the darkness. Almost as if they were following the dragon as he tumbled through the sky.

Faster than thought, a strand of lightning lashed out from the clouds and struck the hatchling dead-on. Remy gave a wordless cry, but his voice was drowned out by the Vortex and he couldn't even hear himself. Tears filled his eyes, blurring his vision as he watched Storm continue to drop, barely visible now through the swirling clouds.

Another fork of lightning lashed out and struck the dragon, but this one didn't immediately vanish. More strands appeared, attaching themselves to Storm, until the dragon resembled a glowing ball in the center of a flickering web. As Remy watched, the dragon drew farther and farther away, seemingly frozen within the lightning web. Until he was nothing but a speck against the darkening sky, and lost from view.

Remy felt numb, and not from the icy wind freezing the tears to his cheeks. His dragon was gone. Storm had been special, a True Dragon, maybe the first hatchling to ever rise above the Maelstrom. He had trusted Remy; Remy had promised to keep the dragon safe, and he had failed. And now they would both perish in the Maelstrom.

Remy slumped, not even feeling the cold wind anymore. He had lost his dragon, but at least in a few moments, it wouldn't matter. The roar of the Maelstrom was deafening. Chunks of wood and other debris spun around him, and lightning seared the air, so bright it was nearly blinding. Remy covered his face and squeezed his eyes shut, hoping that—however it happened—the end would be quick.

Hang on, Remy!

The voice flashed through his head, so fast he thought he had imagined it. Cracking an eyelid, he peeked through his fingers and saw two pinpricks of purple light coming toward him through the darkness. The spots grew brighter, brighter . . .

And then a dragon exploded through the darkness and swooped toward him.

Remy's mouth fell open. It was Storm, only . . . *bigger*. Not as large as a True Dragon, but bigger than Cloud. He had the same deep blue scales, the same silvery mane, the same lightning-shaped stripes down his back and wings. Those wings were certainly much larger now; Remy felt the wind buffet him as the dragon dove past. Now beneath Remy, Storm flared his wings, hovering in midair, and Remy braced himself as he dropped onto the dragon's back. His arms encircled the dragon's neck, and he squeezed with his legs as Storm gave a bellow of defiance and surged into the air, flying up toward the edge of the Vortex.

Shaking, Remy sat up, watching ship chunks drop past them, watching the rise and fall of the dragon's lightning-marked wings.

"Is this real?" he whispered. "Am I dreaming?"

Storm looked back at him, the expression on his reptilian face one of amusement and exasperation. It was that look, instantly familiar and completely Storm, that told Remy that he wasn't dreaming. That he was on his dragon's back, and somehow, impossibly, Storm had become the size of an adult dragon.

But they weren't safe yet.

Above them the clouds parted, and the *Windshark* loomed overhead, grinning and ominous against the sky. In the distance, Remy could also see the *Queen's Blade* circling awkwardly with its shredded wing.

"Cutlass is still there," Remy muttered. "She hasn't left yet. That's means Gem and Bart must still be on the *Windshark*. With Jhaeros." He clenched his fists in Storm's mane. "They must be in trouble! Let's go, Storm!"

Storm let out a bugle, making Remy jump with how loud the dragon's voice was now, and flapped his wings, surging up toward the enemy ship. As they rose toward the hull, Remy saw flashes of lightning coming off the deck, and his stomach clenched. Rising above the side of the ship, he looked down and saw Gem sitting against the railing, looking hurt and scared. Jhaeros stood in front of her, arm raised, his eyes glowing with power. The mage dropped his arm, gazing up at Remy and Storm, and his face went slack with shock.

"A . . . True Dragon," he whispered. "At last, one has appeared. Your power will be mine!"

Raising his hand again, he sent a streak of lightning at the dragon, and the bolt slammed directly into Storm's chest. Storm bellowed, and Remy cried out as crackling strands crawled over the dragon's body. But they didn't seem to hurt him. They crawled over his scales, buzzing and flickering wildly, and sizzled out. Storm shook his head, glaring down at Jhaeros, and for the first time, a shadow of fear crossed the pirate mage's face.

The dragon roared, his booming voice rising over the Maelstrom. Blue light glowed between his jaws, and a streak of lightning arced toward the pirate mage. Jhaeros was flung back, hitting the deck and twitching frantically as strands crawled over his body. Bile rose in Remy's throat, and he turned away as Storm gave a bellow of triumph and surged into the air.

Chaos broke over the *Windshark*. Seeing their captain fall, the pirates abandoned whatever they were doing and scrambled for cover as the dragon swooped over the deck. Storm turned on the pirates with a snarl. Lightning shot from his jaws, slamming into the ship and igniting the wood in a flash of heat and light. In the confusion, Remy watched Bart grab a discarded cutlass and run to Cloud, slicing through the ropes tying the white dragon down. As they circled back, he saw Gem racing across the deck toward the sky knight. A pair of pirates chased her, swords raised above their heads, and Remy gasped.

"Gem, look out! Storm, help—"

Storm was already diving. As Gem passed beneath them, he landed on the deck with a crash and a roar. The pirates immediately skidded to a halt, their eyes wide with terror. They threw themselves aside as Storm spat lightning, igniting another section of the ship.

"Remy!"

He turned. Cloud was on his feet, with Gem and Bart already on his back. The princess's eyes were huge, filled with amazement and a little fear as she stared at them.

"Is that Storm?" she gasped.

"Go!" Remy called back. "Get back to the *Queen's Blade*! We'll be right behind you!"

She blinked, seeming to shake herself out of her daze, and nodded. "Cloud, up!" she cried, and the white dragon launched himself skyward. They rose swiftly into the air with the smoke and swirling embers and flapped away out of sight.

Remy slumped in relief. "All right, they're gone," he breathed, and slapped the dragon's shoulder to get his attention. "It's our turn now. Come on, Storm. Let's get out of here."

Storm opened his wings but froze, every muscle in his body coiling tight. "Storm," Remy urged as the dragon continued to stand there, staring at something in the flames. "Come on. What are you looking . . . ?"

He trailed off, his insides going cold. Through the smoke and flames, he saw something that made his blood freeze. A shadow in the darkness, bulky and hunched over as if in pain. The gleam of a cold blue eye glaring at them through the haze.

Jhaeros. He was still alive.

A billow of smoke gusted between them, and when it cleared, the silhouette was gone. Pirates were shouting, a few of them running toward them with their swords raised.

"Storm, let's go!" Remy shouted, and the dragon jerked up. With a final roar of defiance, he sprang into the air, flapping his wings to gain altitude, and the deck swiftly fell away. Remy watched the *Windshark* grow smaller and smaller beneath him, watched the pirates scrambling to put out flames and recover from the rampage of an angry lightning dragon. He searched for Jhaeros among the flames and wreckage, but the pirate mage, if that shadow *had* been him after all, was nowhere to be seen.

Storm leveled out, flaring his wings to the side as he glided on the air currents. In the distance, near the edge of the Vortex, Remy saw the sleek outline of the *Queen's Blade*. The right wing had been shredded, and smoke curled from several holes in the hull, but it flew straight and true, injured but unbowed, and his heart lifted at the sight of it.

Blowing out a breath, he slumped against his dragon, thinking back to everything that had happened. He remembered then that moment in the Vortex when he thought he was going to die, hearing a voice in his head telling him to hold on. Of course, with all the chaos and weird things happening around him, it might've just been his imagination.

With a sigh, he patted the dragon's shoulder, causing Storm to peer back at him. "Well, that was a wild day," he muttered, and the dragon blinked. "But everyone is all right. And you're big now. I have no idea how *that* happened, but at least now I can ride you."

Storm let out a snort and rolled his eyes. And a voice, perfectly clear and acerbic, echoed in Remy's head. *Don't make me dump you into the Maelstrom*, it said. *Also, I hope there's food on that ship. I'm starving.*

EPILOGUE

They were waiting for him on the *Queen's Blade*: Gem, Bart, Cloud, and Captain Cutlass, all looking relieved as Storm swooped down and landed on the deck. When Remy slid from the dragon's back, stumbling a bit as he hit solid ground, Gem strode forward and threw her arms around him. He froze in shock as the princess of Gallecia hugged him tightly, wondering if it was okay to hug her back. But before he could do anything, she pulled away, her smile shaky with relief.

"I thought you were dead," she whispered. "When you and Storm fell, I thought . . ." She trailed off, then looked past him at the dragon, her gaze shifting to amazement. "Is that really him?" she asked in awe. "How did he get so big?"

"Maelstrom magic," Bart said, stepping forward. "The beast is a True Dragon, after all. Or at least, Jhaeros seemed to think it was."

Storm flared his nostrils. *Who are you calling a beast, old human?*

Everyone except Bart started. Even Remy. He still wasn't used to hearing his dragon's voice in his head. But Bart simply smiled. "It's been a long time since I've heard voices in my mind speaking to me," he mused. "Sometimes, I wondered if I had gone sky-mad, after all." He shook his head, then gave the dragon a very serious look. "Treat the boy well," he said. "Don't break his heart, like mine was broken all those decades ago."

Storm blinked but didn't answer. Captain Cutlass cleared her throat. "Well," she stated, "this has all been very exciting, but I have a ship to look after. The *Queen's Blade* took quite the beating, which I expect to be fully compensated for, *Princess*." She gave Gem a pointed look, and Gem grimaced. "We'll be heading back to port to get her patched up," the captain went on, pragmatic and composed as always. "Dragons, sky knights, and talking lizards aside, I suggest you all decide what you want to do from there."

Remy shared a glance with Storm and found the dragon thinking the same thing he was. What did they do now? Go back to Cutthroat Wedge like nothing had happened? Return to a life of stealing, begging, and scrounging to survive? He didn't think that was possible anymore. Not with a dragon who, though not a full-sized True Dragon, was still as big as any normal adult.

Besides, he thought with a chill, Jhaeros was still out there. And he didn't think the pirate mage was the type who would just give up and forget. If he and Storm stayed in one place, he was certain that Jhaeros would eventually find them.

"Boy," the captain said, making him jump. "Your dragon can stay in the hold with the other one," she told him, giving Storm a scrutinizing look. "With the same conditions I gave the princess: Don't set my ship on fire, and don't eat my crew. Do that, and I won't even ask how in the Great Abyss a dragon you told me was no bigger than a dog got this big this fast."

"You don't have to tell me," Remy said. "He can understand you."

"Can he." Captain Cutlass turned to Storm. "Very well. Dragon, don't set my ship on fire. Do that one thing and we'll get along, understand?"

Storm blinked, thumping his tail against the deck in contemplation. *As long as I get fed.*

"I'm sure we can spare something." Without missing a beat, the unflappable captain of the *Queen's Blade* took a step back. "Now, if you'll excuse me, the crew is waiting for orders. Blackmailed by a kid and a talking dragon," Remy heard her mutter as she strode away. "I'll need a vacation after this for sure."

Bart watched Cutlass leave, then turned back to Remy and Gem. "So," he began, as if preparing for one of his long stories, "I think it's high time someone told me what is going on. Princess"—he bowed his grizzled head to Gem, putting a fist over his heart—"why have you come? I appreciate the rescue, but I am not a fool. That you are here at all, away from the king and the capital, means something big is happening. Otherwise, why go through all the trouble to rescue a washed-up old sky knight?"

Remy's heart beat faster. Was she finally going to tell them? Explain why a princess had come way out here to the Fringe, fighting pirates and mages and warships, all to rescue Bart? Gem paused, putting a hand on Cloud's shoulder as she seemed to gather her thoughts. Her gaze strayed to Remy and Storm, and her lips tightened, as if she were trying to come to a hard decision. Finally, she sighed. Raising her head, she squared her shoulders and gave all of them a grave look.

"This stays between the three of us," she said. Beside Remy, Storm gave an indignant snort and thumped his tail, making the princess blink. "Sorry, the *four* of us," she amended, gazing at them all in turn. "You must promise not to tell another soul," she continued solemnly. "I trust you all, but this is something that could destroy the kingdom if it got out. So swear an oath to me right here, right now, that you will not tell anyone what I am about to reveal."

Bart stepped forward and immediately lowered himself

to a knee. "I swear to you, my princess," he said, bowing his head, "I have not forgotten my oath as a sky knight, to protect the kingdom and the royal family at all costs. I will not tell a soul of what transpired here; you have my word."

Gem gave a solemn nod, then glanced at Remy. He bobbed his head. "I promise, too," he said. "I won't tell anyone. You can trust me."

"I do," Gem said, and her gaze flicked to Storm, watching the conversation in silence. "Storm," she murmured, and the dragon tilted his head. "You are a True Dragon," she said. "That in itself gives me hope. Will you help us? Will you lend your strength to this mission, even though we are practically strangers, and the world itself is new to you?"

Storm regarded Gem with glowing purple eyes, seeming to ponder the question seriously. *Human princess*, he said, his voice echoing clearly in Remy's mind. *I don't know you, or your world. So far it has not been kind to me. But Remy is my friend, and Bart was . . . helpful enough, I suppose. Even if it was begrudging.* Bart gave a very dragon-like snort at that but didn't say anything. Storm ignored him.

I have nowhere to go, the dragon went on, making Remy's stomach clench. He knew that feeling all too well. *But more than that, I want to know where I came from. There are other True Dragons out there, of this I am sure. I will agree to help you and hope that our paths bring us closer to meeting them. But only if Remy agrees as well.*

"You don't have to worry about me," Remy said, and put

a hand on the dragon's neck, causing him to peer down at him. "I want to help you find where you came from. We're in this together; I'm not going anywhere."

The dragon sniffed. *I suppose that means I'm going to have to let you ride me*, he sighed.

Bart shook his head. "I get the feeling I'm going to have to remember my dragon skills," he muttered, and turned back to Gem. "Regardless, you have our oaths, Princess. Now, if you can, please tell us what is going on."

Gem took a deep breath, briefly closed her eyes, and opened them again. Remy braced himself for bad news, but the princess's next words caused everything inside him to freeze in absolute terror, a chunk of ice settling in the pit of his stomach.

"All the islands are in danger," the princess said solemnly. "The crystals keeping them afloat are failing. If we don't do something to stop it, everything we know will fall into the Maelstrom and be lost. Sir Bartello, you might be the only person alive with the knowledge of how to save the world."

ACKNOWLEDGMENTS

Anyone who has ever known me knows that I love dragons, so working on this book was an absolute dream. Thank you to my editor, Kieran, for giving me the opportunity not only to write about dragons, but to create a world that was completely new and filled with all the things I love. Without you, Storm, Remy, Gem, and Bart's story would never have been possible.

And, as always, thank you to my first editor, sounding board, plot developer, and logic-hole spotter, Nick. For all the times you drive me crazy insisting the world in the book actually makes sense.

READ ON

FOR AN EXCITING SNEAK PEEK

AT THE NEXT BOOK IN THE

SAGA!

FIREBRED

CHAPTER ONE

"All the islands are in danger," the princess said solemnly. "The crystals keeping them afloat are failing. If we don't do something to stop it, everything we know will fall into the Maelstrom and be lost. Sir Bartello, you might be the only person alive with the knowledge of how to save the world."

Remy felt his stomach drop at the declaration. Beside him, Bart and Storm gaped at Gem in shock, waiting to see if this was a joke. The princess of the kingdom, Gemillia Sunwind Gallecia XIV, faced them grimly on the deck of the ship, the wind tugging at her dark hair. Her face was serious, her blue eyes solemn, and nothing about her said that she was joking.

They were standing on the forecastle of the *Queen's Blade*, having just escaped from Jhaeros, the terrible pirate who had kidnapped two of Remy's friends. One of them had been Bartello, the old man who Remy had known for years as Crusty Bart, a storyteller at the Salty Barrel tavern.

The other was Storm.

Storm was a dragon. A blue-and-silver dragon with brilliant lightning bolt markings down his back and wings. Jhaeros had kidnapped both Storm and Bart from the pirate town of Cutthroat Wedge and had flown away on his sky ship, the *Windshark*. Remy had vowed to get them back and had joined another pirate crew in order to chase them down. He didn't know that the princess of the kingdom was aboard the same ship, looking for Bart. Together, they had snuck aboard the *Windshark*, found Bart and Storm, and managed to escape. Of course, there had been a few hiccups where both of them had nearly died, but they had made it back. They were safe.

Or so he thought.

"The crystals are failing?" Bart repeated, sounding numb. The white-haired old man in the tattered captain's coat stared at the princess in alarm. "How? Why? What has happened to them?"

"We don't know," Gem replied. "My father . . . the king . . ." Her voice dropped as she said those words, as if she didn't want anyone else to hear. "The king and the archmage have been looking into it. It's become a secret emergency of the crown. They've pulled all available storm mages to the capital to help charge the storm crystals, but the crystals continue to fail. The islands are sinking into the Maelstrom." She paused, biting her lip, then continued in a soft voice: "Archmage Aetrius thinks they could fail completely within a year."

"But—" Remy sucked in a horrified breath, and a chill crept over his whole body. The Maelstrom was the roiling, crackling sea of clouds, wind, and arcane lightning that covered the world. You could not escape it. You could not outrun it. No matter where you went, the Maelstrom was there, lurking below every island, every ship, every rock, as far as the eye could see. "If the islands fall into the Maelstrom . . ."

"Everyone will die," Gem finished softly. "Yes. We are aware of the situation." She glanced at Bart. "Now you know why I had to come find you, Sir Bartello. My father is doing everything he can to help the mages at the capital and, of course, to find a solution, but his position keeps him busy there. Which is why I have taken it upon myself to seek answers. The more people we have working to find a solution, the better."

"Princess . . ." Bart slowly shook his head. His voice was faint, and his skin had gone ashen. He suddenly looked very old and frail, braced against the chill wind sweeping across the deck. "Why do you think I can help with this?" he asked. "I am no mage. I know very little of magic, and even less about the storm crystals."

"But you know about dragons," Gem said. "True Dragons. You've spoken with them. On an island out in the Maelstrom."

Beside Remy, Storm raised his head, purple eyes widening. *True Dragons?* he repeated, his voice echoing clearly in Remy's head. *Like me?*

Remy's stomach tightened. The longing in Storm's voice was palpable. "I thought the True Dragons were extinct," Remy said. "Everyone says they died out with the Shattering two thousand years ago."

"Or so we've all been led to believe," said Bart, still looking pale. "But no, the princess is correct. The True Dragons do exist. No one knows where they are or how they survive, but they are not extinct. Storm is proof of that."

Remy felt dazed. This was unreal. Up until very, very recently, the only dragons he had ever heard of were smaller and less intelligent and didn't talk. They were used as mounts for rich nobles and sky knights, more akin to horses than the ancient True Dragons of legend. Much like Tendril, the gargantuan monster who lived in the Maelstrom, True Dragons existed only in myth and wild tales of the sky.

Storm was the first True Dragon he had seen, the first True Dragon *anyone*—except maybe Bart—had seen in two thousand years. But if what Gem was saying was true, there were others out there. Somewhere.

"The island." If possible, Bart's complexion went even paler. His eyes grew distant and haunted, and for a moment,

Remy was afraid he would either collapse or stand there frozen, saying nothing. When he finally did speak, his voice was a shaky whisper. "That was . . . a very long time ago," he breathed. "I . . . I have tried to forget that part of my life. Those memories bring me nothing but pain." He glanced at Storm suddenly, his lips tightening. "You have a True Dragon right there," he said, gesturing to Storm. "I can hear his voice as clearly as any of yours. You don't need me to take you into the Maelstrom looking for another one."

"Storm is still a baby," Gem said, and the blue dragon immediately snorted.

I am not, he retorted, half flaring his wings. *Look, I'm big now. If I tried sitting on Remy, I would squash him.*

Remy almost smiled. Hard to believe that when he first found the baby dragon, not very long ago, Storm had been the size of a cat. So small he would curl around Remy's shoulders, weighing almost nothing. "Too bad," he told the dragon. "You looked good as a scarf."

I am not a scarf. Storm wrinkled his snout at him. *Not a scarf, not a lizard, not a baby. I'm a dragon.*

"I'm sorry, Storm," Gem said quickly. "I didn't mean to call you a baby. I just meant that you're still a very young True Dragon. You don't have the knowledge that the ancient True Dragons possess. Unless . . . you do?" She tilted her head, cautiously hopeful. "*Do* you have the knowledge we're looking for?"

Storm blinked at her. *I don't understand.*

"The True Dragons were around in the time before the Shattering," the princess went on. "They are said to possess ancient knowledge and are the ones who taught magic to humans. They might be the only ones who know how to stop the crystals from failing and the islands from falling to their destruction." She leaned forward, her expression suddenly intense. "Storm, if you know anything about how to stop it, we wouldn't have to go to the island," she said. "We could take that knowledge back and save the kingdom right now."

But the dragon shook his head. *I don't even know where I came from*, he said in a plaintive voice. *I barely remember anything before I met Remy. I just know that I was scared and . . . running away from something.* He sighed a curl of smoke into the air, watching the sun slowly sinking over the horizon. *I have lots of questions I want to ask another True Dragon*, he said, and even his mind voice sounded tired, *but I don't know where to find them. I don't even know where to look.*

Remy put a hand on the dragon's scaly blue shoulder. "We'll find one," he said as the dragon glanced at him mournfully. "We already know where to go, right, Bart?" He looked up at the old man, though Bart didn't meet his gaze. "The island where you were stranded; you said there were True Dragons there."

"One," Bart whispered. "There was one True Dragon on that island. He was . . ." Briefly, his eyes closed, before his expression hardened. "I don't want to talk about it," he said flatly.

"You must, Sir Bartello." The princess's voice was sympathetic, but her expression was unyielding. "I understand that it was a very difficult time in your life, being stranded on that island, but this is for the sake of the kingdom. Please. We need to speak to a True Dragon. We need to find that island, and you are the only one who can show us the way."

For a long moment, Bart was silent. Remy glanced down and saw that his hands were trembling.

Finally, Bart dragged in a long, shaky breath. "It appears I have no choice," he whispered harshly. "If the princess of the kingdom demands it, and the fate of the kingdom depends on it . . ." His frail hands clenched into fists. "I will return to the island," he continued in a hushed voice. "And face the consequences of what I left behind."

What he left behind? Remy exchanged a look with Storm and he knew the dragon wondered the same thing. What was Bart hiding? What had he left behind? This was yet another secret from his past, another piece that he hadn't shared with anyone. Remy thought he knew Crusty Bart, the old storyteller of the Salty Barrel tavern. But now he realized that he didn't know Bart at all.

"Thank you, Sir Bartello." Gem's voice was subdued. "I can never hope to understand what you've been through, but I am grateful for your help."

"Do not thank me yet, Princess," Bart said. "I am afraid this is no easy task." He turned and gestured to the horizon, to the sun sinking below the clouds. "The stretch of sky the island resides in is treacherous and nearly impossible to get to. Storms surround it constantly, and the island itself does not stay in one place but drifts around. I spent weeks trying to find a captain who would fly me back to the island, but everyone in the capital refused. They thought I was sky mad." Bart's lips twisted in a humorless smile. "Perhaps I was.

"Eventually, I ended up at Cutthroat Wedge," he finished. "And had the misfortune of passing out on Ferus's doorstep." His mouth thinned, as if remembering something unpleasant, before he shook it off. "The point is, Princess, there are not many captains who would risk the journey to that island. They would either have to be exceedingly brave, or reckless, or desperate. Or perhaps all three."

Remy glanced over at a red-haired woman in a purple-and-black coat who was shouting orders to the rest of the crew. "Captain Cutlass would be able to," he said, seeing Gem's lips tighten. "She was brave enough to take on Jhaeros and the *Windshark*. We wouldn't have gotten Storm back if she hadn't agreed to help. If anyone can fly through a dangerous part of the sky, she can."

"She probably could." Gem didn't sound convinced, crossing her arms in thought. "The trick will be getting her to agree to do it. *Without* having to promise half the riches of the kingdom." She rolled her eyes. "But it should be easier now that Jhaeros is dead."

Storm let out a hiss, curling his muzzle back from his teeth. *Nasty pirate isn't dead*, he growled.

"What?" Gem glanced at Remy, wide-eyed. "Jhaeros is still alive? But I thought Storm . . ."

Remy winced. When Jhaeros had kidnapped Storm, the dragon had still been a baby. His goal was to use Storm to lure a True Dragon into the open so he could it kill it and drain it of its magic. Remy had rescued Storm before the pirate mage could enact his terrible plan, but they had been discovered, and in the ensuing chaos, Remy and Storm had been knocked overboard and had fallen into the Maelstrom.

Remy could still hear the Maelstrom roaring in his ears, the purple arcane lightning flashing all around him. He'd thought he was going to die. But instead of frying them to a crisp, the wild energies of the Maelstrom had somehow changed Storm from a baby dragon to a young adult. Now able to fly, Storm had carried Remy back to Jhaeros's ship and had taken the fight directly to the pirate mage.

"I saw Storm hit Jhaeros with a lightning bolt," Gem said, looking from Remy to the dragon and back again. "It flung him halfway across the deck. Didn't that . . . kill him?"

"I don't know," Remy admitted. "When we were leaving, Storm and I saw . . . a shadow across the deck. It was hard to see clearly, with all the smoke and flames, but . . . I think it was Jhaeros."

Bart stirred, looking back in the direction they last saw the *Windshark*. "If Jhaeros is alive," he said in a grim voice, "then we need to move quickly. That man will not forget what we've done. As soon as his ship is able to fly again, he will be coming for us. And for Storm."

Storm hissed again, baring his fangs, and Remy's stomach twisted. They had all made an extremely powerful enemy who would stop at nothing until he got what he wanted. He'd wanted Storm, but now he probably also wanted revenge against the ones who had ruined his plans.

Gem nodded. "We can't afford to be caught now," she murmured. "We're going to need a fast ship and a skilled captain to outrun Jhaeros and find the island." She paused a moment, then sighed. "I guess it's time we let Captain Cutlass know what's going on."

"Agreed," said a voice behind them. They turned to see the captain herself standing at the stairs to the forecastle, her long coat and crimson hair snapping in the wind. "I think it is high time you do that."